THE LAST PRETENCE

Sarayu Srivatsa trained as an architect and city planner at the Madras and Tokyo universities. She was the editor of *Indian Architect and Builder* and has written extensively on the evolution and growth of cities in newspapers and journals. In 2002 she won the Picador-Outlook non-fiction writing award. She has co-authored two books with Dom Moraes – *The Long Strider* and *Out of God's Oven*. *Out of God's Oven* was nominated for the Kiriyama Prize.

The Last Pretence is Sarayu Srivatsa's first work of fiction. It was longlisted for the Man Asian Literary Prize 2008. She is currently working on her next novel.

The Last Pretence

SARAYU SRIVATSA

HarperCollins *Publishers* India

First published in India in 2010 by
HarperCollins *Publishers* India
A-75, Sector 57, Noida, Uttar Pradesh 201301, India
www.harpercollins.co.in

1 2 3 4 5 6 7 8 9 10

ISBN: 978-81-7223-933-6

Typeset in Joanna MT Std 11/13
InoSoft Systems

For Amma, Anshu and Ayush

I shall be he whom you will never find,
Except in me: I am the last pretence:
Dark angel of the world, who moves behind
Dayfall, and whispers truth into innocence,
Hurting it into tears: yet I am kind.

From the 'Visitor'
Dom Moraes

Book One

One

THE SILK COTTON TREES BURST their pods before their time. Tiny parachutes of silk sailed in the wind, scattering colonies of seeds all over the red soil. The sun lay on the crops, roasting them crisp, sucking all the moisture out of them. The land, like a square of leather, shrank and curled up. The wind howled in pain and when it could suffer the heat no more, it abducted straying rain clouds and steered them towards Machilipatnam.

It was the hottest summer in the six years since the English left the country. Frogs leapt into mirage puddles, pretending to wade in circles, dogs ran about zigzaggedly, their tails between their legs, tongues hanging out of their mouths.

The heat now cast its eyes on people. It squeezed them dry until their eyes wore a permanent squint, and their brows, a lasting frown, as the sweat poured from their bodies.

In the heat of the night, in a room full of shifting shadows cast by a solitary oil lamp, Sumitra gave birth to a baby. The midwife lifted the child in her arms. 'It's a girl,' she said to Munniamma, the maidservant, who was then not a year over twenty.

Sumitra held out her arms for the child. 'Wait ma, don't be so impatient,' the midwife said. She slapped the baby hard on her buttocks. She didn't cry as babies do; instead she rounded her mouth and let out a tune – oo-oo-oo – and her eyes glittered with newborn tears.

The midwife saw a flash of lightning outside the window. It was only May; too early for rain. She looked up at the windowpane etched with hyphenated lines of water and a cold knot turned in her stomach. It was then that she knew. It was a sign, this early rain. It meant that something untoward was about to happen.

The midwife pressed the baby to Sumitra's breast. 'You must give her a name soon, ma,' she said.

Sumitra smiled and touched the baby's hair, stiff with birthblood. She bent down and kissed her head.

The midwife called out to Sumitra's husband; her voice was hoarse, and even before Vishnu had rushed into the room she grabbed Munniamma's arm and slipped out of the door.

Vishnu held his wife in his arms. He could see the pain in her eyes: dark, spreading like an inkdrop in water. Disbelieving, yearning, her eyes were locked with his. Then with an effort, she smiled at him. 'Our daughter, Mallika,' she said. She laid down the child beside her, then slid back to the floor and looked up at him.

He had never seen such radiance in her eyes. And then, with his hands soldered to her face, he lost her. His eyes had already memorised her smile and the glow in her eyes. He would never forget that moment: mother and child – one, newly born; the other, recently dead.

It would live in him for all the years to come.

Vishnu was tall. He had a sharp face with deep penetrating eyes. His hair was long, tied into a ponytail. His smile was almost angelic, as though he wished something good for everyone, until tragedy struck him.

Vishnu was a classical singer and musician. He had fallen in love with Sumitra – a singer herself – and despite the disdain of half the town, he had married her. She was twenty years younger than him.

He put away his violin and didn't play a single note after the night Sumitra died. Munniamma looked after Mallika. Whenever she brought Mallika to Vishnu he refused to look at his daughter. 'Take her away,' he said bitterly, 'she killed my wife.' He stayed in his room, sitting in an old rocking chair, rocking his grief away. But it wouldn't leave him.

Every month, on the same day, Vishnu drove his second-hand car to the market. He bought flowers from Ranga's Roses, a roadside stall that sold strings of jasmine and roses in newspaper cones, and cage of lovebirds from Yusuf's pet store next door. He drove all the way to the end of the woods, then climbed up a hill on foot. Under a parijat tree, where he had buried his wife's ashes, he laid the flowers with a prayer and a song. Then let the birds out of the cage one by one.

Munniamma felt terribly sorry for Vishnu but sorrier for little Mallika. On the eve of the fourth anniversary of his wife's death, Munniamma said to Vishnu, 'It's not as if only you have lost a dear one. Mallika has lost her mother even before she could know her.'

Coerced by Munniamma, Vishnu agreed to take Mallika with him to her mother's grave the next day. However, on their way back, he brought his foot down on the accelerator and crashed the car into a tree with a singular purpose. The tree was dead and it toppled over. It was a bad accident: Vishnu's head slammed against the steering wheel; it cut deep into his forehead and blood streamed down his eyes. His right leg crashed against the dashboard. A passer-by found him unconscious.

Mallika was unhurt. But the terror she felt minutes before the car hit the tree instilled a fear in her for ever. Her small body was pitched out of the seat and her head banged against the windscreen. She could hear the sound of glass cracking. It played again and again in her ears. For some years, whenever she was nervous, she would hear the sound of shattering glass.

It was a week before Vishnu was brought home from the hospital and when he saw Mallika, he smiled awkwardly at her. A dimple dented his left cheek. Mallika longed to touch the dimple and then touch the same finger to her own cheek. But she didn't. She was scared of him. He had a scar just above his right eye, near the eyebrow, and he limped slightly on his right leg. Both the scar and the limp would be reminders of the accident and, for Vishnu, remembrance of a deeper pain.

When Mallika was seven years old and asked Munniamma about her mother, Munniamma told her that minutes after she was born her mother had bled and died. Mallika felt a sadness she had not felt before. She tried to understand her father's grief and, overcoming her fear, she held his face in her little hands and saw him smile; his eyes turned brighter and his dimple quivered. But only for a moment. A moment, and then gloom swelled in his eyes.

Two years passed and Vishnu grew weak and pale. Munniamma dressed Mallika in her mother's sari one morning. She coiled her hair into a bun and strung parijat flowers in it. She applied red kumkum on her forehead and lined her eyes with kohl. Then she took Mallika to her father, and endearingly said, 'Look, Mallika looks just like her mother.'

Vishnu glanced at Mallika and saw his wife's face in hers, her eyes in her eyes. He seemed to come alive. The same day he retrieved the violin from its case and began to play. He sang late into the night. And the next day, and the days after.

He taught Mallika music. He did this with patience and affection at first. He was thrilled to hear her sing so well. She had her mother's voice. But later he became irate and demanding. He insisted that she wear a string of parijat flowers in her hair, kohl and a large red bindi just as her mother had done. Then he demanded that she wear a sari although she was only nine. He woke her at dawn to sing or, late in the night, whenever he needed to hear his wife's voice. Then he drank. Both the drink and Mallika's song aggravated his pain, made it unmistakable.

Once when Vishnu asked Mallika to sing, she refused. She pulled out the flowers from her hair, smudged the kohl in her eyes and smeared the pottu on her forehead. Vishnu stared at her, then got up and walked away to his room. He locked himself in and did not come out. He sat in his rocking chair, consumed by grief and rum.

The next morning Mallika dressed up like her mother, complete with the flowers and red pottu, and knocked at the door. 'Please open the door, Appa, I will sing for you.'

It was Mallika's birthday and not a day she liked to remember. What was worse, her father drank all day and the house was filled with an eerie gloom.

Mallika stayed in her room. When Munniamma arrived she went up to Mallika and waved her hands over Mallika's head and then, making fists of her hands, pressed her knuckles to her own head and cracked them.

'Why did you do that?' Mallika asked.

'So that I take away any blemish in you into myself,' Munniamma said. 'It's your birthday today, kanna,' Munniamma said, 'and you are eleven years old.'

'Let's go to the market and buy a cake,' Mallika said. 'And candles and balloons and I will call my friends home.'

'We can't do that ma,' Munniamma shook her head.

'Why not? Meena had a cake on her birthday last week and Anita's mother had baked a cake for her birthday. Why can't I have a cake too? Why can't I call my friends home?'

'You know why we can't celebrate your birthday. Let's go to the temple.'

'I don't want to go to temple.' Mallika ran out of her room, out of the house and up Gibbs Road.

Munniamma ran after Mallika. At the point where the road turned she caught up with Mallika in front of the gates of a large house.

'Whose house is this?' Mallika asked. 'Victorian Villa.'

'Who lives here?'

'No one. It was built many years ago by an English man. Gorgee Gibbs. He lived here with his sister Elisbet. She died. The house is haunted by her ghost. Never go inside.'

Mallika opened the gate and ran towards the house even as Munniamma shouted after her. A part of the wall had crumbled and wild creepers had made it their home. The tall trees around cast ghostlike shadows on the ground. Their leaves rustled in the wind. A window rattled.

Mallika walked around the side and peeped in from the window that had come unlatched. Copper and brass utensils lined the shelves on the wall, cobwebs hanging over them; and the floor was covered in pigeon shit. All of a sudden a pigeon flew out of the window and startled, Mallika turned and ran out through the gates. She threw her arms around Munniamma's waist and pressed her body close to hers.

'Stupid girl,' Munniamma said, 'don't ever go into that house.'

Holding Mallika's hand Munniamma walked through the woods to the lake. They sat under an old chakka tree. With both her hands Munniamma scooped out damp soil. She patted the soil in the shape of a round and then picking up dried twigs she stuck them in a circle into the mud cake.

She said, 'Appy baday to yoo, Mallika.' And then she leant across and hugged Mallika.

Vishnu had been drinking at a local liquor shop since evening. It was past 9 when he returned home. He banged at the door with his fist and when Mallika opened it he staggered in clutching something wrapped in newspaper. He looked at her, slurred something under his breath, then collapsed on the floor.

Mallika knelt beside him, caught his arm and struggled to pull him up. Vishnu caught hold of her shoulders and with dazed eyes he stared at her. His voice trembled as he called out his wife's name. 'Oh Sumitra, my Sumi,' he said.

Mallika's stomach churned. Every muscle in her frail limbs contracted. She crouched on the floor next to him. 'I am Mallika, Appa,' she uttered. She stroked his hair. She touched the dimple on his cheek. Her finger caressed the scar above his right eye.

He smelled of day-old aftershave and sweat; his breath stank of rum. Spit bubbled at the corners of his mouth, a metronome timing his exhalations. He passed out.

Mallika stood up and looked at her father with her huge fringed eyes. Then she ran to her room, lay down in bed and wept. She called out to her mother. But she knew that like her father, although for a totally different reason, her mother wouldn't hear her.

Vishnu woke up an hour later, patted his heart where his ache resided, and gently mumbled to it. Pain was his constant companion. He sat up and looked around him, wondering where he was. Straining his eyes, he curiously stared at the newspaper parcel beside him. Lifting the edge of the newspaper between his fingers he yanked at it hard. 'Papaya,' he said aloud and clasped his hands together. 'Oh yes, the papaya.' His eyes grew misty as he held the fruit against his chest. He remembered he had brought one for his wife whenever she had a cold. It was a hot fruit, she would explain to him, and the heat would melt the phlegm in her lungs.

Holding the wall with one hand for support, the papaya in the other, Vishnu staggered to the kitchen. He picked up a knife and a plate from the shelf and walked into Mallika's room. Leaving the fruit, knife and plate on the bedside table, he sat beside Mallika on the bed and shook her awake. He held her chin with his fingers. 'Sing, my dearest, sing for me, Sumi.'

Vishnu pressed Mallika's head to his chest where it hurt, stroked her hair and kissed her head. His face was flushed. His sweat had gone rancid and his breath smelled stale. The warmth of her flesh, the smell of her hair stirred feelings deep in him. He looked into her eyes; they reminded him of his wife.

He held up the fruit like a trophy. 'I got it for you, Sumi. You like papaya, sweet one, don't you?' Grief had hardened the veins on his temples and neck, turning them blue. He cut the fruit in half, put the knife and the remaining papaya down on the plate and held out the bigger half towards Mallika. She took the fruit from him. 'Sing ma, sing for me, Sumi.'

Mallika looked at him, her eyes vacant. She said, 'I am Mallika, I am your daughter.'

Feelings shackled within Vishnu seemed to break free. 'It is because of you that Sumi died,' he said bitterly.

Mallika hurled the fruit across the room. Vishnu stared at the orange blood of the fruit on the floor where it had landed. His eyes contorted with a deeper pain. He stood up abruptly, rushed to the window and drew the curtains apart, yanking the cloth hard. Then he paced the room, trying to control the pain. But when he couldn't, he flung the cupboard doors open and threw Mallika's clothes out of it. He pulled his wife's sari out, balled it in his hands, and then hid his face in it. He collapsed on the floor and started to wail, rocking to and fro, the sari held to his chest.

Mallika covered her face with her hands and crawled to the corner of the bed. She pushed her face into the pillow and wept.

It was past midday when Mallika woke up. The curtains were still drawn apart. The sun shone through the window. Her head ached. Sunlight hurt her eyes and an odd smell rose in her nose – bitter, sour and fruity.

She looked around the room. Her clothes were neatly piled in the cupboard. The squashed half of the fruit had been removed from the floor. Was it a bad dream? Then she saw her father on the floor on the other side of the bed, froth lining his mouth. An empty rum bottle lay beside him. Clutched in his hand was the other half of the papaya. It was the smaller half.

For some reason Mallika always remembered this.

Two

THE RAINS, AT ALL TIMES, come tentatively to Machilipatnam. By the middle of June the sky grows wishy-washy. Clouds dangle from it, dark, the colour squeezed out of them. Then at night the rains come, sputtering as if from a tap that has remained unopened for a long time.

The monsoon winds rage over the coast. The leafy fingers of palm trees serrate these winds, which now assuming a se-rr-at-ed whine blow over oilseed knolls and proceed over paddy fields and part the wet grass thisway-thatway before they swish away to the dry plains beyond.

Then for days on end the rains lash down on the parched red earth with repressed fury. Tree-branches flap, vines reel out their tendrils. The wet spindles of cobwebs snap. Flowers fluff out their scent and bees suck the wetness out of them. Rain-moths fly up into the air, flutter their wings with such ecstasy that they come apart and their limp bodies fall to the ground — wings falling after them like miniature parachutes made of eiderdown.

It was raining hard when the ship of the British East India Company brought its agent George Gibbs to Machilipatnam. The year was 1838. About this time the town exported the finest muslins, chintz and natural dyes to Egypt, Rome, Athens and Arabia. The British East India Company had established their first trading post in the country in Machilipatnam.

Within a year after his arrival George bought an old dye factory, from a local trader, which had closed down. George repaired it and renamed it Victoria Dyes. He hired local artisans who toiled all day long. They squeezed colour out of vegetables, leaves and roots and made dyes out of them. They dipped tufts of goat hair, held in slit bamboo sticks, into basins of dyes, and then worked fine lines on yards of cloth. This fabric-dying craft later came to be known as Kalamkari.

Some distance from Victoria Dyes, where the swamps gave way to grainy red soil, George built a villa. The roof was cut at the top in notches, arches and pinnacles, falling off in graceful sweeps like a voluminous Victorian skirt with starched ruffles. This was his home. It had no name and came to be known simply as Victorian Villa.

He built an oval garden in front of it. He planted English-looking trees, weepy with pale peeling barks and insufficient leaves. They drooped over a shallow pond that bred mosquitoes. Pleased with himself, George raised a glass of rum to his reigning English Queen and, with his left hand thumping his chest, christened the garden Victoria Park.

Alongside his villa George laid a gravelly path, lined with bricks, curling like an uncoiled ribbon that, with its own English destiny, rambled all the way east to the sea. After his death, this path would be known by his name: Gibbs Road.

He built a four-foot bitumen road on the other side of his villa connecting it to the factory. He planted chakka trees alongside the road and when they had grown he painted lower part of their trunks in red-and-white stripes.

The chakka trees swayed in the sea breeze. Their moist leaves made strange noises. Milky sap oozed from their trunk. And jackfruits, like big, bloated balls, grew perversely from the wrong places. Not from the branch ends or the branch middles. But some place in between. To George Gibbs's pragmatic

English mind, this seemed an aberration of sorts. And the oddness of it all excited him.

One rainy night, illuminated by roulettes of lightning, George ran to the lake in the woods behind his villa. Sweating, panting, aching, he rubbed his taut body against the old chakka tree. His sweat wet the trunk. With eyes closed, he clutched the voluptuous jackfruit in his hands, rubbed his cheek on its porcupine skin and inhaled its aphrodisiac smell deep into his armpits and groin. Amidst gasps and moans he kissed the clefts in the bark for a long time. He imagined the tree to be infested with a surfeit of passion. Slick with sweat and swollen with thirst, he savagely thrust himself against the tree, uttering obscenities in a language the tree couldn't understand, and then George gasped in pleasure. After patting the tree with a co-conspirator's caress, he walked away.

Alone and lonely George turned into a chronic second-hand magazine reader, getting a regular ration whenever the Company ship arrived. He sat in the room at the back of his villa, which was cobwebbed with spiders and mosquitoes were trapped in the spittle-nets. George looked at the pictures in the magazines, of English women, touching them, scratching them, smelling them. They smelled of Englishness. Or old paper. Or of the spit of all those who had thumbed these pages before him.

Respite from his lonesomeness came in the summer of 1842. The East India Company ship brought Elizabeth, George's young sister, from London to Machilipatnam. In the months to come, Elizabeth looked after the house and her brother. She rarely went out. But one rainy evening when George stepped out, she insisted on going with him. They walked to the lake at the back of their home.

The chakka tree cast expectant shadows on the water. Wild creepers crept over its branches and its leaves rustled rapturously in the light drizzle.

Elizabeth sat under the tree; a peculiar odour enveloped her. Her head spun, she closed her eyes and collapsed on the ground and began to moan.

The mushroomy odour of the earth infused with the aphrodisiac smell of the chakka fruit went to George's head that night. It seemed to affect the moon too as it wandered out of the trees and cast its light on Elizabeth's face. A gust of wind tossed up her ruffled skirt. The moon moved hastily to illuminate her thighs. They were plump and white and waiting. The wind grew innumerable hands; a pair cupped her breasts, another kneaded her thighs, pressing up until she separated her legs and the whiff of quite something else tickled George's nostrils. He stroked her breasts, the furrows of her flesh, until her body arched with pleasure. And in her intoxicated state when he heard Elizabeth whisper his name, George fell upon her and consumed her.

And when this aberrant lovemaking came to its end the moon moved away and it was dark all over again.

In the following months Elizabeth bloomed and ballooned and gave birth to what she thought was a boy. But when she looked again she thought it was a girl. Or was it both? She didn't know.

Elizabeth was so distraught that the shock dried up her maternal milk and instincts, and her nipples cracked like parched earth. George handed over the baby to a wet nurse and the sight and sound of her pale child slurping at a brown bosom filled Elizabeth with such disgust that she locked herself in her room and rarely ventured out of it.

Within a year of his birth, the hermaphrodite offspring, the consequence of the passion of two very bored English siblings, disappeared. It was rumoured that the local eunuchs, as is the custom, had spirited him away. This whole episode became a historical omen and social cannon about incest in Machilipatnam.

Elizabeth, who never recovered from the deep ache of the loss of her child, was bitten by a mosquito and died of malaria. George closed down Victoria Dyes and went on a long trip to Africa.

He returned with pyrethrum seeds. He sowed the seeds in the fields between Victoria Dyes and his villa. Soon the patches of land were covered with short feathery plants clinging to the ground. Some of them had white-yellow flower heads that resembled painted daisies and emitted a rancid vomit smell. Mosquitoes were drawn to these flowers, but the smell choked the breath out of them.

George built an institute for mosquito research in his sister's name – the Elizabeth Gibbs Institute. Next to it he set up a small shed and enrolled jobless workers to work in it. They were made to grind the pyrethrum leaves to paste, its seeds to powders, flowers to essence, and roots to dust. They squeezed the dust and powders into pellets that could be burnt, mixed petroleum jelly with the paste, and soaked the essences in oil.

The packets for these creams, powders and pellets were branded with the face of Queen Victoria and called Queen's Mosquito Repellent. They repelled the fiercest of mosquitoes and Queen's became a household name in Machilipatnam.

Twenty long years later, when his war against mosquitoes and the disease they spread had tired him out, George shut down the institute and returned home to England where he eventually died.

Nayantara's house stood on a large plot on Gibbs Road at the other end from Mallika's house. Except for the old Victorian Villa Nayantara's house was the most prominent structure on the road.

Her grandfather, V.R. Rao, had built the house some years after he bought over Victoria Dyes, which had been acquired by the Indian government after the British left the country in 1947.

The house was a hybrid copy of George's Victorian Villa with a steep pitched roof, grouped chimneys, pinnacles, shaped parapets, and old carved temple pillars and brackets all along the veranda.

Nayantara's mother Saroja had inherited the house, and factory with all its English history. And in the years she spent in them, they afforded her both happy and sad memories.

From the time she was a young girl, Saroja helped her father dye cloth in the factory. Even when she was nearly thirty years old, marriage was far from her mind. Her father was sickly and he needed her even more since his wife's death. He hired a young man, Ravi, to help Saroja.

Books were Ravi's passion and he was remarkably wise. Built big at six-feet-four, what Saroja liked most about him were his blue-green eyes, the colour of the sea. And despite what Saroja's father felt, by the end of the year they were married. Eventually, on her father's demand, Ravi moved into their home.

Ravi was Saroja's strength in more ways than one. He helped her modernise the factory and evolve the Kalamkari craft. He was good with the workers. He was kind to her ailing father. Still, Saroja's father died a year after her wedding.

Despite her grief, Saroja's joy was immeasurable when a daughter was born to her a year later. The baby had inherited her father's blue-green eyes. Ravi named her Nayantara. 'Because her eyes shine like stars,' he told his wife.

Ravi was as happy at work as he was at home. He travelled to neighbouring states in search of new fabrics, craft and technique. In a few years Victoria Dyes came to be sought after in the textile trade business. Its dyed fabrics were exported to England under special names: Victoria Muslin, Victoria Linen and Victoria Chintz.

A consignment of fabric had arrived late one night and Ravi was in the factory. The members of the Hindu Nationalist Party started rioting once more. It had been a few years since such troubles had plagued the town.

In the year after India's independence, the Hindu Nationalist Party was founded following a terrible communal riot that had broken out between the Muslims and Hindus in Machilipatnam. The party's main agenda was to keep the Muslims in their place. They could not do away with the Muslims since many of them were artisans who were employed in the old craft of Kalamkari. Their skills were indispensable.

On this particular night, however, the riots were not aimed at the Muslims – the party wanted to erase the remains of all that was English. The rioters set fire to the abandoned Victorian Villa, Elizabeth Gibbs Institute and Victoria Dyes factory.

The fire in the villa and institute was quickly brought under control before it could do much damage. But the fire that had been started in the storeroom of Victoria Dyes raged for hours, and Ravi was trapped in it. He was badly burnt.

With each week, his skin peeled off like the skin of new potatoes; his eyes filled with white pus. Ravi hardly spoke. His face was bloated and he refused to come out of his room. With his mind truncated, and his hands covering his face, he wept through the night.

In the days to come, his flesh rotted; it smelled of curdled vomit. One morning he screamed. A lost and hapless prisoner of his pain, Ravi screamed and banged his head on the wall and then suffered a stroke after which he was rendered speechless. He died speechlessly, his breath curling out of him in spasms.

The funeral was a simple ceremony. There were no display of emotions, no words spoken. When everyone had left, Nayantara lingered at the doorway clutching her mother's hand.

She was six.

When she was all of fifteen, Nayantara was unusually tall just like her father had been and, like him, she was of an awkward, big build. Her skin, the colour of wheat husk, was smooth and unblemished. Delicate peach fuzz lined her upper lip.

Since her father's death, Nayantara had taken on chores in the house. At first she ran errands for her mother, and when she was older she took on more difficult tasks. She retrieved heavy suitcases from the attic, changed lightbulbs, repaired window hinges, or hammered a nail into the wall, as required. She did not help with the cooking, did not clean the house or sew buttons or hooks that had come off her clothes. Those were her mother Saroja's jobs.

Her daughter had grown up like a son.

Saroja was in the garden at the back of the house. The paving stones were covered with a film of early dew. And the flowerbeds blossomed at the right places and the trees around them grew to the right height, flowered in the right colours. Saroja sighed. The cicadas in the trees chirped in harmony.

Saroja lit a bowl of mosquito repellent powder and it shone luminescent-red in the shadows. Its fragrant fumes bewildered the mosquitoes; they buzzed away.

Saroja sat down on the steps. Nayantara came to Saroja dressed in a pair of jeans and a shirt that was too big for her.

'That was your father's shirt,' Saroja said.

Nayantara sat down beside her mother and hugged her.

'How did Appa die?' Nayantara asked for the hundredth time.

Even after all these years, Saroja was pained to talk about her husband's untimely death. Her voice broke as she told Nayantara about him.

Three

Nayantara's school was on Gibbs Road, across the path that led to the woods. Mallika went to the same school. Two years older than Mallika, Nayantara was the house prefect. She was strict and the younger students were scared of her. Mallika was particularly terrified by her.

It was a hot April day in the last week of school that summer. The schoolgirls were out on the grounds playing throw ball. The school sports uniform consisted of a white skirt and a short blouse whose colour was determined by the house the student belonged to: red, green, yellow or blue. Mallika's blouse was green, the same as Nayantara's.

'Mallika! Go join the girls,' Nayantara yelled at Mallika standing by the tree.

'Mallika, you serve,' Nayantara said.

Mallika took her position at the end of the court and with the ball held in one hand she crouched low, then with a burst of energy jumped up in the air and swung the ball across the net. The force of the throw propelled her body around and her back faced the court.

There on her white skirt was a crimson stain.

The girl closest to her whispered in her ear and giggled. Mallika pulled at her skirt, trying to look behind her. Then on her left leg she noticed a rivulet of blood. She ran out of the court. Nayantara screamed behind her, 'Mallika, where do you think you're going?'

Ensconced in the toilet Mallika slid her panties down and when she saw the blood on them she moaned. She was going to die, just like her mother did because of her. She was being punished. She balled the bloodied garment and hid it in the corner of the toilet.

She stepped out into the girls' room, covered her face with her hands and slid to the floor, lying against the curve of the wall, her body taking on the angular shape of an L.

Half an hour later Mallika was still on the floor. She had pulled her knees up to her chin and resembled an apostrophe lying down.

That was how Nayantara found her.

'Mallika, why are you lying on the floor?' Nayantara asked in a hoarse voice. It was then that she noticed that Mallika was crying.

'What's wrong?'

'I am bleeding. I think I am going to die,' Mallika said, trembling.

Nayantara laughed aloud. 'Has your mother not told you about periods?'

Mallika didn't reply. She shrank each time somebody mentioned her mother. She became nervous when anyone asked about her father. Unable to comprehend her father's grief and the absence of a mother, or death itself, Mallika had withdrawn into herself.

Nayantara raised an eyebrow at her, then without another word she led Mallika to the storeroom, and from a cupboard she took out a square of muslin, folded it and gave it to Mallika. She explained its requirement each month, and the persistence of those bloody days.

Nayantara stroked Mallika's hair. 'Your tummy will hurt,' she said. 'Don't be afraid. It will last no more than a day or two.'

But she didn't know then that Mallika wasn't afraid of hurting. She had gotten used to pain.

It was early May but it had rained all week. Mallika was in the attic of her house. She stuck her head out of the tiny window. She could see the grey folds of the sky. She looked to her left, where the chakka tree was entwined with the peepal tree. The chakka leaves were fleshy, a darker shade of green than normal leaves. When clean they shone like the Rexine sofa in her living room. But the chakka leaves just outside the window were covered with dust and the grey-white droppings of pigeons and the black waste of bats.

Kuttan, the chakka man was under the chakka tree, in a green-checked lungi and a black singlet. A gold pendant on a string hung from his neck. He parked his cart there every day. The tree did not belong to him but long ago he'd claimed it as his. The shade of the tree was his. The tree's fruits were his. He did not own anything else, other than the stray dog that slept under the tree.

Every day Kuttan wheeled a cartful of bulging jackfruits; he placed a large, dissected one on top, its entrails exposed. As he dug in with his fingers and prised the nugget-like seeds from its sticky tentacles, it made noises. And Kuttan made obscene noises with his tongue. Mallika was afraid of him.

Only a week earlier, Kuttan had stood at the front door holding a large jackfruit in his hands. Mallika's father was out and Munniamma had gone to the market.

'Munniamma asked me to deliver the fruit,' he said.

Mallika looked up at his face; his eyes were lewd, his smile, leering, and he made those squishy noises with his mouth. He left the fruit by the door, and then shifted his lungi, pointing between his legs where, it seemed to Mallika, a branch had grown. His hand moved over it. Slowly. Then faster and faster. Mallika didn't quite understand but instinct warned her what he was doing was wrong. She shut the door, ran to her room, crouched in a corner and wept.

Now Mallika looked at him from her window and her stomach churned. As the rain came down hard, it glistened wetly on his skin and on the blue plastic sheet that covered the chakkas beneath it. The dog sleeping beside him woke and shook the rain from its skin.

The rain stopped as tentatively as it had started. Mallika leant to the right of the window. She saw electrical cables dividing the sky: up and down, untidy lines. She saw buses: horizontal red bands through the vertical lines of rain. Taxis moved in queues like yellow bugs on a mission. Another bus, a moving red curtain, hid the people across the street.

Mallika peered at the advertisement on it: Godrej Hair Dye, with the picture of a woman with lustrous, jet-black hair. Miss Lobo, her teacher, also had boot-polish shine in her hair. When freshly dyed, her hairline was lower like the new watermarks on old buildings. The Godrej Hair Dye bus passed.

Mallika could hear Munniamma calling out to her.

'Here you are, Mallika,' Munniamma said, as she entered the room in her floral nylex sari. Her long black hair was combed back and tied into a knot covered with a shiny black nylon net. Two golden pins with fake rubies held wisps of hair behind her ears.

'Come along.' Munniamma rushed towards Mallika with a comb in her hand. 'We have to go to the temple.'

'Why must we go to the temple?'

'So that we can find a nice boy for you to marry.'

'Will he be at the temple?'

'No, stupid girl. We will pray to Lord Shiva for a nice Brahmin boy for you.'

'Why Brahmin?'

'Because you are a Brahmin. You belong to the highest caste, ma. A caste made of fair, tall, intelligent people. You can't marry below your caste. That's why. Come on now.'

Mallika turned back, stuck out her tongue at Munniamma and scrambled down the stairs to her room. Munniamma ran after her and caught her. She grabbed Mallika's arm and pushed her on the floor. She sat down behind her and combed her hair, gathering it into a tight plait. She twisted a string of jasmine around the plait. She rubbed talcum powder on Mallika's face and with her middle finger stained her eyes with kohl. She pushed Mallika in front of the mirror.

'See, see how pretty you look, my kanna.' She made a kissing sound with her lips. She held Mallika's chin and turned her face. At the bottom of her lower lip, to one side, with an eye pencil, she twirled a large black spot.

'Now this will keep the evil eyes away, Mallika.' She patted her back. 'Hurry up now, it has stopped raining. Let's go.'

Munniamma held Mallika's hand and walked out of the gate. As they passed Kuttan, he whistled. Munniamma stopped and brandished her arm in the air.

'Did you just whistle at me eh?' she hissed through her teeth.

Kuttan grinned.

'Go on, look, look at me,' Munniamma said as she wiped the back of her neck with the end of her sari. It was hot after the rain. 'I am not young any more. What are you whistling at me for eh?'

Kuttan whistled once again.

'How old do you think I am?' Munniamma poked her finger into his ribs. She leant closer to him. 'I am going to be 104,' she whispered, tipping her head back, laughing.

Kuttan slapped her arm playfully.

'You don't look a year more than twenty,' he said. 'Anyway I am not whistling at you.' He pointed to Mallika. 'I am whistling at her; she is a beauty.'

Kuttan blew kisses at Mallika.

Munniamma slapped his chest.

'I'll pull your tongue out and you'll never whistle again.'

She pulled Mallika across the road and they walked down the market street.

Bare-chested pujaris in white lungis passed by them. They would amble to the end of Gibbs Road and wait outside the temple gates, check their ledgers for auspicious times and look for ardent believers. Drops of spittle would land on their bloated bellies, as they spoke with their mouths wide open.

Closer to the temple, Munniamma stopped at Ranga's Roses. 'Leave your slippers here, Mallika,' she said as she shoved her own inside the stall. 'Ranga will look after them.'

Mallika took her slippers off and dropped them on top of Munniamma's.

Munniamma bought a cone of roses.

'Oh, Mallika, hello,' a voice said.

Mallika turned around. A tall girl in brown trousers and a baggy shirt stood smiling at her. Her hair was combed tightly back from her forehead and held with a clip. A bit flustered, Mallika made arcs on the ground with her big toe.

'Hello Nayantara,' Mallika said, looking up shyly.

Munniamma greeted Nayantara's mother Saroja. She was carrying a basket of vegetables. 'Not going to the factory today, ma?' Munniamma asked her.

'I will go as soon as I finish the shopping.'

'Shopping. Factory. What all will you do? Your daughter could have done the shopping for you, ma.'

'Her?' Saroja smirked pointing to Nayantara. 'She won't lift a finger even to do these household things.'

'You must make her do them, ma. What will she do after her marriage?'

'After her marriage? I can only hope that she gets married in the first place.'

'Don't say that, ma. All girls must get married. My husband, he is a drunkard and an oaf, but I am married at least.' Pointing at Mallika, Munniamma said, 'This is Vishnu-aiyah's daughter.'

'Yes, I know,' Saroja said. 'She looks just like her mother. I met her mother a long time ago. What a good singer she was. It is terrible to die so young.' With a delicate movement of her hand, she caressed Mallika's arm.

A woman ambled over to Saroja clapping her hands. 'Amma, spare me five rupees, ma. The good lord will bless you with a grandson.'

'Grandson?' Saroja laughed. 'Bless me with a good son-in-law first. I am not giving you any money, Kamala. How many times have I told you not to beg? Why don't you work?'

Kamala pouted. 'Who will give me work, ma?' She patted her cheek with her finger. 'Look at me.'

Her face was hard, hard as a man's: square with a broad forehead, angular cheekbones, and a blue-green stubble around it. Her skin was dark-brown, almost black. Dull, as though the colour had been blotted with the wooden English blotter. She was dressed in a red nylon sari with silver sequins. Red was her favourite colour. Her hair was coiled at the top of her head. Her thin, flat lips were painted blood-red. She was a eunuch.

Kamala leant toward Mallika and circled her hands over Mallika's head and then, making fists, she touched her knuckles to her own head and cracked them. 'May God bless you with many sons.' She sauntered to a group of women to continue her begging.

Mallika clutched Munniamma's arm. 'Is she a man?' Mallika whispered to Munniamma.

'Yes.'

'Then why is he wearing a sari?'

'Because he is also a woman.'

'How can he be both? A he and a she?'

'Ssh. I will tell you later.' Then turning to Saroja, 'We must go, ma. We are going to the temple,' Munniamma said.

'I'll go with you,' Nayantara said.

'Okay, you go with them,' Saroja said, 'I will go to the factory.'

'Leave your slippers here,' Munniamma said to Nayantara. 'At the temple you will have to pay two rupees to that woman who keeps them safe.'

Nayantara removed her slippers and pushed them into the stall with her foot. Then holding Mallika's hand she walked towards the temple. Munniamma followed them.

The temple was like a house with a tiled roof, except its outer walls were painted a yellow-ochre with a band of red at the bottom. The main hall was noisy; there were too many people praying in it with raised voices so that the gods could hear them. Nayantara pulled Mallika through the crowd to the front.

Mallika looked up at the painting of Lord Shiva framed in glass. Two bulbs were reflected in his eyes. They turned yellow: strangely shiny. The temple always smelled the same, she thought, a mixed-up pious smell: jasmine-rose-milk-ghee-sandalwood-jaggery-incense-camphor.

Munniamma, not too far behind them, shut her eyes and chanted aloud. She opened one eye and saw Nayantara's arm around Mallika's waist. She heaved a sigh, smiled and chanted once more.

When Munniamma and the girls were out of the temple they collected their slippers from Ranga's stall. Munniamma hurried down the road. Nayantara and Mallika ambled behind her. Closer to home Munniamma stopped at Kuttan's cart under the chakka tree. He cut a large fruit in half. Munniamma smelled it, and then nodding her head she paid for it, picked up half the fruit and walked towards the house.

As the girls approached Kuttan, he whistled. Mallika clutched Nayantara's hand. The dog stirred, opened one eye and settled back to sleep again.

Nayantara picked up a large fruit and crashed it to the ground. Kuttan let out a stream of abuse. Nayantara picked up another fruit with both her hands.

'Mallika catch,' she said and tossed it in the air. Mallika put out her hands but the fruit landed on the road and split into three pieces. Nayantara clutched Mallika's hand and they ran laughing to the house.

Munniamma was in the kitchen steaming the jackfruit. Nayantara and Mallika watched her as she pulped the steamed fruit, then added jaggery, coconut milk and ghee, and put it on the stove to reduce. As the sweet concoction squelched and popped, strains of a violin filled the house.

'Who is playing?' Nayantara asked

'Mallika's father,' Munniamma said. 'It was her mother's favourite song. You should have heard her sing, ma. Even the rain would have stopped to listen to her voice.' She turned to Mallika, 'Take your friend to your room and I'll bring the payasam when it is ready.'

Up in the room the girls stood by the window. Mallika peeped further out so she could see the jamun tree with its delicate leaves. The chakka leaves made a swish-swish sound in the breeze, like the skirt she had on. The peepal leaves made a sis-sis sound, similar to the sound Munniamma made when she was furious; some of her teeth were missing.

Nayantara saw a man on a cycle grab the back bar of a bus and steer through the crowd, steel bands on his ankles holding up his trousers. He was getting his ride free; he seemed happy. And then the bus went over a pothole and the man lost control of his cycle and fell. Nayantara pointed to him and laughed.

Mallika glanced at her. Nayantara wrapped her arm around Mallika's waist.

'Want to come to my house tomorrow?'

It started to rain.

Saroja's heart went out to Mallika when Nayantara brought her home the next afternoon. She held Mallika close against her bosom.

Saroja had always dreamed of a beautiful daughter like Mallika. Though Saroja loved her daughter dearly, she did not fail to see how absurdly the different parts of her body were put together, like Tanjore dolls whose necks, waists, hips and limbs moved in uncoordinated directions as though different lobes of the brain controlled them.

'Why don't you take Mallika to your room,' Saroja told Nayantara. 'I'll make something for you to eat.'

Cocooned in the bedroom, while Saroja interrupted them with savouries and sweets, Nayantara read aloud from her father's books; Mallika sang songs; and they spun stories out of stories they had read. They surrendered themselves to fantasy worlds and believed every fabric of their creation.

One afternoon the girls walked down the mudtrack to the lake. They removed their slippers and sat down on the shore, their legs dangling in the water. Mallika kicked the water with her feet and Nayantara threw stones into it, as far as she could.

All of a sudden Nayantara shed her clothes and dived into the water. She swam across and in a circle, then back to where Mallika was and grabbed her feet, pulling her in the water.

Mallika's skirt swelled like a gas balloon. She dunked, sputtered and screamed. Nayantara held her arms and hauled her up to the shore. Mallika scrambled out of the water and ran to the chakka tree, crouching down under it.

Nayantara went to her. 'Mallika! I didn't know you couldn't swim! I am sorry.' She undid Mallika's braid. She spread her wet hair, picked fistfuls of it, and shook it dry.

There had been a strong wind through the night and the ground under the chakka tree was covered with leaves. Nayantara held Mallika's shoulders and pushed her down on the ground, and then lay close to her. The earth below them smelled odd – a mixed up storm-smell: the ground smelled nutty and the leaves smelled of flowers. The insects stank; a bitter smell. Nayantara propped her body up on an arm and moved her finger from Mallika's toe, up her legs to her navel. Mallika giggled because it tickled. She giggled a lot.

Nayantara moved her finger from Mallika's navel to her breast. She said, 'It's time you wore a bra, Mallika.'

Mallika covered her breasts with her hands. Nayantara's eyes went suddenly wistful. 'My chest is like half a carom board, my mother says. My armpits are the holes.' She laughed. 'Tomorrow we will go shopping for bras. I need one too.' She scooped Mallika's face in her hands and kissed her forehead.

'Come, let's go the beach,' Nayantara said as she pulled Mallika up by her arm.

They walked down Gibbs Road, down the market, past the Shiva temple towards the sea beyond.

Mallika sat on the sand and raising her face to the evening sky, she hummed a happy tune her father had recently taught her.

Nayantara walked to the sea. The wind made her shudder and the salt spray hit her eyes. Water licked at her feet and bits of paper, plastic, flowers floated around her. She hitched her trousers up, walked further into the sea. She stood knee-deep in the water as the waves thrashed against her groin, sprayed all over her chest and fondled her face. Her jeans were wet, her face oiled with sea salt and sweat.

The muezzin's voice could be heard over a loudspeaker from the old mosque. It wailed into the moist atmosphere: 'La ilaha ila allah.' Not far away, the bells in the Shiva temple clanged. Fifteen minutes late. To make up for lost time, the devotees chanted in one seamless voice: 'Shiva-Shiva-Shiva-Shiva ...' And through the clamour for the gods, from a fisherman's boat, an old film song played from the radio, '*Ajeeb dastan hai yeh, kahan shuru kahan khatam ...*'

The sky turned orange in the sunset. Wild orange. Red dancing. Yellow dancing. Nayantara called out to Mallika who went to her. In the water Mallika stood still, not daring to breathe. The sand beneath her feet shifted, caved out and sifted away. She felt the sea wind slaver. She tossed her head back and her body shook as though she was suppressing a giant giggle because the water and sand tickled her soles. And then ever so slowly, using every tremor in her body, she laughed.

On an unspoken command the sound of the waves intensified. Mallika looked around her: the wind, the water, the trees. They appeared to her to be laughing in chorus. A piece of paper fluttering in the sky seemed to her to join in the laughter.

Mallika may have been mistaken but she felt then that the fulfilment of friendship was pure laughter. She shut her eyes and when she opened them she saw Nayantara, laughing. She laughed with her.

Four

EARLY NEXT MORNING MALLIKA MET Nayantara in the market. The air was awash with the smells of the marketplace: fresh vegetables and fruits, stinking fish, chicken feathers, the whiff of roasted peanuts and pungent chillies; and flies that buzzed over sacks of brown jaggery. Joined to the smells were the sounds of the market: the bickering, the haggling and the shouting, voices sweet and harsh. Through it all came the sounds of dogs barking, the mewing of cats, mooing cows, and the squeaking of rats as they moved one behind the other through gaps in the walls.

Ranga had opened his shop. He held out a rose and Nayantara fixed it to Mallika's hair. They walked on towards Mohan's Juice stall sheltered under a large banyan tree.

Kamala was at the stall. She poked her long reddened fingernail into Mohan's side. 'I'll have two glasses today sweetie,' she said, learning close. 'I am so thirsty,' she laughed and whacked her cunt.

Mohan playfully rode his hand over her thigh. Kamala slapped the back of his hand. 'You won't spare a eunuch even, will you?'

Mohan laughed as he fed sweet limes into the mincing machine, pushing them down with a rounded stick, collecting the frothy juice in a steel jug, then scraping handfuls of pith, which he flung into the bucket crying 'six' if all went in, 'four' if half went in and 'no-ball' if all dropped out. He was mad about cricket and he played his game substituting the pith for the ball and the bucket for the cricket stumps. Flies swarmed around the sixes and fours, a cow looked up from its bundle of grass and licked the no-balls.

Mohan handed over the two glasses to Kamala. She drank them one after the other in a long swallow and, wiping her lips with her sari, jerked her head in appreciation. She looked up at the pigeons as they drifted in the breeze as if they were fluffs of soiled cotton. By some freak of weather the sky was cloudless at first; freakish for it was the monsoon season. Then all at once without any advance indication, it began to rain. The birds flew in a clutter, found shelter in the banyan tree.

The rain stopped. Kamala stretched her arms above her head and squeezed the air with her fingers. She shouted, 'Come on you impotent clouds. Rain, you dried up sisterfucker!' She clapped her hands harder. 'Come, come. Rain all over our parched red earth and wet me now!'

Nayantara laughed.

Kamala turned around and saw the girls. Mallika clutched Nayantara's hand and pressed her body to hers. Kamala stepped up to them. She held Mallika's chin between her fingers and kissed the air. 'So beautiful,' she sighed, and cracking her knuckles on either side of her head, she ambled past them.

The girls crossed the road and stopped at Good Morning Café for a quick snack and later walked towards Eros Cinema. It was the only theatre in town that screened English films. It had a matinee show on – Alfred Hitchcock's *To Catch a Thief*. Outside the cinema house Nayantara bought some purple berries from the jamun-seller. Mallika stared curiously at the poster of Cary Grant kissing Grace Kelly against the backdrop of the French Riviera. She ran a finger over the mouths trying to determine which lips were whose.

She looked up at another poster of Grace Kelly with blonde hair and light eyes. She had on a short dress and her lips were painted a dark maroon, almost purple. 'She is so beautiful,' Mallika said.

Nayantara hitched up Mallika's skirt to make it shorter, unfastened two buttons of Mallika's blouse, tucked the collar in so her cleavage was visible. She bit a jamun and rubbed its flesh hard on Mallika's lips to make them purple. 'Look, you are just like Grace Kelly,' she said, 'beautiful.'

After the film Nayantara took Mallika to a novelty shop that, besides cosmetics, sold hairclips and ribbons, bras and panties. It had a show window with a buxom mannequin, its plaster-of-Paris hair slapped into a bun. Its candy-pink body was dressed in a pointed bra and flimsy lace panties, and covered with a see-through nylon wrap.

Inside the shop Nayantara tried out hairclips and ribbons on Mallika's hair, and glass bangles on her wrists. She bought two silver rings, slipped one onto Mallika's finger and the other onto her own. 'Friendship rings,' she said. 'Never remove them.' She bought two bras for Mallika and one for herself. She also purchased a bottle of eyeliner, a tube of lipstick, a box of rouge and a pair of tweezers. They walked back to Nayantara's house.

Saroja was at the factory. The girls were alone in the house. In her room Nayantara pulled Mallika's head into her lap and plucked her eyebrows into two thin arcs. Then pulling Mallika up Nayantara made up her eyes with the liner and her cheeks with rouge. She smeared lipstick carefully on her lips. 'Now smack your lips,' she said. Mallika licked her lips. 'Not like that, silly,' Nayantara laughed, and bending closer she gently pressed her lips to Mallika's and smacked the colour in.

Mallika looked aghast. 'Why did you kiss me on my lips? Now we'll get pregnant.'

Nayantara held her stomach and roared with mirth. Her eyes filled up with tears.

'It's true,' Mallika replied seriously. 'After a girl gets her period it is not safe to kiss.'

'Who told you that?'

'Munniamma.'

'What did she say?'

'She said if a girl kisses a girl, then both get daughters. And if a boy kisses a girl then a son is born to her. And, and,' she clasped her hands and looked down at them.

Nayantara asked, 'And, and what?'

'It seems if a brother and sister kiss like that then she gives birth to a he-she child.'

'A what?'

'A child that is both – a girl and a boy together. Like that Kamala. I asked Munniamma why Kamala looked like a man but was dressed as a woman. Munniamma told me that is what happens when a brother does it to his sister.'

'Rubbish! You will get pregnant only when you marry a man and do that stuff.'

'Do what stuff?'

'You don't know?'

'Don't know what?'

'About making love?'

'Making love?' Mallika looked confused. But her body seemed to understand. It trembled with unknown, unfelt rapture.

'How does love feel?' Mallika tugged at Nayantara's arm.

Nayantara looked at her and spoke softly. 'When you are in love your head feels light and you can't think straight. Your heart trembles. You feel as if there are butterflies in your stomach. And your fingers and toes tingle and your eyes go zzzinnng.'

'Zzzzinnng?'

'Yes, zzzinnng.'

Mallika clutched her hands together. 'So you've been in love?'

'I've kissed a boy.'

'Who?'

'Siddhartha. Dr Kuruvilla's son. He's in Madras now. He is training to be a doctor.' Nayantara held her own hands together with the palms facing up and the lines on them aligned. She said, 'Look, my husband is going to be handsome.'

Mallika asked, 'How do you know?'

'See this curve; it is deep like a bowl. Nayantara giggled. 'Had it been flat I would have got an ugly man. Show me your hands.' She looked at them. 'Your man will be more handsome than mine.' She plucked a long hair from Mallika's head.

'Aaaow! What are you doing?'

'Stop screaming,' Nayantara said as she took off the silver ring from her finger. She tied the hair to the ring and held it over Mallika's left palm. 'Be still now,' she said as she watched the ring. It began to circle. 'Ah, you will have a boy!' she exclaimed. 'Now you do it for me.' Mallika held the ring over Nayantara's palm. The ring started to move back and forth. 'I am going to have a daughter,' Nayantara squealed.

'But I want a daughter too,' Mallika complained. 'Like my mother, I want a daughter.'

'Oh don't sulk.' Nayantara held Mallika's hand and repeated the trick. 'See, now you will also have a girl.'

The room had become dim. The musty smell of the walls hung in the air. Nayantara took her shirt off and then her trousers and slid her panties down. Turning to Mallika, she started to undress her. Mallika protested and held her arms out to stop Nayantara. 'Oh, don't be shy, it's only me. What will you do when you marry eh?' Nayantara slipped Mallika's clothes off one by one.

The spread of Mallika's hips was different from Nayantara's, rounded and shaped like a large peepal leaf on which syrupy sweets are offered to the gods. She let her eyes wander upwards over the soft pucker of Mallika's belly around the navel, past the broomsticks of her ribcage to the gentle seawave of flesh before it moulded into twin mounds peaked with nipples.

Nayantara undid Mallika's hair and it tumbled down and covered her two dumplings of flesh. She pushed Mallika down on the bed, then with her finger between Mallika's eyebrows she made tiny circles. She moved her finger over the bulge of Mallika's cheek, along the curve of her chin, down her neck and over her left collarbone. Her finger glided down to the dark purple berry of Mallika's left breast.

Each time Nayantara's finger lost its contact with her skin Mallika felt giddy from the separation. But as soon as the touch was restored she could hear the murmur of the seas inside her.

Nayantara lay on top of Mallika and held the back of Mallika's thighs in her hands. Wrapping Mallika's legs around her, she pushed against her and then pulled her up against her crotch. She did this repeatedly and a rhythmic responsiveness entered Mallika's body and she flexed her abdomen to an inner tune and was wet with sweat and other fluids she did not know were concealed within her. Mallika moaned.

'Yes, oh yes, that's it, yes, yes, yes.' Nayantara felt a spring become loose between her legs and she heard its zzzinnnng in her head. She felt dizzy. Mallika opened her eyes a little and through the slits saw Nayantara gazing at her. The room smelled different from before. It smelled of hair, skin, flesh, sweat, saliva and a moist mulchy smell – all mixed, it became a single compelling smell.

'Did you feel it?' Nayantara asked in a heavy perspiring voice.

'Feel what?''

'That amaz-ing zi-nn-ing feeling?'

Mallika wound her arms around her friend and hugged her tight. Nayantara kissed Mallika on her lips. 'Now we will both have girls,' she said. 'And I will call my daughter after you. Malli.'

Mallika looked deep into her friend's blue-green eyes. 'And I will call mine Tara.'

It was the happiest year for Mallika. A year filled with friendship, affection, laughter and song. What was more, she was no longer wary of her father despite the fact that he drank, though not as obsessively as before. They continued their music lessons in the mornings before school and in the evenings before bedtime. Vishnu was pleased with her singing and Mallika was only too glad to spend time with her father.

One evening, after the music lesson Mallika asked her father, 'Did Amma love me?'

Vishnu looked out of the window. The moon was round and yellow. A bird flew across it and for an instant split it in two. Mallika sat at her father's feet, looking up at him. 'Yes, she loved you very much.' He stroked her forehead, then held her face between his hands and kissed her on her head.

Mallika couldn't sleep that night. She couldn't stop thinking of her mother and at dawn when she could no longer bear the cramped feeling in her heart she walked out of her room, out of the hall, out of the door, to the end of the street, past trees, to the pond in the woods.

Mallika sat down near the water and wrapped her body with her arms. Through the trellis of her hair she looked up at the moon. 'I love you, Amma,' she whispered to the breeze.

A bird chirped in its sleep; Mallika felt consolation in its voice. The sound broke the spell and everything quivered and rustled with life. Feeling tranquil, she walked back home.

Another summer. Nayantara had finished school. She helped her mother at the factory. School was closed for the season and Mallika often went to meet her. Saroja taught the girls all she could about dyeing.

Soon they learnt to extract the dye pigment from plant fibre and wheat husk. They mixed crushed limestone, ash and toddy with it in a large vat to make a liquid dye. After a week when the dye had fermented they soaked fabrics in the dye twenty times to deepen the colour. They hung the dyed cloth to dry in the room with the skylight so that the dye impregnated the cloth and deepened in its veins. It was called the blue room as its walls were stained indigo.

This room fascinated Mallika. It was filled with bales of dyed silk, muslin and chiffon. It smelled moist, woody and strangely tart. Endless yards of cloth were hung from the roof to get rid of the folds and creases in them. Light from a glass tile above shone on the dyed cloth and gave the room an ethereal feel. Mallika sat in it and dreamed of floating in the blue sky.

Sometimes she wrapped the silk around her, round and round, until she was cocooned from neck to toe. When Saroja found her, 'Oh my beautiful silkworm,' she said as she held the end of the cloth and spun her around like a top. Then Saroja hugged her.

Once Mallika had impulsively said, 'I wish you were my mother.'

Saroja had replied, 'You *are* my daughter.'

Mallika met Nayantara at Eros Cinema one afternoon.

Nayantara pointed to the young man standing in the queue for tickets. 'Oh my God, he's back.'

'Who?'

'Siddhartha.'

Six-feet-three, his jet-black eyes were seeped in mystery and his teeth glistened as though he rubbed them several times a day with tooth powder. His moustache and beard were of a lighter colour than his hair as though a different sun had shone on them and his hair curled like a seagull's wings. This is what Nayantara had liked most about his appearance. He turned and she waved and walked up to him.

'Hello Siddhartha.'

'Oh hi Nayantara. How are you?'

'When did you come?'

'A week ago.'

'And you didn't come to see me?' Nayantara whacked his arm.

'I had to go to Kanuru every day with my father.'

'Where?'

'It is a little fishing village not far from here.'

'Why?'

'The rains had flooded the village and there was an outbreak of malaria.'

'Is it bad?'

'Yes it was. Many fishermen died. Relief workers and doctors have come down from Madras. Thank God the epidemic is in control now. Or else it would have spread to other villages and Machilipatnam. Honestly, the government should revive the old Elizabeth Gibbs Institute and start some active malaria research in it.'

'Do you have to go to that village again?'

'No, I don't think so. My work there is done.' Siddhartha sighed. 'The whole week has been so exhausting, I thought I'd see a film this afternoon. Are you here to see the film?'

'Yes.'

'Oh good. I'll buy a ticket for you.'

'My friend Mallika is with me.' Nayantara pointed to her.

Siddhartha waved his hand at Mallika. 'I'll buy her a ticket too.'

Inside the theatre Siddhartha sat next to Nayantara and Mallika sat beside her. Nayantara inhaled the smell of Siddhartha's aftershave: lemony and sharp. Now and then during the film he leant closer to her to talk. His elbow stuck out of the armrest so that when she moved towards him it brushed her arm or breast. Halfway into the film Mallika saw Nayantara reach out and hold Siddhartha's hand.

Mallika sank deeper into the seat, moved uncomfortably, then sat up and crossed her arms tightly across her breast. Her nails dug into her flesh. She looked up at the screen. All she could see was a blur of colours. Tears, for reasons she couldn't find, streamed down her cheeks. A sniffle escaped her.

Nayantara glanced at Mallika. 'What's wrong Mallika? Why are you crying?'

Mallika held her face in both her hands and her heart beat wildly and her breath came out in spasms. Then without saying a word she left the cinema hall.

Munniamma was surprised when Mallika burst into the kitchen. She looked towards the door. 'Where's Nayantara?'

'Don't talk to me about her,' Mallika fumed and ran to her room.

Five

IT WAS LATE AFTERNOON AND the wind was damp; it seemed like more rain. Mallika was in the market. It was crowded with people packed so close that Mallika could smell their sweat, which smelled, like everything else around, of the sea.

Mallika walked up Gibbs Road. When she reached Victorian Villa she wandered down the mudpath to the lake in the woods. She stopped in her tracks when she heard voices, and hid behind a bush. It was Nayantara and Siddhartha. His arms were around her waist. Overcome with shyness Mallika turned away, looked at the pond and started counting.

Two large lilies ...

One toad...

Out of the corner of her eye she saw Siddhartha undo Nayantara's hair. He spread it all over her face and shoulders.

Mallika counted:

Two buds.

Two more toads.

Siddhartha lifted a fistful of Nayantara's hair, kissed it.

One more half-bloomed lily.

And a toad on a wet leaf.

Nayantara put her arms around his shoulder.

Another lily in the corner.

Siddhartha pulled her closer to him.

And one more lily.

Then he kissed her head.

And one more toad.

He kissed her eyes.

And another one.

And kissed her forehead. And one more time. He caressed her face and arms. He kissed her shoulders, left, then right. He rubbed the small mounds of her breasts, stroked her ribs, and his hand moved over her navel, then down to her thighs. He held her close and kissed her hard on her lips.

Mallika stood still, still counting.

Fourteen full-bloomed lilies.

Four half-blooms.

Six buds.

And seven toads.

Mallika held her breath, pressed a hand on her breast to stop its heaving. Then she turned and ran through the trees. Sparrows fluttered into the air. A lone butterfly flapped its wings, and flew away.

She ran down the narrow strip of bitumen on the other side of the woods. The oilseed plants on either sides of it squeaked as the branches rubbed against one another. Bushes trembled with life: the flutter of a sleeping bird, zipping dragonflies and the scamper of mice. A large grey rat shot across, a dark bundle from one field to another. Mallika walked on towards the beach.

The air was full of the smell of sea, sand and earthmusk. She looked up at the sun and then into the sea, translucent as the sky. It seemed to her like a big field with opaque cloud-like flowers, the sky and the sea, the clouds and the froth, together. She ran into the blue field of flowery froth.

Clouds began to gently tumble and roll; they started to drizzle on Mallika's face. Her skin gleamed as if the rain had nuzzled it with stars, and a knot of warmth quivered under the tendons of her breast. Lapped by the waves her body seemed to swell, and her breasts under the damp blouse were ruled by a reverse gravity: pushing up instead of down. She pulled at her long hair, spread it around her shoulders. It fell like rapture, like mercury, like the happy dope of delight. Something stirred in her: a feeling she had never felt before unfolded gently like the whorl of a flower and then violently like the centre of a typhoon.

The conniving breeze blew Mallika's hair all over her face. Thus veiled, for the first time she imagined being held in a man's arms. She pictured herself reaching up slowly, kissing his lips – like in an invocation, as though to make him stay. To make him hers. Her imaginary lover clutched her hair in his hand and yanking it back he reached down to her upturned face and kissed her on the lips. She clutched his shirt as she sank into the ground. She felt as though the sand below her feet was sucked into her body, swirled in the pit of her stomach, blasted against the walls of her heart, then gently poured out from her pores, dribbled out of her fingertips. She soared into the sky like a bird. She shut her eyes. When she opened them she could faintly see the rainbow's seven-coloured arms hugging the clouds. Then the colours mixed violently and spread, swirled in an intense primitive and flawless rhythm as they were sucked into the sky.

More than discomfited with the intensity of her thoughts, Mallika walked out of the water and ran past the palm trees, across parcelled fields and, like an errant girl, parted the wet paddy leaves thisway-thatway before she swishawayed to the road beyond.

The rain came swishingly now. So did her tears.

It rained heavily all of the next day and Mallika stayed at home. When she sang for her father that evening her eyes were melancholic. Because it worried him to see his daughter like this, withdrawn and seeped in misery, Vishnu confided in Munniamma.

'Her heart is not in her music. She looks so sad.'

'She must be thinking of her mother,' Munniamma replied.

The next day Vishnu saw Mallika sitting under a tree looking up at the sky. Curious, he looked up. There were no fruits, no birds, no clouds, no airplane. Not even stars; it was too early for them to come out.

He spoke to Munniamma once again. 'I don't know what is wrong with her. She sat for hours looking up at the sky. She looked so sad.'

'I wish she would cry,' Munniamma said. 'Girls should cry. Sadness is like a bad cold; it congests the chest. And then it will go and occupy her head and that will make her mad. She must get the sadness off her chest before it goes to her head. She is of that age, after all, when every girl needs a mother,' she hesitated, 'or a man.'

'A man?' Vishnu was startled.

'Yes-yes, a man,' Munniamma said. 'She will finish school next year. How long will she live in this house with you. You must find a man for her to marry.'

Vishnu walked away, his eyes sad.

Mallika was surprised to see Nayantara and Siddhartha at her door the next afternoon. They forced Mallika to go with them for ice cream.

The ice cream parlour was not far from Ranga's flower shop. The old tables and benches outside it were painted in bright green-and-red watermelon stripes. The sign on the shop read:

Pinto's
Juice / Ice Cream Centre

And below, underlined:

No Water Pure Juice Only and No Ice Pure Ice Cream Only.

Siddhartha bought ice cream cones and they stood under a tree and licked the ice cream. Mallika couldn't have hers fast enough and the cream trickled down her arm. Siddhartha laughed as she licked her arm clean.

They went into Sunrise Studio next door. Siddhartha asked Bala to take a photograph of them. Bala showed them the three backdrops that he had. Plain black, for passport, he said. Another was of a blue Eiffel Tower in stormy Indian weather. The third one was with a tree with Japanese cherry blossoms and a full moon.

'This one,' Bala declared, 'is for lovers.'

Bala had special clothes that they could wear to pose for the photograph. Nayantara selected a red shirt and a cowboy hat. Mallika, a flamenco skirt and blouse. Bala handed them a comb and a box of talcum powder. Siddhartha patted the girls' faces with the powder and ran the comb through their hair. He twirled a lock of Mallika's hair and gently pressed it behind her ear. Then he stood between the girls, his arms around their shoulders, in front of the pink blossoms and the full moon. Two copies. One for Nayantara and one for Mallika.

Later that evening, when she got home, Mallika hummed a tune as she studied her face in the mirror. She patted her face with talcum powder. She mixed red pottu with cream, then applied it on her cheeks, rubbing it into her skin. She mixed more red powder into the cream and applied it to her lips. With a brush she drew thick lines of kohl around her eyes. She wrapped her mother's sari around her and pulling the palav over her head, she sang.

Mallika caressed her face, her arms, held herself, kissed her shoulders, left, then right, rubbed her breasts, stroked her ribs, and her hand moved over her flat navel, then into her panties. She breathed hard, then sighed. She felt giddy. Leaning towards the mirror, she kissed her lips in the reflection. Luminous colours seemed to swirl in front of her eyes and deep inside her body she felt the pangs of self-love.

A few days later Siddhartha and Nayantara were at the Maginapudi Beach some 10km from Machilipatnam. Siddhartha, his body covered only by a pair of trunks, came to Nayantara where she sat in the shade of a fisherman's boat. He shook the water from his hair. Seawater dripped off his body. He smelled of salt and fish. His smile showed off his white teeth. With a compelling look in his eyes, he held Nayantara's hand and ran to a grove of palm trees in a hurry, urgently as though the trees were waiting for them, she was waiting for him and he couldn't hold back.

Under a bent coconut palm his brown body leant over her, pushing her against the curve, pressed between the tree-curve and his body-curve, wet, tasting of the sea, smelling of saltyfish, he flung one leg around the tree pinning her against it, then squeezed her breasts with his hands. With an urgent tug he pulled several branches of the coconut tree, laid them on the ground, then laid Nayantara over them, and kissed her with urgency.

'Let's get married,' Siddhartha mumbled into her mouth.

Siddhartha and Nayantara were married in the Shiva Temple five months later. They were leaving for Madras in a week. On her last evening in Machilipatnam Nayantara met Mallika on the beach. Mallika wept like a child.

'Don't forget our pact,' Nayantara said, 'when I have a daughter I will name her Malli.'

A colossal sigh escaped Mallika's throat; a feeling similar to thawing spread slowly through her. She laughed through her tears.

'And I will call mine Tara.'

On a mad impulse Nayantara spun around, then ushered by the breeze, moistened by the seaspray, laughing, she ran towards the sea.

She raised her arms to the sky. It was a gesture in the face of fate. Joy lit her eyes. She bent down, scooped the water in both her hands, filled her mouth with the brine. Mallika did the same and like two wayward children, hand in hand, they spat at the setting sun.

Book Two

Six

It was when the heat was oppressive and sweat clung to the body like a second skin, that an old Ambassador drove into Machilipatnam. In it was P.S. Raman Iyer. Seated next to him was Ammamai, his widowed mother.

Raman Iyer held a Masters in Biological Sciences from the University of Sussex. He was part of a research team known as the Mosquito Behaviour Unit, which was responsible for extensive studies on the mosquito's behaviour.

Some years after his return from England, Raman was appointed the deputy director of the Malaria Research Centre in Madras. Here he experimented on a new anti-malaria technique using genetically altered mosquitoes. By using a micro-manipulator, he attempted to inject new genes into mosquito embryos. He hoped to create new strains of mosquitoes capable of delivering anti-malaria vaccines instead of infecting people with the fearsome disease.

The Indian government, in support of his research, repaired and revived the old Elizabeth Gibbs Institute, which had been inoperative for many years. It appointed Raman as its director and relocated him to Machilipatnam.

Raman was excited about his new posting. Machilipatnam was known for its vigorous mosquitoes and he could make good progress with his research.

Raman's mother accompanied him with a stainless-steel tiffin-carrier, a small khaki-covered suitcase, an old English holdall, a lantern, and an old mosquito net that had been darned in a number of places. These five items represented the essentials of her life of forty-six years: food, clothes, sleep, light and good health.

The Ambassador car drove towards a pair of rickety old gates. Embossed on a square of wood nailed to the gatepost was the name: Victorian Villa.

Ammamai looked up at the house in disbelief. It was haggard and there were holes in the roof and missing windowpanes. The windows were covered only by thin bamboo screens that let the wind blow through, orchestrating its lonely and empty state.

'Ye da, is this where we are going to live? In this dump?' Ammamai asked her son. 'It looks like a haunted house.'

'Don't be silly, ma,' Raman retorted. 'It just needs a few repairs and then it will be fine.'

'Yes-yes, everything with you is fine-fine all the time,' Ammamai snapped back. 'And I am not silly okay. You are the one who is stupid to take this job.'

However, over the next few weeks Ammamai got busy around the house. She fixed two layers of curtains on each of the windows, the shorter inner one fixed by a spring that went drrriiiiiing when stretched. She hung khus mats in the old veranda, and on the floor a pai woven with thin silky reeds.

She converted the small room next to the kitchen into a prayer room. She set her gods out: a plaster-of-Paris idol of Rama and thumb-sized idols in silver and brass of various other gods and goddesses. Beside them she set a lamp, a bowl for flowers, a jar of holy ash, a packet of incense, and a brass pot the size of a fist filled with rice grains, into which she would insert the joss sticks to be burnt morning and evening.

Ammamai was short. She was stumpy, but not fat. She was solid with hard work and childbearing, although only one of her children had survived; three others had died in different positions in her womb. Her umbilical cord was a loop of tragedy, she joked. It coiled itself around a baby-arm, baby-leg, baby-neck and coaxed the life out of them.

Ammamai was always dressed in nine yards of cotton, the colour of an aged deer's skin, which she wrapped around her body and twisted between her legs. Somewhat like frilled trousers, her sari reached her ankles and her bare feet moved quickly and deftly through each day. She wore no blouse because she was a widow and for the same reason her head was tonsured. So she pulled the sari tightly over her bosom and her head. Still one could decipher the shape of her enormous breasts, each of which she confessed, rather comically, she had to swing over both her shoulders to scrub clean the skin under them.

Ammamai was in the garden watering the plants. Raman had just left for the institute. The gates rattled.

'Amma, Amma,' a high-pitched voice rang out.

Ammamai turned around to see a tall manly woman in a bright-yellow sari. She had flowers in her hair.

Ammamai slapped her head with her hands. 'Work, work all day long and this is all I need to add to my chores, a eunuch at my gate,' she said aloud.

'May the good lord bless the house and your family,' Kamala shouted, 'and may you be blessed with many grandsons.'

Ammamai slapped her head once more. 'And who is going to produce these grandsons eh? You?'

Kamala laughed. 'May you find a good wife for your son,' she said clapping her hands.

'That's better. You should put some logic in your blessings. You wait there.'

'I will not move an inch until you give me fifty-one rupees.'

'Fifty-one rupees? You think my son is working hard so I can pay you fifty-one rupees?'

'May God bless your son with a lot of wealth,' Kamala said. 'Fifty-one rupees is the rate ma, for house-blessing.'

Ammamai made a face at her and disappeared into the house. She returned shortly with an old fifty-rupee note and a shining new one-rupee coin. She walked over to the gate and gave them to Kamala through the bars.

'They do, do they? Then go to them and collect your rice.' Ammamai clapped her hands dismissing Kamala. 'Go on, go. I am not giving you anything more.'

Kamala looked at her gold-rimmed men's wristwatch and then with a swirl of her head she walked away.

Ammamai opened the gate a little and sat down on the bench by the pond to wait for Thambi. He was the local barber and every Tuesday he came to shave the stubble from Ammamai's head.

He arrived shortly with his tools and began his task. Ammamai shut her eyes as Thambi touched the blade to her scalp.

'Not that I have any reason to complain, Amma, but tell me what do you eat that your hair grows so quickly?' Thambi giggled. 'I will give you a free head shave if you tell me your secret. Then I can tell my customers at the shop and make more money.'

'Thambi, you idiot! What are you giggling like a donkey for? Have you opened a barber shop to get rid of hair or grow it?' Ammamai laughed, amused at her own wit.

Ammamai had spread the word that she was looking for a cook. A week later, a short young man stood at the gates of the house. Ammamai saw him from the kitchen window as he leant on one hip against the gate, scrutinizing the property. One arm was flung carelessly behind his head.

Ammamai walked to the gates. 'Eh, who do you think you are? A film star?'

He laughed and displayed his teeth; they were white and even. 'My name is Mani. I was a cook in the Indian army. I know English cooking very well.'

Ammamai grinned. 'There is no army here. Just two of us,' she said. 'English cooking? Look at me. Do I look like some pale English woman to you? Who sent you?'

'My uncle, Ranga. He has a shop near the temple. He sells flowers.'

Ammamai remembered him. Only a few days ago she had bought flowers from him on her way to the temple. She had in fact asked him to find her a cook.

'So you are Ranga's nephew then.' Ammamai looked at Mani with evident distrust.

'You can ask him, ma. I am his nephew.'

'Okay, okay. If I find out you are lying I will break your legs. You get all your things tomorrow. You will stay in the room behind the kitchen. I don't want a part-time cook.'

'Okay, ma,' Mani said, and with a wave of his hand he walked away.

As soon as he was out of her sight Ammamai hurried to the market. She walked down Gibbs Road to Ranga's Roses.

Ranga, a short and plump man, was plucking thorns from the rose stems. He looked up from his task and beamed at Ammamai.

'Ye da Ranga, do you have a nephew called Mani,' Ammamai asked.

'Yes, ma. He came to see you?'

'He did. I have asked him to come tomorrow.'

'Don't worry, ma. He is a good cook.'

'That we will see. Ye da, do you know anyone who will clean the house?'

A woman standing nearby leant over to Ammamai.

'You have just moved into that Victorian Villa, no?'

Ammamai turned to her, her hands on her hips. 'And who are you?'

'Munniamma. I work at Vishnu-aiyah's house, down this road. I don't mind working for you, Amma.'

'A-ha-ha. You are a maharani or what eh? Why should you mind working for me? It's not as though you are going to work for free, is it?'

'It's not like that, Amma. I am saying this only because nobody will be willing to work in that house.'

'Not work in that house? Why? It eats people up or what?'

'Have you not heard? That house is haunted by the ghost of that English woman.'

'What English woman?'

'Eliss-bet. Sister of Geogee Gib.'

'What sister? What Gib?'

'It's all nonsense, ma,' Ranga said. 'Don't listen to the rumours.'

Ammamai scowled. 'Ye da Ranga, do you know this woman?'

'Very well, ma. Vishnu-aiyah leaves the entire house in her care. And she ...'

'Enough-enough. I don't need to hear about all her virtues.' Ammamai turned to Munniamma, 'Start tomorrow. 8 sharp. No in-between in-between stuff! You come here first and then go to that Vishnu fellow's house. And I will not tolerate late-coming or bad work. And if I catch you stealing even a pin I will break both your legs.'

'Chi-chi-chi, what you are saying, Amma. Not a grain of rice have I stolen in my life!'

'We will see about that,' Ammamai grimaced and turned away.

Mani arrived next morning with a tattered suitcase. He called out to Ammamai from the gates. She let him in.

'Is this the time to come? Aiyah has already left for work. Go to the kitchen and start cooking lunch.'

While Mani was busy in the kitchen, still anxious over what Munniamma had told her about the English ghost, Ammamai surveyed the entire house, peering behind doors, peeping into corners, cupboards, cobwebs, all the time chanting the thousand names of her God. Then she took her God for a stroll in the garden. She inspected every tree, plant, stone and hole. She came to the pond in front of the house, spread out like a crumpled sheet without a ripple disturbing its surface. She peered into the water. The light through the trees provided an eerie deceit. She didn't trust the pond, she decided.

She went into the kitchen. Mani was steaming rice. He was dressed in a lungi and his chest was bare. Ammamai stared at the blue-black tattoo of a heart on his arm.

'What happened to your shirt eh?'

'It's so hot, Amma.'

'You can roast to death in the heat. But what I don't want is that your sweat and hair should fall into my food. Go, wear a shirt and then get me a plate of steamed rice.'

'A plate of rice?'

'Yes, you idiot. I want to feed the crows. Crows are the spirits of the ancestors and feeding them brings good fortune and peace to the family. Don't you even know this, you fool.'

Mani disappeared into the room at the back and put on his shirt. He returned to the kitchen and heaped steamed rice on a plate and held it out to Ammamai.

She stepped out of the kitchen with the plate of rice, rolled the rice into balls and placed them in a row on the compound wall. She called out to the crows. 'Ka-ka-ka.' Ammamai looked up at a large black crow with a cut near its left eye.

'Oh. It's you. Don't worry now. Your son is doing well. He has become the director of the Elizabeth Gibbs Institute here. You would have been proud, had you been alive. Now don't worry about me. Your son is looking after me well. When he is not running after those mosquitoes that is.'

She then hurried back into the kitchen and returned to present the waiting crow with another ball of rice. 'Here, eat this one. I have mixed it with fresh home-made butter that I churned only this morning.'

The crow flew over the palm trees. 'Ka-ka-ka,' Ammamai shouted to it as she walked to the back of the trees, the ball of rice held high in her hand. There, hidden by Lantana bushes she saw a tomb. The grave, built of laterite stone, had crumbled and grass grew out of its pores. The withered headstone spelled out a name: Elizabeth Gibbs, and a part of the date of her death. Ammamai dropped the rice ball and covered her mouth with her hands.

'Ma, Amma,' Munniamma shouted from the gates. 'Amma, ma.'

'Okay-okay, I am coming. I am not deaf. I have a pair of ears not buttons.' Ammamai rushed to the gates and let Munniamma in.

'Is it 8 o'clock on your watch or what,' Ammamai yelled. 'Is this the time to show up?'

'There was some problem in the slum where I live.'

'What problem?'

'The usual, ma. The Muslim-Hindu problem. It never ends. There was a quarrel at the municipal water-tap and ...'

'Enough-enough. I don't want to hear about all your problems. I have problems of my own. A big one.'

'What happened, ma?'

'Ye di, that English woman was buried here?'

'Yes, ma. That is why her ghost is here, no? And it's an evil ghost, ma. Every family who lived here, something terrible happened to them. And there was always death. That is why this house was locked for over twenty years.'

Munniamma stepped closer to Ammamai and said in a hushed voice, 'You know what happened to the Kumars who lived here last? Tch-tch, poor Kumar-aiyah, his wife stabbed herself with a kitchen knife. And do you know what happened to the Menons who lived here before the Kumars? And to Venktesh-aiyah? That was horrible. He fell down from the roof.' Munniamma held her face in her hands. 'Yes ma, strange-strange things would happen. The doors would fall off, windowpanes would crack and sometimes things would go missing even.'

Ammamai slapped her head with both her hands and called out to all her gods. 'Yesterday I am sure I had filled the bucket for my bath. But when I went into the bathroom the bucket was empty. And this morning I found my slippers in my bedroom. I always leave them outside the front door. The slippers can't have walked on their own, could they?'

'I am telling you, ma,' Munniamma said with a nod of her head, 'it is all because of the ghost of that Gib woman.'

'I told my son so many times, don't take the job, don't take the job, but he wouldn't listen to me. Now what am I going to do?'

Munniamma stood with her hands on her hips. 'Don't you worry ma, I know someone who can drive her ghost away all the way to England.'

'Then go! Why are you standing here gawking at me like I am the ghost! I have enough on my hands in this big house, and the last thing I need now is some female ghost who babbles in English.'

Munniamma promptly returned half an hour later with an old man wrapped in too much cloth.

'Munniamma, who is this human cocoon?' Ammamai asked.

'He is the Muslim fakir who sits near the mosque.' Munniamma rubbed her hands together. 'He will drive away the evil spirit.'

'Ye di Munniamma, could you only get a half-starved man to do the work? And he is Muslim.'

'With ghosts, religion doesn't matter, Amma,' she whispered. 'And it is an English ghost after all. I can tell you this much, Amma: the spirit will be gone like that,' Munniamma clicked her fingers in the air. 'Githa-amma who lives near Gemini Talkies, her daughter was possessed by a spirit. Chi-chi-chi, absolutely filthy words spewed out of her mouth. Githa-amma tried so many things but nothing worked. But this fakir made her daughter all right. He says he will do it for just 100 rupees.'

'Hundred rupees! To drive away a weak ghost of an English woman who died so many years ago! What does he think money grows on? My head? Not more than twenty-five.'

The fakir raised three fingers and shook them in front of Ammamai's face. 'Thirty rupees. You have to pay first.'

Ammamai pushed his hand away and then wiped her hand on her sari. 'Why should I pay first? How will I know the ghost has gone? I will pay only when I know it is gone.'

The fakir shook his head and started walking away. 'I can't start until you give the money.'

'Come back,' Ammamai grunted. She opened the knot she had tied with the end of her sari. From it she retrieved several notes, counted them and then gave them to the fakir. 'Five I will give later.'

The fakir spread a black cloth on the ground. He arranged coins, stones and bits of wood in a circle, then shut his eyes and made a whining sound. He swayed back and forth and began to mumble. His arms flapped about and spit spewed out of his mouth. His body shook and he began to wail as if in terrible pain.

Ammamai asked, 'Why is this man howling like a mad dog?'

Munniamma raised a finger to her lips. 'Sshh, it is the English ghost tormenting him.'

From his bag the fakir took out a small roll of cloth no bigger than his palm. He wound a piece of twine tightly around it and placed it in the middle of the circle. He thrashed the floor with a broom made of leaves.

The wind became steadily fierce. The fakir shrieked and started to shiver. He stood up and with his arms flailing above his head he circled round and round. He rushed to the pond and just when it seemed to Ammamai that he was about to jump into it, a branch of a palm tree snapped and fell into the water.

The fakir crashed down in a heap on the ground. He foamed at the mouth and his body shook.

'Achicho, he's having fits or what?' Ammamai screamed. 'Munniamma, go get some water. And get my old slippers and leave them next to him and, yes, get the iron key and shove it into his mouth. What are you gawking for eh?'

Munniamma cupped her hands and filled them with water from the pond and sprinkled the water on the fakir's face. She held him by his shoulders and shook him.

'Why are you shaking him like that? He's already shaking.'

The fakir opened his eyes, wiped his mouth with the back of his hand and with the other hand he pointed to the branch fallen in the pond. 'That was the ghost,' he said. 'She's gone.'

Ammamai looked into the pond, at the branch fallen in it. She was not entirely convinced. Although she believed in supernatural matters, logic was stamped in her Tamil brain and it often intercepted her blind faith.

Yet it appeared that the spirit had entered the fakir, then flown to the tree, slid down its branch and dropped into the pond.

So the spirit was still in the pond. Floating. It was an English spirit after all and it could certainly swim.

'Rubbish,' Ammamai snorted out the word at the fakir, 'the ghost is still here. I am not going to give you the balance five rupees.'

Through the night Ammamai was certain she heard a wheezing sound.

'It must be the ghost, I am certain of it,' she told Munniamma the next morning. 'I think the ghost was resting all this time and that Muslim fakir of yours only managed to awaken it.' She grunted. 'I told you didn't I, these Muslims can't do anything right.'

Munniamma slapped her thigh. 'Don't worry, ma, I will get it out of the water or my name is not Munniamma.'

'Po di! If your name should change why ever should that matter to me eh?'

Munniamma ignored that remark. But Mani who had stepped up to them with a plate of boiled rice roared with mirth.

Munniamma made a broom of neem branches, thrashed it around the pond and generally brandished it about in the air. She cut a ripe lemon with a knife, then with her back to the pond she threw the lemon halves over her head into the water. 'Now Amma, no evil spirit is going to harm this house.' She rubbed her hands together. 'Lemons have magical powers. They can keep away evil.'

'You should get a dog, ma,' Mani said. 'They can actually see spirits and they bark so loud that the spirits are afraid and they stay away. Yusuf has a pet store in the market. But he is a cheat, Ranga uncle says.'

'Why get a dog from Yusuf eh?' Ammamai asked. 'So many of them running about in the streets. Go look for one and bring it here and feed it for a few days, then it will remain faithful and guard the house and keep the ghost away. Go now.'

Half an hour later, Mani returned holding a rope tied to the neck of a mangy white dog.

Ammamai inspected the dog, walking around it. She slapped her forehead. 'Aiyooo Rama. Why is it so thin and white? Those English people left behind their dogs or what? Chi-chi, God only knows what illness it has. Feed it outside the gate. So it will stay there, under that tree.

'What to call it?' Mani asked.

Ammamai thought for a bit. 'A nice English name. A name of a king perhaps. Or a hero. Yes, I know. We will call it Churchill.'

Mani patted the dog's head. He pulled the dog by the rope, calling out,'Cha-chi, Cha-chi.' He tied it to the tree.

Ammamai was still not convinced the dog would do the trick. She decided to send for the local astrologer.

Perumal Swamy was tall and extremely lean. His chest had caved in. His cheeks were twin moon-crescents. His mouth was more like a snout and his teeth stuck out like a horse's.

Ammamai and Perumal sat on the pai in the veranda. Perumal studied Raman's horoscope that Ammamai had given him. His nose twitched now and again as he referred to his charts and notes to check the position of planets, the celestial houses they occupied and their transition between houses.

'Scorpio is the ascendant,' Perumal declared, 'the Sun is in Pisces and Saturn is in Gemini.' He looked at Raman's horoscope again. 'Saturn will cause a lot of damage when it transits from the house of Gemini.'

Perumal looked up at Ammamai with weary eyes. 'You must perform a ritual prayer to ward off the evils of Saturn, ma.'

'Then fix an auspicious date and get me a pujari to perform it.' Ammamai said.

The pujari arrived a few days later. He sat in the veranda, lit a fire in a square, tin box that he had purified by water and sanctified with turmeric and kumkum. Smoke rose into the air as he chanted. Ammamai closed her eyes and prayed to the gods and her ancestors to keep them safe.

Crows circled above the trees. Ammamai opened one eye and looked for the crow with the cut under its eye. It wasn't there. She sighed and closed her eye and prayed to the spirit of her husband to look after her and, more specifically, their son Raman.

Raman was lean, tall and dark-skinned, and wore gold-rimmed glasses. Hair sprouted out of his ears. His white teeth were crooked and when he concentrated on something he ground them.

He did this now, as he stood in front of the bathroom and toilet at the back of the house, detached from it.

Ammamai shouted out to him from the kitchen window. 'Go have your bath, da. Breakfast will be ready soon.'

When Raman was seated at the dining table, he announced, 'I am going to convert the storeroom next to my room upstairs into a toilet and bathroom.'

'What for?' Ammamai raised an eyebrow.

'The bathroom at the back is not convenient and it is too dark in it.'

'You are some great maharaja or what? The bathroom and toilet is good enough for me. And I don't want all those workers in the house. There's enough work in the house as it is.'

Raman didn't reply. He had made up his mind. He hired a contractor to build the toilet cum bathroom on the first floor. When the work was done, the contactor had the bathroom fitted with a cupboard and a mirror. The commode was pink. Ammamai was wonderstruck when she saw it – gleaming like a pearl with a wide-open mouth.

But next morning, as she was in the prayer room right below the new toilet on the first floor, she heard the flush and gurgle of a giant. She rushed up the stairs and knocked on the bathroom door.

'Raman, come out, this very minute. Whatever you are doing in there, come out now!'

She punched Raman on his chest as he emerged out of the bathroom, a towel around his waist, and shaving cream on his face.

'Aiyoo da, that shit seat is right over the prayer room. You are shitting on top of gods' heads.'

Raman tried to explain to her about modern plumbing and how the gods were safe from its exigencies, but Ammamai slapped her cheeks and wept.

'Aiyoo Shiva-Shiva ... No one will use this as long as I am alive,' she declared. 'Upon my dead body will anyone use this dirty seat. Otherwise I will pack all my gods and leave this wretched house where gods can't even reside in peace without worrying what is happening over their heads.'

'You are so silly, ma,' Raman said. 'You don't have to worry about the gods. They can look after themselves.'

He walked into the bathroom and locked the door.

The evening air was hot and moist. Ammamai stepped out of the front door looking for Raman.

Raman was in the garden bending over the pond collecting a sample of its water in a dish. It was full of larvae.

'It's so hot,' Ammamai said wiping the sweat on her neck with the end of her sari. 'And so much work all day long. It's tiring me out. Now if I had a daughter-in-law she could be of some use and relieve me of this responsibility. When do you think you are going to get married, eh?'

Raman didn't reply. Ammamai slapped her arm and brushed off a dead mosquito. 'All you are interested in are these blood-sucking mosquitoes. Do you know what is happening in the house even? You are away all the time and that Mani is hopeless. Do you know he eats all our rice and takes away all the papayas from the tree? Then tells me that it is a male tree; it doesn't grow fruit.'

A mosquito whined near her ear.

'And what if I die suddenly of malaria, like that English woman? Who will look after the house? Who will look after you? And that Mani will eat all the rice. And all my jewellery I haven't worn for years? Who will look after that? As it is I have to check the lock on my trunk every morning and evening. And next year you will be twenty-six and which father do you think will agree to give his daughter to you?'

Raman shook his hand firmly in front of her face. 'Look at this place swarming with mosquitoes. Twenty-five years since our independence and look at the state of our mosquito-ridden country.'

'Why? This country has only you to fight mosquitoes or what? You don't have to take full responsibility on your head. And what about me? Do you have no responsibility towards me? If only your father had been alive. Seeing me in this wretched state he would have promptly died.'

Raman looked at her. 'Oh stop all this,' he snapped. 'Let me be. I have a lot to do. The last thing I need now is a wife.'

When Raman returned from a trip to London two weeks later he brought with him a vacuum cleaner. 'This is for you, ma,' he said and showed her the way to work it. 'This will help you keep the house clean.'

Ammamai suspiciously looked at the gleaming red thing with a long elephant's trunk. She slapped her forehead. 'I asked you to get a wife and you get me this! Aiyoo kadvale.'

She wrapped the machine in an old silk sari and left it in the storeroom. On occasion, she would use it, the button in normal position, to vacuum the prayer room so her gods remained tidy. And she learned to use it, in the reverse position, to blow the husk of new rice. As she blew and blew the husk away, she kept at her refrain whenever Raman was within earshot.

'And what if I die suddenly? Who will look after the house? And the servants will eat all the rice. And my jewellery? Who will look after that?'

She would pause, then drive home the punch: 'Look at your hair; it has already started greying. Soon you will go bald even. You are getting old, Raman, very, very old.'

Outside the gate Churchill barked into the night.

Seven

Ammamai had procured from Perumal Swamy a list of suitable girls in town and every other evening with a plate of sweets and flowers she visited the girls' parents to check them out. She attended, without fail, dance and music concerts, went to women's haldi-kumkum gatherings and prayer meets.

Through the weeks, Ammamai told Raman about her joint pains; also about all the girls she had seen for him: a too-dark one, a too-fat one, a too-poor one, a too-thin one; either a friend's uncle's daughter or an uncle's friend's daughter …

'And don't you go about fixing any matrimonial matches for me,' Raman warned Ammamai one evening as she got ready for one of her rounds. 'I am telling you, I will not get married.'

'About that we will see,' Ammamai retorted with an equally fierce look and walked out of the door.

As soon as word got around that Ammamai was looking for a bride for her only son, she was invited by mothers and fathers to look at their girls. These young girls had been carefully tutored. After all Raman, though a bit old, was an eligible bachelor. He was a Brahmin, the head of a government institute, and lived in a big house – he was a good catch. The girls' mothers were eager about the match. So the girls, following their mothers' instructions, knew the precise moment to raise their eyes from Ammamai's feet, the exact minute to smother a smile and when to nod, and when to dance and break into a God-loving song.

One afternoon when Ammamai was out on her mission with Perumal, he stopped to post a letter. He noticed an old election campaign poster stuck on the red letter box. It had endured for over a decade, because the glue was strong. The party had lost and the ex-corporator had resigned. Still his features remained pasted to the letter box.

'How silly of me,' Perumal said pointing to the face. 'I know him well. His youngest daughter is unmarried.'

'You mean you have run out of girls for me to see? You want me to meet people whose faces are glued to a postbox!' Ammamai looked at the poster. 'He's not blind, is he?' She pointed to his gouged-out eye.

'Of course not. And his daughter is fair as milk and highly educated. Double graduate and all that.'

Ammamai told Raman that evening, 'She is beautiful. And fair as cow's milk. Graduate twice. And a Brahmin. What more can we ask. Not often can we get an opportunity like this one. I am meeting them tomorrow.'

Ammamai went with Perumal to meet the ex-corporator's daughter. The young girl was dressed in white and gold, jasmine flowers in her long hair. She stood with a tray of silver tumblers.

'Take, ma,' the girl's mother said as the girl stood before Ammamai, 'she has made the coffee with her own hands.'

The young girl was very tall, taller than Raman. This wouldn't do. Men didn't like their women to be taller than them, Ammamai thought as she raised the tumbler over her lips, swirled the coffee around in her mouth and swallowed it. She frowned.

The girl's mother cast a worried look. 'Ye ma, not good?'

Ammamai set the tumbler on the table. Then looking up at the girl, said, 'Too much milk. And too sweet.'

Ammamai stared at the girl. Her spectacles were thick and behind them her eyes appeared small and worn out. What was worse, now and then she appeared to Ammamai to be cock-eyed.

'She is double MA. English and Philosophy,' the mother said following Ammamai's gaze. 'Now she's doing Ph.D. Reading-reading all the time. Even her eyes got spoiled. That is why the spectacles. And reading two books side by side at the same time has ... well never mind that, what can we do? What's done is done. But the good news is that she has got a letter from the government for a post she had applied for.' She looked at her daughter with pride.

Even more learned than Raman, Ammamai thought. Aichicho, this won't do. This won't do at all. No man likes a woman who is cleverer than him. And joining the government, no-no, too pushy.

'She sings very well. Sing, ma,' the girl's mother said.

'Don't trouble her,' Ammamai said hastily. 'It's very old-fashioned to make an educated girl sing and dance. One day she will become an important officer in the government. Good luck to her.'

'Oh thanks.' The girl's mother beamed as she placed a plate of coconut barfi on the table in front of Ammamai. 'Please take.'

Ammamai leant forward and picked up a square of coconut barfi. She chucked it into one side of her mouth and as she chewed the sweet she wiped her brow. She told the girl's mother firmly, 'She is too tall for my Raman, ma. Also, I am looking for a younger girl. And not so educated. Just school-pass will do. And unemployed is better even. Women should look after the house and family; why they should look after the country eh? There are so many men to do this.'

Her voice mocking, Ammamai said to Raman that night, 'Sha! She's too tall and too clever for you, and so ambitious. Wanting to work for the government and all that, can you believe? As it is you are hardly at home and what am I going to do with an absentee daughter-in-law as well eh? I will not only have to look after the house single-handed but look after the two of you too. And what if you have children henh? Who will look after them? And even if this is what is written in my fate and I have to stand upside down to rewrite it, I will.'

Soon after that might Ammamai accosted Raman angrily. 'I told you so many times, Raman. Get married, get married. But no, you had time only for your wretched mosquitoes.' She slapped her arm. 'And mind you, it is our blood, our blood that they suck, sha! I should not have listened to one word from you and should have started looking long ago for a bride. Tch-tch. It is your fate. Don't blame me now if you get an old and ugly cock-eyed thing who can't make coffee even.'

She held her head in her hands. 'Think, what will you do after I am dead? Henh? Who will look after you and your house?'

Raman considered her words seriously for the first time. He knew Mani was dumb and impossible to train and Munniamma annoyed him too much. He wondered whether he should get married. Then hastily decided against it.

Prayers were her only resort Ammamai decided, and the minute Raman left for work she rushed to the temple. She took Munniamma with her to carry the purchases from the market.

A chaos of smells filled the air: coffee, curry powder, pickle, sour rice batter, tender shallots roasting in ghee, ripe bananas, jackfruit, and the scents of jasmine, kadamba and roses. It was a mixed-up smell that lingered from the beginning of the market street to its end, and beyond, where the sea claimed its territory.

In the market, old south Indian greengrocers had laid out on the road the countrified vegetables – the snaking gourds, the rolling pumpkins and pimply yams – dull, their dyes derived from dried earth. Amidst them, the younger north Indians had arranged in baskets purple aubergines, red tomatoes, green peppers, each rubbed with oil to make them shine.

The southern fruitsellers had put out a conglomeration of bananas. Beside them, those from the north sold apples, pears and grapes.

'Tch-tch, these south Indian fruitsellers only sell bananas,' Munniamma remarked with a pout.

'Then what?' Ammamai enquired with a raised fist. 'Ye di, you think any nice south Indian will sell apples?'

Old women in nine-yard silk coiled between their legs, and younger women in bright nylex saris, ambled through the market, faces talcumed, half-moons of sweat at the armpits. They bought flowers for their hair and for the gods. They huddled towards the Shiva temple, glowing with the same flamboyant colours as the aubergines, tomatoes, peppers.

Smells of shambrani and incense rose from a window across the way. Its shutters were painted green. Behind the window a young girl combed her long hair. She plucked the hair from the comb, balled it and threw it out of the window.

Screwing up her eyes Ammamai followed the hairball as it floated in the air, whirled, down, down, got caught on a branch of a tree, slipped, fell on a lamp post, slipped, and then rolled down the pavement like a coiled insect. Ammamai heard a girl singing.

'Ye di Munniamma, who is that singing like a koyal?' she asked.

'That's our Mallika. Vishnu-aiyah's daughter.' Munniamma pointed to the house.

'I told you, didn't I, that I work there?' She frowned and slapped her head. 'Her father, poor man, he lost his wife. He should get Mallika married. I have said this to him so many times. Not nice, you know, to have an unmarried daughter living alone with her father. People talk. They talk and talk. I told him to get her married soon. Every day I tell him.'

'What does this Vishnu do?' Ammamai asked.

'He is a musician. He and his wife used to have many radio programmes. But he stopped all that when his wife died.'

Ammamai had a gleam in her eye. 'How old is his daughter?'

'Nineteen. '

Ammamai frowned. 'Much too young for Raman.'

Munniamma's eye glinted. 'She is beautiful, ma. You should look at her. Come with me, I will take you to Vishnu-aiyah.'

'No need.' Ammamai undid the knot at the end of her saree and gave Munniamma some notes she had secured in its fold.

'You go buy a head of cabbage and a snake gourd,' Ammamai said. 'And don't forget to get ginger, chillies and curry leaves. And get some ration rice for that Churchill. Such a thin dog but how much he eats.'

After Munniamma had left her side, Ammamai crossed the street to Mallika's house. She knocked on the door.

A young girl now stood before her. Her skin was the colour of moist cashew, her eyes the lustrous purple of an aubergine.

Her hair, soft like fleece of corn, fell to below her knees. She smelled of jasmine.

'Who is that?' an abrasive voice of a man called out. Ammamai could see him sitting near the window, dressed in a white shirt over a veshti. She walked over to him.

'My son and I live down the road, in Victorian Villa. I was in the market; I heard your daughter sing. She sings so well.'

Vishnu tied his hair into a ponytail and secured it with a rubberband. 'Just like her mother.'

Ammamai turned to Mallika who stood behind them. 'Please sing, ma.'

'Sing Mallika,' Vishnu prodded.

Mallika sat cross-legged on a mat on the floor. She patted her thigh with her hand, then with her face raised to the air, in a voice that rang through space and walls, she sang. Her eyes were shut and, in the morning light, her face was laced with rose and gold. With her other hand she caressed the air, fondling it, curling it up and up and out of the windowpane.

Ammamai was under a spell, touched by an unknown bliss. Mallika's song followed her all the way back to the house.

When Raman sat down to dinner he was surprised to hear his mother humming.

'You seem very happy tonight,' he said.

Ammamai sat in the chair next to him, and leaned forward.

'I have found her, Raman. Can you believe it? She was right under my nose all along.'

'Under your nose? Where?' Raman bent his head and looked up at Ammamai. He laughed.

Ammamai ignored him. 'She sings. Aiyooo, how she sings, pure 24-carat gold drips out of her mouth. And Raman, you will drown in her eyes. My God what heavenly eyes!'

'But I don't like drowning, ma,' Raman teased. He couldn't help smiling.

'Now don't refuse. You will never get a girl so young, so beautiful. And her mother was a good singer too.' Ammamai clasped her hands. 'Gods heard my prayers after all.'

'I am sure they did. But I am not getting married even for gods' sake.'

'Then do so for my sake. Now fulfil an old woman's wish or I will not eat a single morsel after this moment, and I will surely die.'

Raman threw back his head and laughed.

'People who talk of killing themselves often call a doctor if they cut their finger,' he said. 'Now don't be foolish. I am not getting married. There are around 300 million cases of malaria in our country and about 3 million die every year. I have a lot to do.'

'Do it then. It's your life, why should I care,' Ammamai said with a grimace.

Churchill howled.

'See, even the dog is howling at your fate,' she said and got up from the table.

The next day, Vishnu told Munniamma about Ammamai's visit to the house.

Munniamma's eyes glinted. 'Now why didn't I think of this before,' she said. 'You must go and talk to her.'

'About what?'

'About Mallika. Don't you see, her son is the perfect man for our Mallika.' Munniamma clasped her hands to her chest. 'You must not waste any time. Eligible men are like ripe fruits. You must pluck them or others will. Go talk to her today.'

Vishnu considered what she had said. 'I don't know about this. What will I say to her?'

Munniamma smiled. 'You don't worry; I have another idea. There's no time to lose. I must go now.'

She rushed to Saroja's house and told her what had happened. 'You go ma, and meet the mosquito scientist's mother and talk to her about Mallika. After all Mallika is like your own daughter. It's pure destiny, ma. That's the real reason the Iyers came to Machilipatnam. I am sure of this.'

'Shouldn't Vishnu go?'

'Sha! These men know nothing about such matters, ma. You go. Mallika is lucky to get a man like Raman.'

'How old is he?' Saroja asked.

'He looks about thirty.'

'Mallika is eleven years younger. He's too old.'

'How does young or old matter ma, as long as the man is good? Mallika has become so thin. So alone she is after Nayantara left, ma.'

'Yes, but perhaps she will find someone younger.'

'Nice young men drop from the skies or what? Her father will die soon and Mallika will be totally alone. Then what? I am telling you ma, it is all destiny.'

Saroja didn't believe in destiny or fate. She was far too pragmatic for such matters. But ever since Nayantara went away, it was true that Mallika had become a recluse. She stayed at home practising music and song. Whenever she visited the poor girl, she seemed distant and lost.

The next day Saroja carried a silver plate with a coconut, betel leaf, bananas and flowers, and went to see Ammamai at Victorian Villa.

Munniamma was at the gates when Saroja arrived. She took Saroja to Ammamai who was reclining on the pai in the veranda.

'This is Saroja-ma. She runs the dye factory,' Munniamma said.

Ammamai took the plate Saroja held out and turning around she gave it to Mani who stood by the front door.

'What are you posing like some actor for eh? Go get us coffee,' Ammamai barked at him. 'And Munniamma don't you have work to do? Go on, don't waste time.' Then turning to Saroja, 'Come ma, sit down,' she said patting the pai.

'You have a daughter?' Ammamai, who had got used to mothers trying to meet her, asked.

'Yes. Nayantara.'

'What does she do?'

'She's in Madras. She's married to a nice doctor.'

'Oh she's married,' Ammamai looked at Saroja, puzzled. 'That's good, very good.'

Mani returned with two tumblers of coffee set in bowls. He offered one to Saroja. Ammamai took the other from him, poured the coffee out into the bowl and back into the tumbler to cool and froth the coffee. She held the tumbler above her mouth and poured a mouthful, then swirled it around. She made a face.

Mani cast a worried look as Ammamai set the tumbler on the floor.

'I asked for coffee not milk. When are you ever going to learn, you fool! How many times must I tell you eh? Put milk in the coffee not coffee in milk. Sha!'

Ammamai wiped her forehead with the end of her sari. 'How long can I manage this house on my own? Oh how I wish I had a daughter-in-law to take over from me.'

Saroja who was unused to such delicate matters blurted out, 'Mallika is a lovely girl. She is my daughter's closest friend. You couldn't find a better wife for your son.'

'Don't I know that? But my stubborn son will not listen to my pleas.'

Mani returned with a plate of murukus. Saroja nibbled a twist.

'Nice ma, nice,' she said. 'Did the cook make this?'

'This fellow?' Ammamai looked behind her at Mani. 'He's good for nothing. All he knows is to eat and eat all day long. I made these murukus.'

'Nice,' Saroja said. 'Not enough salt though.'

'Salt is not good for me. I have high-pressure blood. Have to eat less salt. But how to eat less eh? And oh, pickles I like so much. But how long can I keep making murukus and pickles eh?'

The smell of food had brought Churchill to the steps.

'Mani, ye da Mani,' Ammamai screamed.

Mani came running to them.

'Get this dog out of the gate. Didn't you feed him enough?'

Ammamai turned to Saroja. 'Look at my fate, I have to look after the dog even.'

Saroja smiled. 'Don't worry, ma. I will bring Mallika with me this evening. Everything will work out.'

Raman retuned from work to see two women with Ammamai. They were in the veranda.

Ammamai introduced Saroja and Mallika. Just as Raman turned to step into the house, Ammamai whispered to him, 'Raman, talk to them, I will get you coffee.'

When she returned, Raman was talking to Saroja. Mallika sat quietly, her eyes riveted to her toes.

Ammamai frowned as she set the tray on the floor. 'I'll get something to eat.' She signalled Saroja with her eyes.

'Let me help you,' Saroja quickly said, and followed Ammamai indoors.

Raman glanced at Mallika wondering what to say. A mosquito whined near her cheek.

'Hold still,' he said, and held his hand near her face and slapped her cheek.

Mallika let out a yelp and turned her head away.

'This town is full of mosquitoes,' he said.

Mallika twisted the end of her sari. She was indeed beautiful, as Ammamai had said she was.

'Do you know there are about 3,500 species of mosquitoes in the world?' Raman asked.

Silence.

'You sing?' Raman tried again.

'Yes.'

'What sort of music?'

'Carnatic.'

'Oh, I see.' Raman didn't know much about Indian classical music. 'I hear your mother is a good singer.'

This time Mallika looked up at him with her huge fringed eyes. Raman looked into them and felt a strange sensation.

As he started to speak, Mallika stood up abruptly and left the veranda, heading towards the gates.

Ammamai stood at the door with plates of savouries. 'Where is Mallika going?'

Saroja called out to Mallika and rushed after her.

Ammamai sat on the veranda steps, and set the plates beside her. She nibbled at a twist of muruku. 'What did you say to Mallika?'

'Oh nothing,' Raman said, listening to the buzzing of mosquitoes.

Raman slapped his cheek where a mosquito had just bitten him and walked to the bathroom at the back of the house. He washed his hands and face, then straightened and stared at his reflection in the mirror in the faint light. He checked his hair, turning his face from side to side.

Ammamai was right. The hair just above his ears was turning grey. He rubbed it with his fingers as if to bring the colour back and then he inspected the frown lines on his brow. He rubbed his forehead vigorously and then, slowly, the undersides of his eyes, then his neck. With his fingers he touched the top of his head and located the balding patch.

The bathroom mirror always reduced him to flat, magnified dimensions. It was like looking through a close-up camera lens. He bent closer to the mirror and counted the warts that had begun to appear under his eyes and on his neck. His breath left two dewy appliqués on the glass. He breathed hard; the wet appliqués quivered, then dissolved.

Raman was terrified of becoming old.

Within a month, a rather stupefied and smitten Raman succumbed to his mother's pleas and taunts and agreed to marry Mallika.

Ammamai sent for Saroja and told her the good news. Munniamma was ecstatic. Vishnu was both happy and sad. Mallika was despondent.

Next day Vishnu took Mallika to Ranga's Roses and bought flowers, and at Yusuf's shop next door he bought a cage of lovebirds. With Mallika at his side, under the parijat tree on top of the hill where he had buried his wife's ashes, he laid the flowers with a prayer and a song. He then let the birds out of the cage one by one.

'This is where your mother's ashes are buried,' he told Mallika. 'She would have been so happy today.'

The minute Nayantara heard from her mother about her friend's imminent wedding she was delighted. She phoned Mallika from Madras.

'Why didn't you tell me the good news?'

'I don't want to marry him,' was Mallika's sullen reply.

'Don't be silly. You must marry him. I will come down a week before the wedding. Siddhartha is going to America so he can't come. Everything will be all right. I am so happy for you.'

On the morning of the wedding Munniamma fixed strings of flowers across the front door of Mallika's house. She drew a kolam of rice flour on the floor.

Nayantara and Saroja were in Mallika's room. Saroja dressed Mallika in a red saree with gold zari. She slipped gold bangles onto her wrists and clasped a gold choker around her neck. They had belonged to Mallika's mother.

Nayantara coiled endless strings of jasmine in Mallika's hair, and then kissed both her cheeks.

'I don't want to marry him,' Mallika said. Her eyes were dry and vacant.

'He's a nice man, Mallika,' Nayantara cajoled her. 'And so educated.'

Mallika pouted. 'He has crooked teeth and hair grows from his ears.'

'Teeth and hair don't matter,' Munniamma said cracking her knuckles on either side of her head. 'It's the best thing that could have happened. Such a big house, and he will look after you like you were his queen.'

Mallika looked at Nayantara, 'But what about love?'

Munniamma slapped her forehead. 'What love? Eh? What love? Love is nothing but smoke. It rises and you rise with it. And when it falls, you fall with it and break your heart. Then what?'

Vishnu walked in through the door. He couldn't take his eyes off Mallika. 'You look so much like your mother,' he said. 'Sing for me one last time, ma.'

Mallika walked to the window, and with her eyes shut tight to hold back the tears, she sang.

Eight

MOSQUITOES WHINED IN FESTIVE CHORUS around the strings of jasmine flowers that Nayantara had hung from the posts of the bed. Moonlight stroked the strings of the mosquito net and under it Mallika lay curled up like a caterpillar. She thought of her imaginary lover: young, handsome and robust, and winced when Raman touched her arm.

When he tried to turn her towards him she clenched her fists and grit her teeth. He slapped her arm and picked up a dead mosquito. Getting out from under the net, he went to the desk and with cellotape fixed the dead insect on the first page of a notebook.

He wrote the date on it: 27th September 1967. For him it was a date to remember.

Mallika got out of bed and sat by the window. Raman came to her and sat down beside her. He slapped his cheek, plucked the squashed mosquito, put the dying insect on the floor and watched it wiggling its life away.

'Did you know Mallika, it is the female mosquito that bites? The female mosquito pierces the skin of people and animals to suck blood. She can't see, but the temperature of our body produces an infrared picture for her and she is attracted to carbon dioxide.

'The male is a vegetarian, poor fellow; he lives on fruit and flower nectar but the female requires a blood meal to develop her eggs. She is called Anopheles.'

Raman paused and looked at Mallika. 'Now tell me what is she called?'

Mallika turned to look at him. In the light of the moon he didn't seem so dreadful.

'Ano-phi-lees,' Mallika repeated.

'Very good.'

Raman bent forward and kissed her cheek.

After her son left for work, Ammamai sat in the garden on the stone bench near the pond watching Mallika watering the plants. Churchill barked and Ammamai turned around to see Kamala at the gates.

'Mallika, let that woman in, will you,' Ammamai said rubbing her aching knees with her hands.

Mallika looked at Kamala and then nervously at Ammamai.

'Don't be afraid,' Ammamai said. 'Eunuchs are the re-incarnation of Lord Krishna. It's good to get their blessings. It's like getting Lord Krishna's blessings by express telegram. You will get a healthy son.'

Mallika walked to the gate and let Kamala in. Kamala pinched Mallika's chin. She traced her finger around Mallika's face and nodded her head in approval. She scrutinized her breasts, waist and hips. She rounded her hands in front of her own chest.

'They are like mountains,' she laughed and patted Mallika on her shoulder. 'Ah, they will give a lot of pleasure to your son.'

Kamala sauntered towards Ammamai. 'And your grandsons will never want to be pulled away from her breasts. Look at her slender waist; I can grab it in both my hands. And those abundant hips.'

Ammamai laughed. 'They will produce big babies.'

Kamala left after coaxing a hundred rupees from Ammamai.

Ammamai turned to Mallika. 'You must give me a grandson soon, Mallika.' Ammamai cracked her knuckles on either side of her own head.

Mallika blushed and covering her face with her hands she ran into the house.

Nayantara had been unwell for a week; she felt listless and languid. Saroja took her daughter to Dr Kuruvilla who gave her the good news. Her daughter was pregnant.

Nayantara went to Mallika's new home that evening to tell her the news. She let herself in through the gates. Ammamai was sitting on the pai in the veranda.

'Come ma, come.' She turned around and shouted, 'Mallika, ye di Mallika, look your friend is here.' Then turning back she asked, 'When are you returning to Madras?'

'Next week.'

'That's good. Not a good idea to leave your husband alone for too long.'

'He's in America.'

'I see,' Ammamai nodded looking up Nayantara as she stood before her. 'Any good news, ma?'

'Yes. I'm five weeks pregnant.'

'That's wonderful. God bless you with a son.'

Nayantara smiled. 'I want a girl.'

'Don't say that, ma. You must have a son.'

'Where's Mallika?'

'Upstairs. Go up ma, and tell your friend the good news. I hope she will give me a grandson soon.'

Nayantara went up to Mallika's room. Mallika who was sitting by the window reading a book was delighted to see her. She rushed to Nayantara and hugged her.

Nayantara laughed and drew away from Mallika's tight embrace. 'I am pregnant,' she said.

'Pregnant? How? I, I mean when?'

Nayantara laughed. 'I must have conceived some five weeks ago. I called Siddhartha this morning to tell him the news. He's so happy.'

Mallika touched Nayantara's belly. 'I am sure this is Malli.'

Nayantara pinched Mallika's cheek. 'So how was it?'

'What?'

'The amaz-ing zi-nn-ing feeling?'

Mallika looked away.

'Didn't you do it?'

Nayantara held both Mallika's hands in hers. 'Don't be shy of your dear husband. Think of something funny. Like this.' She made faces. She stuck her tongue out and rolled her eyes. She hopped around the room on one leg. Then flapped her arms and pretended to fly.

'Like this?' Mallika stuck her tongue out and rolled her eyes. She hopped around the room on one leg. Then flapped her arms and pretended to fly.

Nayantara hugged her. She patted Mallika's stomach.

'And then you will have Tara.'

A week later Nayantara returned to Madras.

Raman's study was at the back of the house. Its furnishings included a mock Elizabethan chair; a rattan chair that had given way in the centre; a moth-ridden table, its crevices filled with the dirt of years; and an old English safe. The safe contained little money, but in it were bundles of Raman's papers and reports he had recently prepared on the behaviour of a certain species of female mosquitoes.

Attached to the study and connected by a door was a garden full of flowering shrubs enclosed by a steel net and partly covered with dark canvas to keep the interior dim and warm. In large glass trays of slimy water, larvae grew into adult mosquitoes. Families of the Aedes, Culex, Culiseta and Anopheles buzzed, copulated and multiplied.

This was Raman's favourite place. The drone and whine of a thousand mosquitoes thrilled his ears. His absolute power over them energised his mind.

Raman did not need to refer to his numerous books about mosquitoes any more or the encyclopaedic tome on the mating ways of insects. Instead, he poured over a third-hand volume of the *Kama Sutra* that he had managed to procure. He turned the pages to the section that offered practical advice on sexual intercourse. Randy mosquitoes whined around him.

It was past 9. Ammamai was in the kitchen, warming milk. She added a few strands of saffron to it, poured the milk into a tall silver tumbler and took it to Raman in his study.

She set it down on the table in front of him. Raman hurriedly put away the book and covered it with a file.

'Aiyoo kadvale! Mosquitoes, mosquitoes. All year long its only mosquitoes. Can you think of nothing else?' Ammamai said. 'Go up to your wife. You are her husband, remember? Here, drink this saffron milk before you sleep.'

Raman grunted and picked up another file. Ammamai slapped her forehead.

'Have I got to teach you everything? Had only your father been alive today, I would not have to face this pitiable moment.

Tchah-tchah-tchah. Muttal, don't you even know that all childless men are condemned to puthu.'

'What puthu?'

'Puthu. *Puthu*. It's a terrible place. A sort of hell. Worse than these trays of mosquito eggs. And if a woman wastes her eggs then there will be tragedy. There will be natural disasters and disease, more deadly than your malaria and it will affect not just you and her, but everyone. As it is, there are enough problems in this world. You are only adding to them.'

Raman laughed despite himself. 'Eggs? Natural disasters? Disease? Such nonsense.'

'What I am telling you is not nonsense. But why should you listen to me? After all I am only a stupid widow. But tomorrow when you suffer you will remember my words.'

Ammamai held out the silver tumbler. 'Here, go up now. Or when your son is born he will mistake you for his grandfather.'

Raman stroked his hair and his fingers located the bald spot on his head. He took the tumbler from his mother and shaking his head, made his way to the bedroom.

White moonlight hit the glass window, then permeated sheet-like into the room. Two squares of light lay prostrate on the floor. It was an ominous spectacle, as though the floor had a pair of eyes and was witness to everything. The curtains shivered in the breeze that escaped through the gaps in the window. It seemed as if the room was alive and breathing and waiting.

Mallika was asleep. Her sari had moved up over her legs and Raman could see her thighs. Desire surged within him. He drank the tumbler of aphrodisiac saffron milk and stood near the bed looking at her, following the slope of her nose and the curve of her cheek, to two mosquitoes perched on the edge of the pillow.

Rounding his mouth he whistled but she did not awaken and the mosquitoes were far too engrossed in one another to bother. He brought his hand a few inches over them and whacked them hard.

Mallika woke up with the sound. He sat beside her and pulled away the palav of her sari. Mallika's breasts heaved and fell. He stroked the hollow of her neck, her breasts and her waist and gently undressed her.

'Oh, my Mallika, Mallika,' he whispered. She did not resist him. Raman picked up a bottle of scented mosquito repellent oil and with tenderness rubbed it all over her body until she was seal-skinned and her face was oily; the hollows of her neck, her shoulders, arms, breasts and nipples, waist and thighs, legs, feet – oily.

Raman held her carefully lest she slip out of his fingers. He turned her over, stroked her back, almond-toned, fruit-smelling, fruit-tasting, no, more pungent, spice-smelling, spice-tasting, all the way down to her buttocks – such harvest-heaps – and before them a triangular fleshpad bordered by three dimples which he kissed: once, twice, thrice. He turned her over and kissed her lips, crushed cherrypads, once, twice, thrice. The corners of her mouth curved upwards, her aubergine eyes smiled. He kissed them one by one.

Mallika thought of what Nayantara had told her and giggled. When Raman kissed her neck, she giggled. When he sucked her nipples, she giggled. When he thrust his tongue into her bellyhole, licked her feet, the insides of her thigh, when he turned her on her stomach once more, ran his thumb down her spine and licked the trail, she giggled.

He kissed her for a long time and a hundred moons spewed out of their orbits and danced in front of his eyes. And the moons melted their gold and they rained drop by drop and coated his tongue, which seemed to have turned solid and erect and strained achingly inside her mouth. Through her nostrils he could smell the damp breath of pent-up longing. Her laughter violated his heart and it beat wildly, recklessly, then missed a beat – he thrust into her savagely and oh, oh my God, my goodness, oh my ... and then he heard a buzzing sound. He rolled over and slapped his cheek. And asked, 'Did you know that the mosquito goes through four stages of life: egg, larva, pupa and an adult. The larva lives in the water and comes to the surface to breathe. It sheds its skin four times, growing larger each time. The larva changes into a pupa. After two days the pupal skin splits and an adult mosquito emerges. It rests on the surface of the water, waiting for the wings to harden. Then it flies in the air.'

He shook her arm. 'Did you hear what I said?'

Mallika covered her face with her hands and giggled.

Nine

IT HAD BEEN FIVE MONTHS since the wedding and Ammamai was anxious as Mallika was still without child. She chose to believe that it was the malicious work of the English ghost rather than fault her son or new daughter-in-law.

Ammamai obtained a special mantra from Perumal Swamy to ward off evil and coaxed Mallika to chant it.

Mallika woke up each morning at 5 as instructed by Ammamai. She bathed and washed her hair. She wore silk saris that smelled of mothballs and old suitcases. With a lamp in her hand she circled around the sacred tulsi plant. Drops of water that dripped down from her long hair made zen-like circles on the ground. From a booklet Ammamai had given her Mallika recited a mantra in a lilting voice that awakened the sparrows in the trees. Churchill barked and the neighbour's buffalo mooed, then chewed moist husk in resigned silence.

As the days passed, Mallika circled the tulsi plant and chanted twice the prescribed number. Ammamai carefully examined her each day to notice any indication of listlessness. There was none. Moreover, Mallika was losing weight and Munniamma was worried.

'Look at her, how thin she has become,' Munniamma said to Ammamai. 'What will her father say? How will you explain to Saroja-ma eh? They will think you are not feeding her properly and you are making her work too hard.'

When Ammamai found Mallika in the kitchen helping Mani she scolded her. 'No need for you to work. Go and read a book, listen to the radio or practise your music and let this lazy Mani do his work. And you must eat properly, ma. Look how thin you have become. What will your father say? That my son is not looking after you?'

So most of the time Mallika remained in her room or in the garden by the pond. As for Raman, he was far away from his women. He toured villages in the district, recording the varieties of mosquitoes. He was gone for many weeks at a time. When he was lonely he drank rum, shook his legs anxiously, thought of his problems, his wife, and masturbated.

Mallika had her own problems. Her period came only once in three or four months and did not last longer than a day or two at the most.

'It's all because you're too thin,' Ammamai complained, 'and not eating is not good for procreation.'

She took Mallika to Dr Jacob Kuruvilla who had long ago returned from Chicago. He was the most reputed doctor in town especially because he was foreign-educated. He was a middle-aged man with a razor-thin moustache. Despite the heat he was habitually dressed in a loose suit and a narrow tie. His eyes were small and intense under bushy eyebrows that he twirled with his fingers now and then.

Dr Kuruvilla had a Ph.D in Human Sexuality and a D.Ed, Masters in Public Health. His entire career had been aimed towards a single set of goals: telling the truth about sexuality, helping people feel sexually normal and powerful, and supporting the healthy sexual expression and exploration of women and men. He wrote extensively for American medical journals and spoke on a popular radio show that aired late in the night. Before his return from America he had studied Dietetics and Physiology. His thesis was: *A study of the relationship between physical activity, dietary factors and sexual disorders in a group of active young women*. He was awarded a D.Sc. in Biochemistry for his research on the nutritional content of rice and its link to sexual dysfunction.

However, despite the sexually overt stone sculptures at the Khajuraho temple, which display heavenly nymphs and their mates joined together in explicit erotic postures, and being in the land of a people whose gods indulged in a form of free sex, Dr Kuruvilla until recently did not have many patients in his clinic in Machilipatnam.

On the day the doctor added Dietician and GP to the sign on his clinic, patients began to flock outside his door as if he was giving away free gold. While some indeed suffered from an illness or some sort of dietary problem – or so they said – once inside Dr Kuruvilla's clinic, they spilled their worrisome problems of sexual this or that.

On the evening Mallika was brought to his clinic by her mother-in-law, Dr Kuruvilla looked at the young woman from under his eyebrows.

'If you ask me, it's all because of the food she eats,' he said to Ammamai, shrugging his shoulders. 'Too much rice. And too many gourds and pumpkins. And no garlic? I haven't ever heard of any meal without garlic. And all those idlis and dosas. She should have no rice. She must have lots of milk, cheese, bread, butter, eggs and of course chicken, pork and juicy steaks would be nice.'

He laughed and twirling his eyebrow, added, 'Tch-tch, but you are vegetarians so the last ones on the list are out. She must eat spinach, tomatoes, peas, cauliflower and yes, potatoes. Fry them, boil them or roast them, she must eat potatoes. Not rice, not curd, but potatoes. And eggs, at least two a day.'

'Eggs. Chi-chi, we don't eat eggs.' Ammamai made a face to emphasise her distaste for eggs.

'But eggs are an excellent source of protein. They are what make young people grow and fill out. They titillate the glands.

Look at the physique of young American girls and you will understand what I am saying. They get their periods at age nine and ten.'

Ammamai was aghast. 'No, no. No way can I have eggs cooked in my kitchen. My kitchen is a pure vegetarian one.'

'Then have her eat raw eggs in milk in the garden,' the doctor suggested.

On Ammamai's orders, Munniamma mixed two eggs in milk and forced Mallika to drink it every morning outside the kitchen. She asked Mani to boil or fry potatoes and insisted that Mallika eat them all day long.

Despite consuming sixty egg yolks in a month, Mallika's period was still irregular. So she faked it. She put a red circle on the 15th of the month on the calendar. Nice number, halfway, she thought.

Four days before this date, she complained of pain in the legs. She pretended to be moody and refused to step out of her room; she didn't eat much, though the lack of appetite was something she found increasingly difficult to fake.

Two days later she lay in bed doubled up with pain and cramps in the stomach.

'It must be something you ate, ma,' Ammamai said.

'No,' Mallika said. 'It hurts here.' She patted her abdomen just below the navel.

'You must be getting your period, ma,' Ammamai said with a smile.

Ammamai was outside the kitchen. She kept looking up at the gates, waiting for Munniamma to arrive. Getting impatient she laid out sheets of old newspaper and on them she spread fistfuls of raw rice to be suncrisped.

The rice was infested with black lice and cobwebbed with obese maggots. The sun's heat flushed the maggots out from the rice. Soon crows would peck at them. Even after the maggots were removed, Ammamai knew, the suncrisped rice would still smell of them. She was afraid she would have to give away all the rice to Munniamma. The thought didn't please her.

Mani watched Ammamai from the kitchen door as he hummed a film song.

'Ye da, you have no work or what? And where is that Munniamma?'

'How should I know, ma? And the dirty vessels are heaped in the sink.'

'Then what are you standing there for eh? Go clean them.'

'That's Munniamma's work.'

'Rubbish. Everything is your work. Understand.'

Just then Munniamma walked through the gates. She walked up to Ammamai. 'Aiyoo, the rice is full of lice.'

'Ah, the maharani has come at last,' Ammamai scolded Munniamma. 'Do you know what the time is?'

'Vishnu-aiyah was not well, ma,' Munniamma said, 'I cooked him some lunch.' She sat down and started to clean the rice.

'What's wrong with him?'

'He coughs a lot. And he's so lonely, poor man. Ever since Mallika left home, he hardly eats. How thin he has become.'

Ammamai grunted, 'Just like his daughter. How will she produce a child when she's so weak eh?'

'You should take her to Ratnamma, the old woman in Chiroor village, near Madras,' Munniamma said. 'She gives away magic seeds from a peepal tree for free. Her seeds are very good for getting children. Men are not even required.'

'Nonsense. If she eats those seeds she will give birth to a peepal tree, that's all.'

Ammamai heard Churchill barking and looked up to see Saroja walk in through the gates. She had sent for her.

Ammamai walked over to the stone platform under the neem tree and sat down on it. Saroja joined her. Ammamai wiped the sweat that had collected on the tip of her nose with the end of her sari. She tucked her large breasts under the palav of her sari.

'It must be so uncomfortable,' Saroja remarked. 'Why don't you wear a blouse, ma?'

'Of course it's uncomfortable.' Ammamai laughed. 'What to do? This is my fate.'

'Wear a blouse. You will feel better.'

'Like me, you are a widow, ma. Then why don't you wear a white sari, or a fawn-coloured one like mine. It is our tradition and it is not dignified to be dressed as you are. And these flowers, jewellery, that pottu on your forehead – they don't suit you at all. What will people say?'

Saroja grunted. 'I don't care what people say.'

'But ma, your clothes don't change your status. Under them you are still a widow.'

'If that is so then why don't you dress up like me? You will still remain a widow.'

Ammamai's hand sprang to her mouth. 'Chi-chi-chi. It's a sin. And God will punish me.'

'Gods exist only in our minds. In any case, if He does exist I would like to face God as a woman and not a widow.'

Ammamai sighed. 'All that is okay. But look here, what I am worried about is Mallika. So many months and she is still without child. I hear there is an old woman in Chiroor village near Madras who gives away seeds that make women pregnant.'

'Seeds? What seeds?'

'The seeds of a magic peepal tree.'

'I don't believe in all this and neither should you. It's just nonsense.'

Munniamma looked up from the rice she had been cleaning. 'It's not nonsense, ma. That Laxmi-amma who lives in the street behind the temple, she told me she got the seeds and within eleven months her daughter had a healthy son. Yes-yes.' Munniamma beamed. 'Also the potters there make big clay idols of the snake goddess. Don't forget to bring back an idol of the snake goddess, ma. Serpents are good for fertility. Ask Mallika to pray to the goddess every day and she will be blessed with not one but four sons.'

Ammamai snorted. 'Ye di, how long will you take to clean a sack of rice eh? If you keep listening to us, all the lice and maggots will have made a feast of it.'

The old Machilipatnam railway station dominated the morning landscape. The tar on the road outside had melted in the heat and crows flew in elliptical circles over the roof. And inside the womb-like station, cobwebs of dust had settled everywhere and the air was infused with its acrid smell. Resident pigeons cooed in the arches. And the caterpillars of locomotion, steel gnawing steel, hissed, as they trundled between platforms strewn with people eating, talking and waiting endlessly.

Ammamai and Mallika sat on a bench and waited; the train was two hours late. The platform was dimly lit but brighter because of all the noise and activity, which heralded the beginning of a show. Vendors tinkled trays of cold drinks, a lone man sweated out his fever, not far from him a pregnant woman vomited, a radio warbled a popular tune, snot-nosed children waved at passing trains, displaced people slept around a crumbling monument of an English man, and unwashed young men with bloodshot eyes watched pigeons defecate in the trusses.

The smells on the platform were overwhelming – of refried snacks, sweaty feet and unwashed mouths, vomit and dust. And a clinging ammonia smell above all else: sharp and pungent.

The train to Madras arrived. People rushed to board it and coolies dawdled between them, carrying tiers of luggage on their heads. Ammamai and Mallika got into their compartment, located their berths, tucked their luggage under them and sat down. Soon they were off.

Ammamai shelled groundnuts and popped the nuts into her mouth. Mallika looked out of the window.

The train hustled through the countryside and the landscapes were frozen for an instant by the square of the window. The fleeting images seemed to Mallika like a stack of photographs:

> A little boy waving.
> Pyrethrum fields.
> A crow perched on a buffalo's back.
> A scarecrow wearing a hat.
> Telephone wires dangling.
> A mother and child.
> An eagle flying high above.
> A squirrel leaping from a tree.
> A cart laden with jackfruits.

A page of a newspaper swirled, spiralled in the air, up up up, reached beyond the window frame and could be seen no more.

One station after another passed. People waited with trunks and cloth bags. Some sat, others stood, expectation sweating on their faces, gazing into the distant space, an emptiness from which the train would emerge. Vendors moved between people, coolies squatted on their haunches, expectant. At the end of the platform on one station, an old man sat holding a bamboo stick and a rope that was tied around a goat's neck, waiting. Further on there were stunted trees, a distant lowing of cattle.

The train pulled into Madras Station the next afternoon. Ammamai and Mallika got on a bus to Chiroor.

It was late evening when they arrived at the village. It was without electricity. In the pale light of the moon Ammamai located Ratnamma, the old woman. She was sitting on a rope cot outside her hut, under a huge peepal tree. Ammamai told Ratnamma the purpose of their visit.

The old woman asked Mallika to sit next to her on the rope cot. Ammamai sat beside her.

Spread out under the tree were several jars containing herbs, seeds and chunks of bark. A large glass bottle contained the skins of dead lizards and snakes. A human skull hung from a branch, the sockets of its eyes large and gleaming in the moonlight. Its jaw was wide open; one tooth was missing.

Mallika looked disbelievingly at the skull, then at the old woman's face. Hers was a worker's face, creased and furrowed by the fears of other women.

At some distance, an old potter turned his wheel. The smell of desiccated mud rose into the night air.

Ratnamma held Mallika's chin and stared into her eyes.

'Look at you. So tender, like a baby cucumber.' The old woman tweaked Mallika's cheek. She stamped her foot. 'Ha! All men want their women to be green, untouched and innocent. But they don't know that women are possessed and revengeful. They wait in the dark, doubtful, without trust, afraid.'

She pointed to the spotted insect next to her. 'Look, a female.'

The bug climbed onto the old woman's lap. It moved under the folds of her sari. She put her hand between her thighs, plucked the insect, pulled out its wings one by one, then crushed it on the mud.

Gravely, she looked into Mallika's eyes. 'You must be careful of men. All men: fathers, brothers, husbands and sons. They will clip your wings so you can't fly any more. Remember, it is a burden to be a woman, a disgrace, because we are always captive in one way or another; large iron locks are clasped to our ankles and we sink deep into dark waters.'

Red ants had appeared out of nowhere. They perambulated around the dead insect. Mallika watched as they disentangled the insect's legs and pulled it towards a rathole.

'See those ants,' the old woman said to Mallika. 'Men are like them. Be careful. Men will wait until you are helpless, and then swarm all over your body.'

She looked up at the moon. Then clapped her hands and laughed loud and shrill. The potter shredded the claybits stuck to his instruments, cleaned them, lifted the wheel and stood it against the mud wall of the hut. He covered the leftover clay with a wet sack, and rubbed his hands together. As the clay tendrils fell at his feet, he looked pleased with his clay gods and goddesses.

'One a day.' The old woman pressed a packet of seeds into Mallika's hand. Raising her finger, she said, 'Eat it fifteen minutes before or after meals. And remember, it is before meals for a boy and after meals for a girl.'

With a month's supply of seeds and a clay idol of the snake goddess, Ammamai and Mallika were on the return train to Machilipatnam the next evening. Halfway, the train attendant came with steel trays of food.

Ammamai said, 'Now don't forget to eat the seed before you start.'

Mallika took a seed out from the packet. She held it between her fingers and raised it to her mouth. Glancing sideways at Ammamai, she dropped the seed in her lap. She ate the rice and potato curry, she finished the pachadi and the sweet, then she swallowed the seed. She patted her stomach.

'Tara,' she said to herself.

Raman had been terribly busy. He came home late each evening. As soon as he was home, he rushed to his study and remained there well past midnight. Ammamai was hardly pleased about this.

On one particular night, it was unusually windy. Mallika rushed up to her room to shut the windows that banged in the breeze. Raman returned from work and hastened to his study. The door was locked. He shouted out to Ammamai for the key.

'Okay-okay, I am coming. Don't scream like the mad wind now.' She stood in front of him, one hand on her hip, the other holding the key tied to the end of her sari. She asked, 'Why?'

'What do you mean why?'

Ammamai gritted her teeth. 'Go up to your wife.' In a cajoling voice she added, 'Poor thing, she has been waiting for you for weeks.'

Raman grunted, then made his way to the room upstairs. Mallika was sitting by the window. She was singing softly. Raman stood by the door, listening to her. When she stopped he walked over to her and, holding her hand, he pulled her up on her feet. With an arm around her waist, he led her to the bed. She lay down on it. He lay next to her staring at the ceiling, breathing hard. Then he turned to her and pulled away her sari. He undid the hooks of her blouse and, lifting her arms one by one, slipped them out of the sleeves, then unclasped her bra. He loosened the string of her petticoat, slid it down her hips. Then, as though he could no longer hold back, he fell upon her body and with pent-up passion, consumed her.

Mallika stared at the ceiling. Her thoughts turned to the dead bug, the red ants tearing its limbs apart.

Ten

IT WAS THE THIRD DAY Munniamma had not showed up for work.

Another riot had started in the slum where she lived. There had been a minor quarrel between Yusuf Ali, the Muslim owner of Yusuf Pet Shop, and Ranga, the Hindu owner of Ranga's Roses.

People on the way to the temple stopped at Ranga Roses to buy flowers for the gods. They also bought grass to feed the holy cow that sat outside the shop. Ranga considered the cow to be lucky for him.

But Yusuf considered the cow to be his worst nightmare. It produced piles of dung. Flies descended on them and then drifted into his shop, parked themselves on his birds and animals. But most of the time they lingered on his glass of tea and fried pakoras he had with it.

Two days ago as Yusuf walked back from his prayers at the mosque, the holy cow that was standing close to his shop let fall a stream of piss. It spattered all over Yusuf's freshly washed salwar. Yusuf cursed and beat the cow fiercely with his fist.

The next morning a pig was found butchered in front of the Mosque. Suddenly what started as a squabble between Ranga and Yusuf had swelled into a bigger and a more dangerous tumult between the Muslims and the Hindus in the locality. At the break of dawn, on the third day of the quarrel, a cow was found slaughtered in front of the Shiva temple.

Their faces distended with rage, a mob of the Hindu National Party set fire to many Muslim houses in the slum including Yusuf's.

Munniamma came to work a few days later. Her face was swollen and her right eye was puffed purple.

'Aiyoo, what happened to you eh?' Ammamai asked.

Munniamma didn't reply. She defiantly tucked her sari palav into her waist and rushed into the kitchen. When most of the work was done she walked up to Ammamai who was sitting on the pai in the veranda. With one hand on her hip, the other raised, Munniamma resentfully said, 'Ye Amma, you want to know what happened, yes?' She pointed to her purpled eye. 'See how the men beat me.'

'What men?'

'Those men in saffron clothes. The men of the Hindu Nationalist Party.'

'Achichoo! Why did they beat you?'

'Because I helped Nafisa.'

'Who?'

'She's Yusuf's wife and my friend. Those scoundrels tried to burn her house down. I stopped them and they beat me up.'

'Aiyoo, why do you interfere in other people's problems,' Ammamai said, slapping her forehead. 'We have enough trouble as it is.'

'What trouble? What happened?'

'Not just any trouble, it is big trouble. It's a month since we went to your Chiroor woman and her seeds are all over and still Mallika is without child.'

'That Chiroor woman's seeds are good only if women have problems, ma,' Munniamma said. 'Maybe there's nothing wrong with Mallika-ma. Something must be wrong with Raman-aiyah.'

'Maybe. Of late I have noticed Raman-aiyah is always grumpy and tired. He sits in his study with his mosquitoes and I am sure they are sucking all the blood out of him. Without enough blood it is natural he will get angry and tired, no?'

Ammamai's eyes became moist. 'I must have committed some grave sin in my last birth to deserve this. Imagine, I am going to die without seeing my grandson.'

'Don't talk like that,' Munniamma said. 'Don't blame yourself, ma.' In a solemn tone she added, 'Gods have a hand in these matters. When they decide Mallika is ready she will have a child.'

Ammamai pressed her knee and stroked her thigh just as a thought formed in her mind: *Why am I blaming myself or my son for the terrible state of affairs and, what is more, exonerating Mallika of her faults? After all you don't get a clap unless there are two hands.* As the thought took full shape, Ammamai clutched Munniamma's wrist.

'It's all Mallika's fault. She is to blame. Women should know how to manage their men and keep them calm. Tell me, why he spends all his time with mosquitoes, tell me eh? There must be something wrong with Mallika, no?'

Munniamma moved closer to Ammamai and whispered, 'Sometimes ma, we have to help our gods in their work. Tell me, what do you do with the jackfruit seeds?'

'Who knows? Maybe that Mani roasts them and eats them all.'

'Next time you get a jackfruit, don't give away the seeds to Mani. God only knows how many women he has got pregnant by now. Roast the seeds, powder them and mix them with sesame seeds and jaggery. Make small laddoos from the mixture and give them to Raman-aiyah after dinner.'

Munniamma beamed and slapped her thigh. 'Then watch. Aiyah may be one mile away from his wife but in the middle of everything, he will run to her. So much thirst, ma, so much heat, he will not be able to control. Nothing can stop that ache between a man's legs. Not even his bad temper.'

No sooner had Munniamma left than Ammamai rushed into the kitchen.

'Ah there you are Mani.'

Mani was boiling rice for lunch.

'Give me fifteen minutes,' he said. He was dressed in a green checked lungi and his chest was bare. The blue-black tattoo on his arm rose and fell. He scratched his hair, inspected the grime in his fingernails, chewed at one, and spat it out.

'Ye da, how many times have I told you to wear a shirt when you are in the kitchen. I don't want the sweat from your armpits to drip into the rice. Chi-chi-chi! Go wear a shirt at once. And don't ever chew your fingernails like that. I'll chop your fingers off.'

Mani reappeared in a bright red shirt. Ammamai shook her head. 'Is this the only shirt you could find? If you walk on the street people will mistake you for a postbox and shove letters into your mouth.'

Mani laughed. He posed with a hand on his hip and a leg stretched out. 'This is the same shirt Susilkant wears in his latest film. It's playing in Gemini Talkies.' Mani had never stopped dreaming of being a film star.

'Okay-okay, don't forget you are a cook; not some great star.'

Mani curled his lip and churned the rice once more before he went to the dining room and spread a cloth stained with turmeric over the old table. He sang a film song as he set steel plates on it. In the centre, he placed a glass containing assorted spoons. He set the bowl of curried snake gourd, a bin of papadams, a bowl of sour curds, lime pickle, and steel tumblers of wellwater. He would bring in the rice, piping hot, when they sat down to eat.

Ammamai pressed some coins into Mani's hand and asked him to get her a ripe jackfruit.

'Now?' Mani looked surprised. 'But lunch is almost ready, Amma.'

'Ye da, the sun has only just risen and you are hungry already. Go on, lunch can wait.'

Mani looked pleased. 'Oh, you are going to make jackfruit payasam.' He caught his reflection in the windowpane, then stroked the side of his head and pushed his hair up to hoist a puff. His face, as though waxed smooth, squeaked whenever he rubbed it. His teeth were so even and white that they put a Colgate smile to disgrace.

'Stop grinning like an idiot,' Ammamai snapped. 'Mention food and your mouth works overtime. And close your mouth. Any second it will be drooling all over the place! Do as you are told without jumping to stupid conclusions. I want each and every seed mind you.'

'What will you do with them?'

'Roast them, silly. What else am I going to do with them henh? Plant them in your head so branches grow out of your dirty ears and nose and big fat fruits dangle out of your mouth?'

'Why are you always making fun of me? I was only asking, Amma. You want me to roast all the seeds? Who will eat so many?'

'I will. You have any problem with that? Doctor said it is good for my knees. It will make me walk properly.'

'When I eat those seeds they stop me from walking. They make me so thirsty that I have to drink gallons of water after eating a few of them. My stomach gets so full that I want to sleep all day. And if I stand all day long all the water rushes to my feet and they swell up. I can hardly walk'. Mani laughed

'What are you laughing like a jackass for? Look at your belly. Anyone would think you are pregnant. What do you know about water in the feet? If you know so much you should have become a doctor. Why are you just a stupid cook then henh? And don't you go about roasting the seeds. I will do that myself. Now don't stand there like a buffoon. Go get that jackfruit and after you have taken out all the seeds, go get yourself a haircut.'

'Haircut? Before lunch? Today is Wednesday; it is not hair-cutting day even.'

'So? Look at you, hair growing all over your head like a paddy field. And get that barber to clip the hair growing out of your ears. Chi-chi-chi.' Ammamai clapped her hands, 'Go, go get me the jackfruit first.'

Kuttan, the chakka-man was asleep under the chakka tree, a wet towel around his face. Flies swarmed over the jackfruit that he had cut in the morning and laid open on the cart. Its sweet smell clung to the hot air around it and quickly curdled in the heat.

Mani shook him awake. 'Lucky fellow,' he said, 'sleeping all the time.'

'I don't feel well,' Kuttan said.

'What's wrong?'

'I get high fever, and my body shakes.'

'You should see the doctor, pa.'

Mani bought the fruit from him and back in the kitchen, he cut it, pried out the nuggets, removed the kidney-shaped seeds and arranged them on a steel tray. He stretched out his hand in front of Ammamai.

'Now what?' she asked.

'Give me money for my haircut.'

'Ye da, your brains have gone for a stroll or what! I have never given you money for a haircut before. Why should I give you money now?'

'Because this time it is you who wants me to cut my hair. I don't think I need a haircut yet. Why should I waste my own money?'

'Po da!' Ammamai grunted as she undid the knot at the end of her sari. She took out five coins from it and gave them to Mani.

He looked at the coins in his hand. 'Just five rupees?'

'Then what? Who do you think you are, a maharaja? No need to go to a barber shop. Just go to that street barber near the temple. Stop making such a disgusting face. That street barber will do fine. You are not some Susilkant. Go, go, and don't waste time. Time doesn't grow long like your hair.'

Mani trotted off, and Ammamai hurriedly roasted the seeds. She ground them to powder and made laddoos just as Munniamma had instructed her. She kept them safe in the steel almirah in her bedroom lest Mani try some.

Ammamai scrutinized Mani when he returned. His ears were thankfully hairless but the hair on his head was not any shorter. 'Ye da, I gave you five rupees for this?'

Mani adjusted his locks and with his hip sticking out, he struck a pose against the door and sniffed the air. 'You have already roasted the seeds? Where have you kept them?'

'I ate them.'

'All?'

'Yes all,' Ammamai sniggered as she walked out of the door.

Each night she gave laddoos to Raman. But they didn't seem to have any effect.

'Your ideas are all so hopeless,' she told Munniamma one morning.

'Learn to be patient, ma. It will happen,' Munniamma assured her.

Ammamai was delirious with joy when two months later she found out that Mallika was pregnant. She informed Vishnu and Saroja. Nayantara called up Mallika as soon as she heard the news.

'Now Malli will have her Tara.'

Ammamai gifted Munniamma a silk sari. 'How can I ever thank you,' she said holding both her hands. 'It worked, Munniamma, it worked.'

'What worked?' Mani asked Ammamai.

She frowned at him. He had had a haircut that morning.

'Aiyoo Rama-Rama. It was much better with all that hair in your ears. At least you couldn't hear well then.'

Eleven

Dr Kuruvilla was alarmed. Kuttan had come to him with high fever, almost 104 degrees. He was covered in sweat. His eyes were swollen and he was barely conscious.

Dr Kuruvilla recognised the symptoms and the blood test had confirmed his fears. It showed the presence of the deadly plasmodium falciparum malaria parasite. Kuttan's haemoglobin was down to 3.4gm/dl.

The next evening Kuttan was found dead under the chakka tree. Flies swarmed all over his face. The jackfruit that he had cut in the morning lay exposed on the cart. Its sweet smell clung to the hot air mixed with the foul smell of death.

Within a week of Kuttan's death Dr Kuruvilla's clinic was full of patients complaining of high fever, nausea, vomiting, sweating, rigours and fatigue. Already, in the other parts of the town, there were reports of 140 deaths due to malaria; an epidemic had broken out in some of the villages in the district.

Soon the lethal parasite spread over miles, across the land and rivers, maiming every organ it infected, defacing each drop of blood it contaminated, even choking foetuses in the womb. People melted as though made of sweat, their skins burned hot when cold and were scalded like milk surface reaching boiling point. Yellow-eyed, they vomited, coughed their plasma out, then flipping like fish out of water, they died. With dilated eyes, like bicycle wheels, families watched the before and after rushes of the obliteration of their kin. All over the countryside people ended in heaps of ashes, crosses, bits of inverted stone rammed into the earth. Or there were corpses in fields, flies humming over them and maggots pouring out of the soil to eat what remained of the flesh.

Newspapers reported the numbers of the dead; not their names. Each day the numbers in the lefthand side column on the front page of the local newspaper increased, under the simple heading: Malaria Victims.

In the eighty-bed Civil Hospital in Machilipatnam, there were more than 400 malaria patients from all over the district. They lay on mattresses, reed-mats and sheets on corridor floors, verandas, under stairways and on the mid-landing, intravenous fluids administered to some of them.

Surveillance workers went house to house and field to field spraying the pesticide DDT. To cope with the situation, the district administration called for special medical teams from Madras, equipped with microscopes and rapid diagnostic kits. They too went from door to door to collect blood samples, which they would deposit in the makeshift laboratory attached to the Civil Hospital.

Saroja manufactured insecticide-treated nets in her factory, dyed them with natural pigments – blue, green, yellow, red – and gave them away for free. Health officials distributed free malaria drugs.

Ammamai boiled turmeric roots in a large iron pot with sea salt and at dusk sprinkled the yellow brine inside and outside the house.

'What are you doing,' Raman asked her when he returned from the institute.

'Turmeric keeps malaria away,' she replied. 'That's what my mother used to say.'

'Rubbish,' Raman said wearily and walked away.

Raman, for reasons both self-interested and public-spirited, toured the district with his team. In every village he went to, chimneys belched carbon-coloured smoke into the air and open sewage drains gushed green slush into the ponds nearby. Buffaloes waddled through the slush with crows perched on their backs. Mosquitoes fed on swampy watery phlegm and bred, such suckers for blood. Invisible to the naked eye, the cauldron of new strains of parasites simmered.

Raman organised camps in affected areas to educate villagers who listened with wide-eyed suspicion. Superstition and panic had spread as rapidly as religion. 'Don't eat too much palm oil, stay out of the sun, and don't eat watermelon or you'll catch malaria,' the villagers warned each other but did not stop throwing their washing water out close to their huts, or rubbish everywhere.

Furthermore, Raman was disturbed to note that the malaria drugs were becoming much less effective and the parasites were showing early stages of resistance. His research on a malaria vaccine was at a foetal stage and would be, for some time to come, of no use to him or anybody else. Desperate and frantic, he laboured late into the night, day after day, week after week to rebut actuality, to refute the laws of the natural world that a thing once dead does not live again.

He contacted the malaria research team in London that was conducting experiments using artemisinin and curcumin. Following their work, Raman injected mice with P. berghei-infected mouse blood. He observed the animals as they developed high parasitemia, twitched and turned, sweated and paled, and then died in about five to eight days. But when he injected the infected mice with the artemisinin derivative and fed them orally with curcumin isolated from the roots of *Curcuma longa* or turmeric, to his astonishment they survived.

Raman submitted his report to the District Health Department that set up provisional clinics in every village and town in the region. They were a success and the lethal parasite was soon brought under control. At a special felicitation, the district collector commended Raman's research and work. A local newspaper carried the story with Raman's photograph. Ammamai was proud of her son.

Raman returned early one evening and saw Mallika curled in bed, her knees pressed against her chin. She trembled and moaned and sweated profusely. He touched her forehead; it was damp and burning. He called Dr Kuruvilla at once.

'There's no doubt,' the doctor said after checking Mallika, 'it's malaria. I am certain of this. She needs a lot of care, she's pregnant.'

Ammamai screamed at Raman after Dr Kuruvilla left. 'Go, work with your mice and mosquitoes and fill the house with parasite. It's because of you that Mallika is sick. Now don't you expect me to look after your wife. You look after her.'

Raman was home early every evening. He rubbed Mallika's forehead with eau de cologne, pressed a cold towel on her forehead and made sure she had her medicines. Three weeks later, although weak, she was well.

The next day, Raman returned late from work. Mallika was in bed, and the sight of her frail body was both touching and unbearable. He opened the packet he had brought with him. 'Here, Mallika, let me put these jasmines in your hair.' He pressed his cheek against hers. 'Look after our child,' he said. Mallika clung to him.

He often got her flowers. He bought her saris and a gold necklace set with nine coloured gems. On the nights he made love to her, Mallika was responsive and seemed happy to him.

The sky was a sheet of wavy blueness and the sea breeze blew warmly. The nights had grown longer, warmer. Nayantara was back in town for the delivery of her child. Mallika was overjoyed.

Nayantara and Mallika went to the market, bought frocks and dolls and other baby-girl things. When Mallika showed them to Ammamai, she slapped her head. 'Aiyoo Rama-Rama. If you keep thinking of a girl then you will get a girl,' she yelled.

'But I want to have a daughter.'

'Shut up. Don't even say that,' Ammamai said covering Mallika's mouth with her hand. 'I want a grandson, understand.'

Mallika insisted with a nervous little laugh, 'But I am certain I am going to have a daughter. And Nayantara is going to have a daughter too.'

Ammamai retorted in a biting tone, 'A daughter! Aa-ha-ha, aa-ha-ha. With all the prayers I am offering at the temple, you think you will have a daughter eh? Never.' She slapped her chest and triumphantly added, 'God will hear my prayers. You will see. Yes, you will see, when you give birth to my grandson.'

One warm and long night Nayantara went into labour and, with Mallika beside her, she gave birth to a beautiful girl at dawn. She handed the baby to Mallika.

'Mallika, here's your Malli,' she said unable to suppress her joy. 'My wish has come true.'

'I told you didn't I, Mallika?' Ammamai said when she heard the news. 'Stop thinking of a daughter or you will also get a daughter like Nayantara. Poor girl.'

A month later Nayantara and Malli were at the station waiting for the train to take them back to Madras. Saroja and Mallika were with them. Mallika hugged her friend. Nayantara patted Mallika's belly and said, 'See you soon, Tara.'

On the start of the seventh month of Mallika's pregnancy Ammamai arranged the valakappu. She invited her women friends and their daughters and daughters-in-law and daughters-in-law to be.

Saroja came with boxes of red and green glass bangles, a garland of roses and a black sari with a blood-red border.

'Mallika, Saroja-ma is here,' Ammamai called out. Mallika waddled into the kitchen holding her bloated belly in her arms. Ammamai patted a fistful of coconut oil on Mallika's head.

'Go and have your bath, Mallika,' Saroja said, as she led her to the bathroom, 'and be careful, the floor is slippery.'

Saroja helped Mallika drape the red sari she had worn on her wedding day, tied a string of kanakabaram in her hair and hung the garland of roses around her neck. Ammamai led her to the prayer room to pray to Lord Ganesha to remove obstacles from her life. With her hand over Mallika's head, she blessed her, 'May you have a healthy son.'

The women who had collected in the hall sang songs, clapping their hands and swaying to the rhythm. Ammamai, a widow, sat at a distance, supervising the event. She gave a young married woman two bangles made out of neem twigs. 'Put these on Mallika's wrists for me,' she said. 'This will protect my grandson from evil spirits.'

The young woman slipped the neem bangles and a pair of red and green glass bangles on Mallika's wrists. Then Saroja walked her away. She dressed her in the black sari and escorted her back to the hall. One by one the married women pushed red and green bangles onto Mallika's wrists. Ammamai watched them. When she saw her neighbour Veena walking over to Mallika's side, she called out, 'Not you Veena. Six years of marriage and no child yet! That's not a good omen, ma.'

When Mallika had nine bangles on the right wrist and eight on the left the women smeared turmeric paste on her arms and feet, around which they had arranged neem leaves and five kinds of flowers.

Munniamma put some sweets and savouries into the palav of Mallika's sari and tied it around her waist. 'This is food for the baby,' she said.

'Not baby,' Ammamai said sternly, 'say son. If we keep talking about a son only then will she have one. With the birth of a son, three generations of the family will cross over from heaven into eternal bliss and they won't be reborn again.'

Churchill howled. Ammamai yelled out to Mani. 'Ye da, Mani, ye Mani, run and shut that dog up! It's a bad omen if it howls.'

Mani smiled. 'It must be hungry, that's all.'

'Donkey! Don't stand there showing me all your thirty-two teeth, grinning like a monkey. Go feed that stupid dog.'

Mani walked away to the kitchen.

Munniamma put a vessel of rice in the middle of the room and the women walked around it, sprinkling flowers and chanting. They clapped their hands so that the baby would not be born deaf. Each of them blessed Mallika with a son.

Ammamai called the astrologer to read the fortunes of the yet-to-be-born child. Perumal Swamy arrived dressed in a starched white veshti, bare-chested, his Brahmin thread looped over his shoulder. He was preoccupied. At least 40 per cent of his predictions had come true in the past, but in the last year each one of them had gone awry. People were losing faith in him and his predictions. He wondered if he had lost the knack. So he came armed with notebooks, charts and a fertile imagination.

Perumal surveyed Raman's and Mallika's horoscopes, matching house for house, planet for planet and star for star. But what was the use? The air inside his stomach tossed violently. He knew something was wrong even before he had started. With a deep sigh he set the frayed textbook with lunar notes in front of him and beside it, several notebooks in which he had made notes of stars.

'What is it?' Ammamai asked. 'Why are you sighing like that? Are you dying or what?'

With a shudder of his chest Perumal blew the air out of his stomach and burped. Then in order to focus on the job he made notations on a page and put down lunar calculations in the margin. 'A girl,' he pronounced with a wavering smile.

Ammamai slapped her thigh. 'A what?' She wiped the sweat under her lip with her sari. 'Look-look, see properly. It has to be a son. I didn't go and offer all those coconuts in the temple just for nothing eh?'

Perumal adjusted the thread over his shoulder. He fanned his armpits with a fan made of dried leaves. The astringent odour of Lifebuoy soap and perspiration wafted towards Ammamai. Her nose twitched and she covered it with the end of her sari. She sniffed to ensure the brief breeze had blown away, before dropping the sari from her nose.

'I am not certain, ma,' Perumal muttered. 'The stars are not in their right positions.'

Ammamai grunted. 'Achicho Perumal, so it's true what people are saying about you,' she said, 'that you have lost your touch.'

Perumal looked up at Ammamai and stared at her open mouth. 'A pure artist,' he said with a hesitant smile.

'A pure what? See properly. Is it going to be a son?'

'A son,' he muttered. 'I am certain.'

Ammamai's mouth closed and then ever so slowly it widened into a smile. She clasped her hands together, stretched them in front of her, and pressed them out until her finger bones cracked. Twin dimples appeared at the back of her elbows.

Perumal looked up from his notes, 'It may also be a girl.'

'Rubbish! What do you mean *also* a girl? You said a boy first.'

'Yes-yes, I know.' He peered into another notebook. 'Maybe it's a boy.' He was losing it, he was certain now.

'What maybe-maybe! If it has to be *maybe* then I can predict it myself. All I am asking is – is it a boy or is it a girl? I am not asking you to choose from one hundred options.'

'Definitely a boy, Amma,' Perumal looked up and beamed, although his eyebrows remained knit together as though they had a mind of their own and they didn't entirely agree. He smoothed out his eyebrows. 'And he will be a fine artist,' he added.

'What fine artist! Bad enough to have a mosquito scientist in the house. And now an artist. No. Never. He will be an engineer like my maternal uncle and build big-big bridges. Or my grandson can be a lawyer even. Our Mahatma Gandhi was a lawyer after all. Oh don't smile like that. I am not being stupid. Tell me, could a simple woman like Gandhi's mother ever have dreamed that one day her son would become the Father of the Nation? See, you can never say. Now tell me the rituals I have to do to negotiate his profession with the gods. Whatever it costs, perform them now only, and don't wait for the child to be born. If we address our grievances in advance I am certain we can redraft our fate.'

At the temple the next day Ammamai offered two coconuts, a basket of flowers, an entire bunch of bananas and fifty-one rupees to Lord Shiva. As he sang the bell, the pujari rotated a plate with burning camphor in front of the idol. Looking intently into Shiva's eyes, Ammamai folded her hands and said, 'Please bless my family.'

When the pujari stood in front of Ammamai with the plate of burning camphor, the sweat on her nose caught the light and glittered. She covered the flame with her hands and touched her eyes and face. She drank the holy water that the pujari dropped into her palm with a silver spoon. She looked back at Lord Shiva and added, 'One more thing, please make my grandson a lawyer.'

Mallika had been pregnant for over nine months, and still hadn't gone into labour. Ammamai grew worried. She touched Mallika's belly, tapped it as though it was a ripe watermelon. 'I hope it's a baby and not all water in there,' she fretted.

One hot and humid day, Mallika was sitting under the cool shade of the neem tree, fanning her face with a book. Suddenly, hugging her belly, she bent double and retched all over the trunk of the tree. The violent heaving and squeezing of her stomach started the pain.

Mallika felt as though her life had turned into water and was oozing out of her. Something grew between her legs and uncoiled like a snake with Messiah-like fervour. She could feel the wetness on the front and back of her sari. Her life-tap dribbled away, leaving a trail of water on the ground, as her stomach seemed to slide down, down. Her lungs emitted a sound that seemed not to come from her. She called out to Ammamai who was resting in the veranda.

Ammamai rushed to Mallika. She panicked and at once sent Munniamma to call Saroja and the midwife. By the time they arrived Ammamai was in a state of alarm. Holding Mallika by the arms, Saroja led her to the dark, windless storeroom so that light and wind wouldn't startle the newborn. The walls of the storeroom were lined with gunny bags containing red rice from the local fields. They diffused a homely starchy smell meant to be good for babies. The midwife helped Mallika sit on the floor and, holding her shoulders, gently laid her down.

Ammamai waited in the veranda. Outside the gate, Churchill set up a howl.

'Mani, get that dog to be quiet. It's a bad omen,' Ammamai screamed.

Mani ran to the dog and Ammamai heard him shouting at it. A few minutes later, it stopped howling.

Mani appeared before Ammamai. He looked bewildered.

'What is it? Have you seen a ghost or what!'

'It was howling one minute Ammamai', Mani stammered, 'and the next minute it fell to the ground and died. Cha-chi died.'

Ammamai's hand flew to her mouth. 'Achicho, death at the time of birth, that's a very bad omen.'

Ammamai had no doubt now that the ghost of Elizabeth Gibbs had cast its evil eyes on her family. She rushed into the kitchen, took an idol of Ganesha from the prayer shelf and two oil lamps. She carried them outside, beyond the grove of palm trees. She set them on Elizabeth's grave. She lit the lamps, shut her eyes and prayed to Ganesha.

Meanwhile, inside the storeroom the midwife grew alarmed.

'Her water is all gone,' she said as she pressed Mallika's stomach. Persuaded, the pain started but lasted over twelve hours. Mallika felt each minute in its entirety, and the separate grain of each second.

Raman, who had been summoned from work, paced up and down in the hall outside just the way he had seen new fathers do in movies, with the clock ticking away the hours: 7-8-9-10-11-12-12.01-12.05 … He clutched his nose, unaccustomed to the smells of birthing: raw birthblood and sweat.

The smell was omnipotent. It filled the stark room and soon everyone, everything, smelled of it. The midwife smelled of it, Mallika, Munniamma, Ammamai, the air and the spitcircles on the towel that Mallika pressed to her mouth and bit at. It smelled of blood and sweat and spit.

It started to rain. For a moment, it was pitch-dark, and then Mallika screamed. Her wail pierced the night like lightning. Ammamai rushed into the storeroom.

A big push and the baby arrived, headlong, the umbilical cord coiled around its neck. The midwife cut the cord and held up the baby to Ammamai.

Ammamai slapped her cheeks. 'Aiyoo kadvale, it's a girl.' She stupidly stared at her granddaughter who was kicking her legs in the air. 'That Perumal was right after all.'

Saroja grabbed the baby from the midwife's hands and held her out for Mallika to see. She said, 'Look Mallika, she has your eyes.'

Mallika looked at her baby fondly. Laughing through her tears, she kissed her daughter's head. She whispered her name in her ears. 'Tara.'

Raman stood at the door, his shirt drenched with sweat. Saroja walked up to him with the baby and raised her into his arms. He looked down at her, wonder in his eyes. The baby twisted, cried, turned blue, and then was still. She was no longer breathing.

For some absolutely mindless reason Raman thought of his notebook in which he had pasted dead mosquitoes with the precise date and time of their demise. The thought amused him; he began to laugh. There were tears in his eyes.

Saroja looked up at Raman and then at the baby. She wrenched the dead child out of his arms, and walked back into the storeroom with uncertain calm. She laid the child next to its mother.

'My Tara, my little Tara,' Mallika cried.

Her voice clear and comforting, Saroja said, 'Yes ma, look at your Tara for the last time, hold her for the last time. She died ma, she died in her father's arms.'

Munniamma crumpled against a wall and wept.

Mallika writhed and moaned with extreme pain. Perplexed, the midwife turned to her, and, pressing Mallika's stomach with her hands, forced the abnormally large placenta out of her womb. Blood tote. Culprit red. It had occupied all the space, pushing the little girl into the coils of the cord of birth and death.

'Oh my God.' The midwife raised her bloody hands to her head. 'It's another baby.'

And thus he was born in a dark room that smelled of raw rice.

Book Three

Twelve

MALLIKA SAT CROUCHED IN A corner of the storeroom. Not once did she ask to see her son. And each time Munniamma brought the baby to her Mallika looked at him; in his eyes she could see her daughter's eyes. Mallika turned her face away.

Old women gossiped on the streets of Machilipatnam. They talked about Mallika, her dead child, and her son whom she refused to see. Stories about Elizabeth's ghost lingered on their tongues.

Ammamai was on the bench in the garden, the newborn in her arms. Kamala arrived at the gate, dressed in red and gold, flowers in her hair, kohl in her eyes, betel-mouthed.

'Come here,' Ammamai called out to her. When she had walked up to the bench Ammamai held the baby out to her. 'Bless my grandson,' she said.

'He looks just like his mother.' Kamala stroked the baby and made a kissing sound with her lips. Then she cracked her knuckles on the sides of her head and blessed the child.

'I am not leaving until you give me a hundred rupees and a sack of rice,' Kamala said with a scowl. 'The poor child needs all the blessings he can have, ma. Specially mine. I hear his mother refuses to see her child eh?'

Ammamai yelled out to Munniamma to get a sack of old rice. 'And get my money purse from under my pillow.'

Munniamma came with the sack and gave it to Kamala. She handed the purse to Ammamai and took charge of the baby. Ammamai retrieved a hundred-rupee note from it and gave it to Kamala.

After Kamala left them Munniamma raised the child up on her shoulder. 'Poor baby,' she sighed. 'Mallika must be made to cry. She will go mad if she keeps her grief inside her.'

'Get a keener,' Ammamai told her.

The next day Munniamma came with a professional keener. Enormously fat, she had reddened hair that was knotted at the top and adorned with flowers. Several necklaces covered her ample bosom. Her eyes, lined with kohl, were large and weepy. She chewed paan.

Munniamma took her to Mallika. 'See, how she keeps staring at the floor like that. Because of not crying, only because of not crying. You must make her cry.'

The keener removed her necklaces one by one, and then the flowers in her hair. She let her hair down, spread it around her face. She walked to the window and spat the paan out, then asked Munniamma to get her a glass of water. After she had drunk the water, she stood for several minutes with her eyes closed. Then, taking a long and deep breath, she wailed – a long, single wail, like the opening note of an orchestra.

Her shoulders grieved, her breasts drooped, she rhythmically beat her chest, again and again, gasping. She shrieked and, still beating her chest, she hollered. Tears ran down her face, turning into rivulets of kohl.

The keener wailed for half an hour. Then, looking at her watch, she stopped. She wiped her face and neck with the end of her sari, knotted her hair and fixed the flowers back, then adjusted her breasts inside the cups of her bra, put on her necklaces one by one. Drinking another glass of water, she collected her fee and left. Mallika stared at a spot on the floor.

'This is not of any use, Munniamma,' Ammamai said, wringing her hands together. 'Only prayers can make her better. Bring her to the prayer room.'

Munniamma escorted Mallika to the prayer room. Mallika was weak and could hardly walk without support. Ammamai lit the lamps, burnt incense sticks and began to chant. Mallika looked at all the gods' pictures, the fresh flowers around them and the bowls of fruits and milk set on the floor. She looked at the clay idol of the snake goddess that Ammamai had brought back from Chiroor. The Goddess's face was black, as was the snake coiled around Her body. Her eyes were algae-green and the tongue sticking out of Her mouth was blood-red. The plaster-of-Paris idol of Rama gleamed in the light from the lamp. His lips were postbox-red, His teeth Colgate-white, and He wore a permanent holy smile. The smile mocked Mallika.

Her breath came out in a tiny gasp and her body shook. She poured the milk over the idols and threw the fruits at them.

'Aichicho, what are you doing!' Ammamai yelled as she held Mallika's hands.

Mallika yanked her hands away. She picked up the empty bowl and banged it hard on the idols. The idols cracked, crumbled bit by bit, and fell, a holy head here, a sacred hand there, the snakehead in that corner, the bloody tongue in another, and at Ammamai's feet, the permanent pious smile.

Mallika ran back to the storeroom and locked herself in.

Raman stood outside the storeroom that evening beseeching Mallika to open the door. When she did he was aghast to see her – her face was swollen and tainted with grime.

At the sight of him, Mallika's eyes widened with rage. She let fly a stream of abuse at him. Raman had never heard her scream or shout before. He could not fathom what it was that angered her. She instilled in him a helplessness that he had never felt before.

'Why are you angry with me? What did I do?' Raman asked. He held her by her shoulders and crushed her to his chest. It was a bad move. Mallika's eyes froze. She pushed him away and retreated into the room and threw all those things that would break: bottles, glasses, an old mirror. And with each throw she screamed, 'You killed her. You killed my baby. You killed Tara.'

Raman turned around and went straight to his study.

Mallika retreated to the corner of the storeroom. She recollected the words of the old woman from Chirror. 'You must be careful of men,' Ratnamma had said, 'you must be careful of fathers, husbands. They will clip your wings so you can't fly anymore.'

It was a burden to be a woman all right. It was a disgrace. Mallika felt as though large iron locks were clasped to her ankles and she was sinking deep into dark waters.

Vishnu came to see his daughter and grandson the next day. Ammamai spread the pai on the floor in the veranda. Vishnu spent a few moments expressing grief and soothing words about the dead twin. After they had sat down Ammamai asked Munniamma to bring the baby and she placed him in Vishnu's lap. He retrieved a silver rattle from his shirt pocket and shook it over the baby's face.

'He's got Mallika's eyes,' he said tickling the baby under his chin. 'Have you thought of a name, ma? When is the naming ceremony?'

Ammamai didn't reply. A gush of shame, like redness, spread over her face and she averted her eyes.

'What's the matter, ma? Where's Mallika.'

Ammamai became stiff and pained.

'She has locked herself in the storeroom. She doesn't look at her baby. She doesn't nurse him even.'

'How can that be possible? Let me talk to her,' Vishnu said. He lifted the child into Ammamai's arms and stood up.

Munniamma led him to the storeroom. She knocked on the door.

'Mallika, open the door, ma. Your father has come to see you.'

Mallika stood at the door and Vishnu held her by both her shoulders, gently shaking her.

'Why are you doing this to your son?'

Mallika looked at him.

'Tara died, Appa.'

'But your son is alive and he needs you.'

Mallika felt hurt and powerless. Her own father, her own flesh and blood couldn't understand her loss. She went back into her corner.

Vishnu moved forward and then with a change of mind he turned to Ammamai who had come to the door with the baby in her arms.

'Look after her nicely, ma. Poor girl, she's in deep grief,' Vishnu said, his voice strange.

'Look after her?' Ammamai retorted. 'Do you think I am not doing anything at all for her? When my son got married I heaved a sigh of relief because I thought my daughter-in-law would take over from me and look after the house. But she's so weak she can't do a single chore. Just look at my fate! I thought she would look after me. And *you* are asking me to look after *her*? *Nicely*? What about all the humiliation I have to bear? And what about this ill-fated child?'

Vishnu didn't reply. He shrugged and with a resigned look in his eyes, he walked out of the house.

Saroja came to see Mallika in the evening. Ammamai poured her grief out to her. Saroja took the baby to Mallika and cajoled her. 'He is your child. He has been crying all day long,' she said. 'His chest is sore. And Ammamai has had to feed him diluted milk and honey.'

Mallika looked at her son. In his eyes she could see her daughter's eyes, before she died. Mallika turned her face away.

'Maybe Nayantara can put some sense into her friend's head,' Ammamai moaned when Saroja returned to her with the child. 'Will you ask her to come?'

'She's having Malli's ear-piercing ceremony next week. I will ask her to come after that,' Saroja assured her.

Days passed and Mallika refused to see her son. She came out of the storeroom early each morning when everyone was asleep. She washed up and ate leftovers, then returned to the room. All day long she sat in a corner and stared at a spot on the floor. Her hair was dishevelled. She had not changed her blood-stained sari and her face was stained with tears.

Ammamai carried on grumbling to Munniamma, 'Oh my wretched fate. Why didn't I die long ago so I didn't have to live through all this?' She slapped her forehead. 'Just look at Mallika's breasts, so full with milk. And the poor child is so weak he can't even suck on the feeding bottle.'

'Why don't I get a wet nurse, ma?' Munniamma said.

'Yes, yes, do that. Or else this child will die.'

The wet nurse came to the house the next day. She held Mallika's boy to her breasts and nursed him. But when Raman saw his son being nursed by a stranger, he was enraged.

'I don't want her here,' he told Ammamai.

'Babies must have mother's milk,' Ammamai said. 'It is good for them.'

She fixed her eyes on Raman, the pupils large and intense and reproachful.

'God only knows with what fate your son has arrived in this world. Mallika hasn't held him since the moment he was born. If this goes on she will be responsible for his death. Can you think of any mother killing her own child? Why don't you do something, Raman? By ignoring the problem it is not going to sprout wings and fly away like one of your mosquitoes.'

Raman was flustered. 'What can I do? What did I do?'

Ammamai settled the baby in Raman's arms. In an altered, almost severe tone, she said, 'Children die at birth all the time. My own children died. My mother had eleven children and four of them died at birth. My brother before me died at birth. Now if my mother had behaved like Mallika and refused to feed me then I wouldn't have been alive to see this day. I wish I had died like my brother! Even the gods have stopped listening to my prayers. Every day I offer one coconut, a dozen bananas, flowers and twenty rupees to Lord Shiva at the temple, but what is the use? It's the eleventh day tomorrow and we must have the naming ceremony. Am I going to have a nameless grandson eh?'

'Forget the ceremony,' Raman snapped. 'You give him a name right now.'

'Now?' Ammamai slapped her chest. 'Ayiyoo! What will people think? No naming ceremony for my first grandchild?'

'You worry too much about people. Forget them.'

Ammamai shook with fury and narrowed her eyes. 'Why should I care what they say? He is your son after all.'

Raman became gentler now. 'Amma, all that is required is for an older member of the family to name my son and bless him. That's all. You do it, Amma,' he said.

Ammamai took the baby from Raman's arms and went to the prayer room. She put him down on the floor. She lit the lamps and incense sticks, chanted the names of her favourite gods, smeared the baby's forehead with holy ash and whispered in his ear. 'I name you after my dead brother. I name you Siva.'

Thirteen

'Eat slowly,' Ammamai said as she served two more idlis on Raman's plate one morning. 'The idlis don't have feet; they are not going to run away. The pujari will be here in half an hour.'

'What pujari?'

'For the naming ceremony.'

'But you already named him.'

'Yes. I named him Siva.'

'That's fine then. No need for any stupid ceremony. And no need to fill the house with people.'

'Who's calling people? Just the pujari to do the rituals to bless your son. You are the father, remember, you have to be present for the ritual.'

'I am leaving right now. I have work to do.' Raman left the room.

'Go, go,' Ammamai screamed after him, 'you think you are some big scientist now and this is all rubbish. Your success has gone to your head. Go, I will do everything myself. He's my grandson after all.'

The pujari arrived on the dot. He hastily set out the things for the ritual fire.

'I have to go to three other homes for child-naming ceremonies,' he said to Ammamai. 'Bring the child and ask the mother and father to come.'

He lit the fire and the room filled with smoke.

On Ammamai's signal Munniamma brought the baby, naked, and laid him on a square of unhusked rice spread on the floor. He was fast asleep.

'Ma, where are his parents?' the pujari asked.

'You just go ahead and do what you have to do,' Ammamai asserted.

'Without the child's parents?'

Ammamai turned to Munniamma. 'Go, get Mallika dressed and bring her,' she said, gritting her teeth. Then turning to the pujari she said, 'Don't you have to go somewhere? Why don't you just start?'

The pujari shut his eyes and started chanting.

Munniamma rushed to the storeroom where Mallika lay on the floor. Munniamma pulled her up by her arm.

'Get up ma, the pujari is here and we have to do a puja for Tara.'

'Tara?' Mallika gaped at Munniamma.

'Yes. So that her soul rests in peace.' Munniamma held her face and kissed her forehead. 'Come with me.'

She led Mallika to her room and helped her change into a fresh sari. She wiped her face with a wet towel, combed her hair, dotted her forehead with fresh pottu and smeared kohl in eyes. She brought her down and made her sit in front of the ritual fire.

The pujari asked Mallika, 'What's your child's name?'

'Tara.'

'My grandson's name is Siva,' Ammamai said almost at once.

The pujari chanted his name out aloud. 'Now whisper the name three times into the child's ear.'

Even as Ammamai bent down towards the baby, as though the events of the day had been orchestrated by some paranormal force, as if Elizabeth's ghost had had her way, Saroja stood at the door, her hair dishevelled, her eyes, red.

Not once did Saroja's eyes move away from Mallika. 'There was an accident, Mallika,' her voice was oddly calm. 'Nayantara had gone to get earstuds for Malli for the ear-piercing ceremony. Her taxi hit a truck. Nayantara died.'

Ammamai got to her feet and rushed over to Saroja. Gripping her arm she hurried her out of the house and towards the gate.

'I am so sorry, ma. And Malli?'

'She's with her father. She's okay.'

'When did it happen?'

'Last evening,' Saroja said. 'I am leaving for Madras and I thought I should tell Mallika.'

'Mallika won't be able to deal with this,' Ammamai said quickly. 'Please. Please go.'

Saroja turned on her heel and walked out of the gate.

When Ammamai returned to the hall Mallika had gone back to the storeroom.

Nayantara's sudden death shattered Mallika; it fractured her. Her skin grew pallid, notched with pain lines, and her eyes, those aubergine eyes, turned muddy brown. Her hair fell off in tufts.

Ammamai was in the kitchen cutting an obese brinjal on a blade shaped like a hook. The blade cut through the brinjal's tight flesh, slicing it; not a drop of sap dripped from it.'

Munniamma ran through the kitchen door, holding out a fistful of hair.

'Look Amma, I just have to run a comb though Mallika's hair and they fall off.'

Ammamai continued to slice the sapless vegetable faster, the slices thinner. When nothing was left in her hands, she raised them and covered her face.

'Enough, enough. I can't take it anymore. Munniamma, take Mallika to her father. Let him look after her.'

'What about Siva?'

'Siva? It's not as if Mallika looks after him.'

'And Raman-aiyah?'

'I will tell him something or the other.'

Munniamma escorted Mallika to her father's home.

Three months after Siva had been introduced into the world, Ammamai pulped a piece of banana into a bowl of milk and fed it to him with a silver spoon. He cried all evening. So the next evening, she crushed a piece of home-grown papaya into the milk and asked Raman to feed it to him. Siva ate it greedily, opening his little mouth for more.

Raman began coming home with different kinds of papaya. The long ones, the round ones and particularly the sweet small ones, which came from the western coast, called disco papaya.

In fact it was the first word baby Siva learnt to speak. Each time Ammamai brought his evening feed, he kicked his legs in the air. 'Pa-pa, pa-pa, yaaaa.' She told Raman Siva was asking for him. Raman liked the sound of that. He liked it very much.

He introduced Siva to the world of insects and worms: flies, moths, butterflies, ants, silkworms and mosquitoes. 'You are telling him about mosquitoes,' Ammamai laughed. 'As if he will understand.' But she could not help smiling at the sight of Siva in his father's arms. It was the only thing that gave her pleasure those days.

Mallika's eyes regained their colour and her hair started to grow, but she spent most of her time in her room in her father's house, where she could be herself. But to be herself was difficult as large images of her past flashed in her mind. They click-clicked, whir-whirred like slides projected on a screen in an ill-fated sequence.

Whir: Her mother died.
Whir: Her father drank.
Whir: Nayantara went away.
Whir: She got married to Raman.
Whir: Tara died.
Whir: Nayantara died.
Whir: She was alone.

Mallika despised everything about being herself.

Ammamai called Vishnu now and again to enquire about Mallika. Raman, although he missed his wife, stayed away from her. When Ammamai called Vishnu one morning he said to her, 'You must take Mallika home, ma. It's been two months since she came to me. She might just get used to living here and she may forget she has a son.'

Vishnu took Mallika to the beach that evening. They sat on the sand and watched the sea.

Mallika rested her chin on her knees that were pulled up to her chest. She turned her face and looked at her father. There was a little scowl on her face, but underlying it was infinite sadness. Her eyes were dark and heavy. Vishnu had never seen such loneliness in a face.

Even with his personal grief, Mallika's pain seemed to vibrate within Vishnu and he was sucked into Mallika's misery. The tremendous fragility of the moment overcame him; he scooped Mallika's face in his hands and kissed her forehead.

'I am sorry Nayantara died. I am so sorry your girl died.' The breeze was damp on his eyelids.

'I named her Tara, after Nayantara...' Mallika's voice broke.

Vishnu pressed her shoulder. 'We have our sorrows, but we must learn to live with them, not to be defeated by them.' He held Mallika's hand, said gently, 'Your mother died, I have accepted this though it took me a long time. You too should accept what has happened. It's been over two months since you came to me. You should go back to Raman's house Mallika. Don't forget, that's where Tara was born.'

Something in the tone of his voice, the finality of it weakened Mallika's resolve. So a week later, when Raman was on a tour and Ammamai came to see her, Mallika willingly went home with her.

Mallika ran up to her room and locked herself in. She picked up the doll she had hidden in the cupboard, sat in a corner of the room and rocked to and fro, holding the doll to her breast.

'Ssshhh, don't cry Tara,' she cooed, 'I am here.'

Ammamai sat on a wooden plank in the bathroom at the back, stretching her legs in front of her. She hitched her sari up to her hips and tucked it under her thighs. Then Munniamma laid the baby face down on Ammamai's legs.

Ammamai rubbed Siva's back with oil, then turning him around she oiled his chest, stomach, arms and legs. She rubbed his body with soap and washed it away with tepid water. The water gurgled around his neck, and then down Ammamai's legs. She wrapped him in a towel and lifted him up into Munniamma's arms.

'I'll take him to Mallika,' Munniamma said. 'She will be happy to see her son.'

'Wipe that grin off your face, Munniamma,' Ammamai said with a sneer. 'When you are as old as me you will know that bad times come to stay as permanent guests.'

'Yes-yes, when I am as old and helpless as you Amma, I will also become pessimistic like you,' Munniamma retorted.

Humming a lullaby Munniamma climbed up to Mallika's room with the baby. Mallika was sitting cross-legged on the bed with the doll clutched to her breast. Her eyes were shut.

Munniamma laid the baby in Mallika's lap. 'Your son,' she said. 'Look at him, how big he has grown.'

Mallika glanced at the child in her lap and her eyes widened with fear, as though she was looking at her dead baby. She screamed, and Siva started to wail. Munniamma picked him up and ran down the stairs into Ammamai's room.

Ammamai was sitting on the floor rubbing her knees with balm. 'What happened, Munniamma, why is the child crying?'

Munniamma put Siva in his cot and patted his chest. 'It's no use, Amma.' She told her what had happened.

'What did I tell you eh?' Ammamai hit her head with her hands. 'These are bad times. And they will stay. I know this in every bone in my body. Can you hear them rattling?'

Munniamma sat down beside her and kneaded Ammamai's legs. 'Don't worry, ma. Mallika is back and this is all that matters. And Raman-aiyah will be back tomorrow and everything will be all right.'

Raman returned late in the evening. Ammamai was waiting for him in the veranda.

'Mallika is back,' Ammamai said.

'She's back.' There was a hint of relief and gladness in Raman's voice. 'How is she?'

'She's worn out, poor thing. I forced her to eat early and go to her room.'

Raman realised just how much he had missed his wife. He rushed up the stairs to his room. Mallika was in bed, fast asleep. He lay down beside her. She stirred and Raman very gently kissed the ends of her hair. Then he kissed little baby kisses all along her hairline from one ear to the other. He saw Mallika's breasts heave, and sighed, 'Oh Mallika.' He undid her blouse and with his tongue he made a trail over the line of thin hair all the way down to her navel. He circled her navel, once, twice, a number of times, round and round and round.

At that very moment the clock in the dining room whirred and struck twelve. For Raman it was a midnight of incontrollable passion. A wild hunger grew in him. 'Oh Mallika,' he said as he undressed. Then just as he positioned himself to feed his urge, he saw his dead child's eyes before his lust-filled ones and every muscle in him went flaccid. He lay back, looking up at the ceiling, his fitful impotence aching like an old scar.

When Mallika awoke beside her snoring and spent husband, she left the house and walked to the seafront. She stood in the water, her legs apart, riding the waves. The sea wrapped its waves around her and between her legs. It fulfilled and calmed her.

Back at home, after Raman had left for work, Mallika went up to her room, opened the cupboard and at the back she found the bottle she was looking for. Unscrewing its cap, she smelled the dark liquid; it was a smell that had wrapped around her since childhood. She tilted her head back and consumed a quarter of the bottle's contents. The fire in her throat seemed to soothe her mind but tears pricked her eyes. She drank more. Then with the doll she sat down in a corner of the room. She crooned to it, over and over again, 'I am here, Tara. Don't cry my baby.'

When Raman returned home he found his wife sitting in the corner with the doll. 'Mallika,' he said gently and when she looked up at him her eyes were glazed. She smelled of rum. The bottle next to her was half empty. He lost control and without thinking he slapped her hard on her cheek with the back of his hand.

That night Mallika moved her things to the spare room upstairs.

Raman let her be. He did not know how to handle her. His mosquitoes were, at least, predictable. They bit. They sucked. They multiplied.

Fourteen

Mallika was in the kitchen chopping tomatoes. She dropped them into the boiling tamarind water and added a spoon of turmeric and sambhar powder to it. Her faded cotton saree had turmeric stains on the front. Her hair was uncombed and her face sweaty.

Raman returned from work with a friend. They went into the living room and then Raman called out to Mani to get two glasses and a jug of water and lime.

Minutes later Mani stepped into the living room with a steel jug of water, steel tumblers and a lime cut in quarters. He stood rooted to the spot as he stared at the woman.

She was tall and fair, with big, bright eyes. Her face was made up like a film star and her hair was cut short in a chic bob. She wore fitting black trousers and a sleeveless blue chiffon blouse that seemed to Mani like she had wrapped the sky around her. And the sky smelled of perfume.

Raman glared at Mani, then looked at the steel tumblers. 'Muttal! Did I ask you to get these? Henh? I said a glass, glass, understand?' He picked up the quarter of lime. 'And what is this? Is this how you cut lime?'

Mani looked confused. 'But saar, that is how I always cut lime.'

'Fool! Go cut them in thin slices and bring them immediately.'

Ammamai stood at the door. 'Amma, this is Rukmini,' Raman said. 'She was in London with me.'

He turned to Rukmini. 'My mother,' he said.

Rukmini rose, looking queenly and radiant, as she held out her hand. 'Good evening, Mrs Iyer.'

'Evenin-evenin.' Ammamai turned on her heel and went back to the kitchen without another word.

Mani returned with the glasses and the slices of lime. Raman poured the dark contents of the rum bottle in two glasses, topped them with water and dropped slices of lime in them. He held out a glass to Rukmini.

She raised the glass up. 'Here's to your experiment.' Then she sipped her drink. Raman gulped his and poured himself another stiff measure. Rukmini looked in her bag for a packet of cigarettes and a lighter. 'Is it okay if I smoke here?'

Raman muttered a reply as she held out the packet to him. He pulled out a cigarette, took the lighter from her hand, lit her cigarette first, then his. Rukmini took a long puff and sat back in the chair.

Mani had remained by the door, gaping at Rukmini, unable to take his eyes off her.

Ammamai sidled up to Mani and said, 'What are you standing there for with your mouth wide open like that? Before you know, a pair of mosquitoes will go in and lay their eggs inside your stomach. Then you will die of malaria of your stomach. Get back to the kitchen.'

Ammamai turned on her heel and followed Mani into the kitchen. She grabbed Mallika by the arm and said bitingly, 'Look what is happening in front of our eyes? Your husband has come home with a woman and she is blowing smoke all over your shameless husband's face. And look at your dirty saree, and your hair all out of place. Have you not even washed your face eh?'

Ammamai hissed through her teeth. 'Have you no idea how to be a proper wife? You have to be cunning. Conniving like a cat. And you have to learn to control your husband without him even knowing it. Men are not as tough as they appear. They are easy to impress and confuse. First whisky and then woman.'

Ammamai dragged Mallika to the corridor. Her eyes went hard with disgust. 'See how he is smiling at her. Ye di, have you ever seen so many of his teeth on display? And crooked ones at that? He had better close his mouth or else his saliva will drool down his chin and flood the room.'

She pinched Mallika's arm. 'You silly thing, you silly thing! At times like this you have to claim what belongs to you. Go and sit with them so that witch knows who his wife is. Don't leave them alone even for a single minute.'

Mallika looked at Raman with a queer, half-bewildered, half-perverse smile. She felt as if her chest was crushed and she couldn't breathe. She gulped the sob that rose in her throat, turned around and ran up to her room.

Ammamai slapped her cheeks and groaning she walked back into the kitchen. Mani arched his eyebrows and asked with a smirk, 'Is she a film actress?'

Ammamai made wild clucking sounds with her tongue. 'How does it matter to you whether she is an actress or a whore, henh? You are getting too big for your slippers!'

Mani reached up to scratch a spot on his scalp. Ammamai shook a finger at him, 'And if even one word leaks out, I will break your legs and hammer your head so bad you won't be able to tell which is which.'

Loud squeals of laughter came from the living room. 'Just listen to her laugh. Chi-chi-chi, these London women have no shame. Did you see what she was wearing? Tight-tight pants and a transparent blouse without sleeves even.' Ammamai flushed so that the veins in her neck stood out.

She clasped her hands. 'Only God can help us now,' she muttered and rushed into the prayer room. She lit the lamp and incense sticks and started to pray.

'She's gone,' Mani said from the door.

Ammamai stood up, tucked the free end of her sari around her waist and rushed to the front door where she confronted Raman.

'How can you bring that woman into this house eh? Who is she?'

'I told you, ma. She was in the London institute with me.'

'So? What is she doing here?'

'She was in Madras. I invited her to come and see my work.'

'And when is she leaving?'

'She is flying back to Madras tomorrow,' Raman said, his one eyebrow raised. 'From there they will fly to Colombo.'

'They?'

'Rukmini and her husband ...'

'She's married?'

'Of course she is married. David, her husband, is a very good friend.'

Ammamai folded her arms in front of her chest and smiled. 'She's very nice, this Rukmini.'

Saroja had brought Malli back with her from Madras. Siddhartha was unable to look after his daughter. He agreed it would be good for Malli if she were to live with her grandmother. Malli was just under a year old.

Some days later Saroja came with her granddaughter to see Mallika.

Mallika heard a knock on her bedroom door the next morning. It was Munniamma. 'Open ma, look Saroja-ma is here,' she shouted.

Mallika flung the door wide open. When she saw the little girl hiding behind Saroja her eyes lit up in amazement. She leaped out of the doorway. 'Tara? Oh, my Tara,' she cried and crushed Malli to her chest.

Saroja looked at Mallika with fear and guilt – guilt for having the one thing that Mallika so needed and fear of the pain that the truth would bring her. She hadn't noticed before but now as she looked at Mallika she thought she could see in her a touch of madness. She was afraid for her, of her. Very gently she pulled Malli out of Mallika's arms. She clasped Mallika's hand and with a voice that shook she said, 'Mallika, this is my granddaughter, Malli.'

Mallika seemed not to have heard her. She beseechingly looked at Saroja sending a shiver down her spine. Saroja patted Mallika's shoulder. 'This is Malli. Nayantara's girl. Not Tara.'

Mallika fixed Saroja with a sort of witch-like glare. Then she did an extraordinary thing. She lifted her face and, staring beyond Saroja, in a clear, brittle voice, she said 'Nayantara's daughter? Poor motherless child.' She shut the door in Saroja's face. Munniamma was witness to this and it was an incident she wasn't going to easily forget. She dressed Siva in one of the frocks that Mallika had got for Tara and smeared his eyes with kohl.

'Why have you dressed him in that frock, Munniamma?' Raman asked when he returned home. He grabbed his son and peeled the frock off and with his handkerchief wiped the kohl from his eyes. 'Don't ever dress him in frocks. He is a boy, not a girl, understand?'

'Why are you shouting, Raman?' Ammamai walked to him with a tumbler of coffee. Munniamma walked away, her face tight.

'Crazy woman, she had dressed Siva in a frock and plastered the poor boy's eyes with kohl.'

'So what?' Ammamai said. 'When you were a baby I dressed you in frocks too. Stop making a hill out of a heap of mustard seeds. It's a minor matter. There are more important matters. It's been three weeks since Mallika returned and not once she has asked about Siva. And you are not bothered about this even. How long will this go on eh? This arrangement of separate rooms and all that? How long will I have to look after your son?'

'I will look after him,' Raman said and hugged his son.

The next morning Munniamma once again dressed Siva in a frock and lined his eyes with kohl. She held him in her arms and walked into the kitchen. Ammamai gave her a tight slap on her back. 'Aiyoo Rama, what's wrong with you, Munniamma? Did you not hear what Raman-aiyah told you? He will skin you alive if you keep on doing this, you crazy woman. Go, take that frock off at once.'

Munniamma struck her tongue to her palette, making a defiant cluck. 'When Saroja-ma came with Malli, Mallika mistook her for Tara. What if we make Mallika believe Siva is Tara,' Manniamma beamed. 'I am telling you, she has to just hold him once and she will be fine.'

Ammamai considered what Munniamma said and her eyes lit up with hope.

'Maybe, maybe.' She clutched her cheeks with both her hands and laughed. 'Take him to Mallika; let's see what she does.'

Munniamma knocked on the door and called out to Mallika. Ammamai stood against the wall, concealed by it. When Mallika opened the door, Munniamma thrust the child in her arms.

Mallika looked at the baby. For a moment she seemed confused. Then smile teased the corners of her mouth, and a tear fell from her eye.

'Tara, my child. Oh Tara.' Mallika kissed Siva on both his cheeks and held him. She walked to the bed and sat down. She felt an unfamiliar sensation in her breasts and her blouse grew wet; there were two damp circles around her nipples. She was lactating.

Mallika held the baby to her breast and, unbuttoning her blouse, thrust her nipple into the baby's mouth.

The night was ink dark. It was Amavas and there was no moon in the sky. Ammamai, her forehead ash-lined, sat in the prayer room. On a silver tray she had placed, as she did every Amavas, a silver lamp, some flowers, a silver bowl of water and a small jar of rice and sesame seeds. She went to the garden and looked up into the moonless sky. Clutching a fistful of jasmine and pointing her hand where the moon should have been, she turned it round and round and dropped the flowers on the ground. She took a pinch at a time of rice and sesame seeds from the jar and sprinkled it on the soil, over which she sprinkled water. Then she sang a song to awaken the dead who, slumber-stirred, sang back to her. Or so she believed. Her eyes closed, hands clasped tight, Ammamai prayed to the moongod for peace and happiness in her home.

Raman was mostly travelling; he didn't have much time for Siva. Mallika spent all her time with her son whom she believed to be her daughter. A pattern had been set and it assumed the guise of everyday routine. Four months passed by, though slowly, routinely, without much incident.

Siva had started to walk. Mallika dressed him in a pink frock with a matching lace trim she had recently got and took him to the pond.

White lilies grew tall and butterflies flitted over each bloom. Green-brown toads croaked in unison. A few cicadas mistook day for night and screeched in chorus. Mallika sat down on a grassy mound under the chakka tree.

She patted her thigh. 'Come, sit on my lap, Tara,' she said, and when Siva did, Mallika covered his head with her sari and, unclasping the hooks of her blouse, thrust her nipple into his mouth. Instinctively he sucked at it, his face concealed under her sari.

Munniamma who had come looking for them slapped her cheeks and shaking her head she walked away. She found Mani in the kitchen chopping onions. She grabbed the knife from him and started to chop the tuber, slicing them frenziedly into thin slices.

'Not so thin. I want them quartered for the sambhar. What's wrong with you eh?' Mani asked her. 'Why don't you leave my job to me?'

Munniamma sighed. She had tears in her eyes.

'Now look, the onion has made you cry,' Mani laughed.

'It's not the onion, idiot,' Munniamma retorted. She put the knife down and told Mani what she had seen. 'Siva's nearly a year old,' she said, 'how long can she keep nursing him!'

Mani laughed. 'Oh that lucky boy!'

Munniamma hit his head and walked away. 'Aren't you going to wash the vessels?' Mani shouted after her.

'Wash them yourself,' she yelled back and went in search of Ammamai.

'How long will Mallika keep thinking her son is Tara?' she asked Ammamai.

'Until she realises he is Siva.'

'She knows he is Siva, ma. She is only pretending. That's why she never gives him a bath or sees him without any clothes. All this pretence is not good for Mallika and not at all good for Siva.'

Ammamai let out a loud moan.

'See what a mess you have got us into. Munniamma, how can we stop all this? Mallika seems so happy and my grandson is content.'

Mallika shook Ammamai awake one afternoon. The first thing Ammamai saw when she opened her eyes was Siva looking adorable in a long silk skirt the colour of wet paddy and a red blouse. His large eyes were kohl-lined and on his little forehead was a vermillion pottu. Mallika had fixed a string of jasmine to his long hair, which she had until now refused to cut.

'I am having Tara's ears pierced today,' Mallika said. She looked radiant in a red silk sari.

Ammamai sat up with a start. 'Ears pierced? Today?'

'I thought of it only this morning and I have been busy making all the arrangements.' Ammamai saw Munniamma at the door signalling to her.

Mallika persisted. 'Come, Amma, the pundit is waiting,' she said.

As soon as Mallika walked out of the room with Siva, Munniamma rushed to Ammamai's bedside. 'What are you going to do, ma? Are you going to let her pierce Siva's ears?'

'Let her do it,' Ammamai said firmly.

'But Ammamai, Raman-aiyah will get very angry.'

'He's not here. He's away all the time, and he may not notice even.'

'But Amma, how long do we go on with this pretence?'

Ammamai held her head in her hands. 'Munniamma, I know we are making a terrible mistake. But just look at Mallika; she is getting better day by day. And imagine how unhappy Siva would have been if Mallika had continued to reject him. I will tell Mallika soon. But until such time let's fulfil all her desires.'

Siva sat on Mallika's lap, sucking a pink lollypop. 'My little princess,' Mallika said bending down to kiss his cheek. The pundit sat in front of the fire, pouring spoonfuls of ghee into the flames. The mole on the tip of his nose grew red as the flames hissed and shot upwards.

Mallika's face and armpits were sweaty. Siva was restless; little beads of sweat collected over his upper lip. He tried to free himself but Mallika held him tight. Sweet syrup trickled down the corners of his mouth, mixed with his sweat.

Mallika bent forward and threw puffed rice into the fire. The pundit continued to feed it as he chanted, one-spoon two-spoons three-spoons of pure home-made ghee. Siva's candy-coated tongue stuck out, lick-licked, then disappeared.

When the man in the white veshti pierced his ear and twisted a gold wire into the hole, Siva screamed. Mallika shoved a spoon of sugar into his mouth. The man quickly pierced his other ear and Siva started to howl. Mallika hugged him. 'Don't cry, Tara. Look at your ears; there are stars in them.'

Siva struggled in Mallika's arms and started to wail. Mallika balled her sari in her hand, blew warm air on it and pressed it to his ears, one at a time. 'Now the hurt will go away,' she said softly.

Fifteen

MALLIKA DESPAIRED AS SIVA GREW slowly. Weak and sickly, he was allergic to dust, sensitive to heat; milk gave him a rash and green vegetables made him itch. He was four years old but he still wet his bed and sucked his thumb.

Ammamai was equally perturbed. 'What is it about this child, so delicate?' she asked Raman. 'And sensitive to heat? Have you ever heard of anything like this? Sensitive to heat? Ha! In Machilipatnam? With the sun blazing 365 days of the year?'

Raman scolded her, 'It's because you are spoiling him. Don't bathe him in warm water. Bathe him in cold water. Let him cry; it's good for his chest. And don't cover him with that silk quilt when he sleeps. Let him get used to the cool breeze. And at night, don't leave the lights on. Let him get used to the dark.'

'Poor child, he's so weak,' Ammamai complained to Munniamma.

'Don't worry, ma,' Munniamma comforted her. 'I'll soak green gram overnight in water and give it to him in the morning. I will get goat's milk for him to drink. And I'll bathe him with moong flour and sesame oil. Don't worry ma, he will soon be all right.'

So Munniamma used moong flour with sesame oil instead of soap when she bathed Siva. She fed him goat's milk, which was difficult to get, and its smell clung to him. She made him chew a fistful of horse gram every morning.

When Raman consulted Dr Kuruvilla about Siva's allergies, bed-wetting and thumb-sucking, he blamed it on congenital fear.

'It will go away,' he said, adding, 'Give him fish liver oil. It will make him strong. And change his diet. Eggs, you must make him eat eggs.'

Mallika fed Siva soft-boiled eggs and, pinching his nostrils with her fingers, she forced down his throat a spoon each of cod and shark liver oil. And when he cried Mallika lifted Siva on her lap, held him to her breasts and gently rocked him.

'Oh my Tara, my sweet Tara,' she cooed.

Siva put his finger on the top of her forehead, then slowly ran it over the ridge of her nose, down its tip, over her lips, her chin and all the way down her neck to the hollow under it. Then he curled his finger into the dip, sheltered and safe.

Siva's health didn't improve much but at five he was a bright and gifted child and Raman was overjoyed about this. He would often be in his study with his son going through a big picture book of insects.

'Tell me, what is this?' Raman asked Siva.

'Ant.'

'Good.' He turned some pages. 'And this one?'

'Butta fly.'

'Very good. Now tell me what this is?'

'Catta pilla.'

'You can't see its legs but it has six in the front and many in the middle. Its head has six eyes on one side. And what is this?'

'Silkworm.'

'Yes. That's correct. Silk is made out of silkworms' homes called cocoon. What is this?'

Siva shook his head.

'This is a praying mantis. It is the only insect fast enough to catch flies and mosquitoes.'

'Pider, pider,' Siva said pointing to the adjoining page.

'Spider, not pider. Spiders are our friends because they eat harmful insects like flies and those horrible mosquitoes that carry disease.'

He turned some more pages. 'What is this?'

'Mus-ki-to.'

'Yes. But which one?'

Siva stuttered. Raman laughed and fondly pinched his ear. 'Silly, you don't even know what this is? It is an a-no-phee-lees. Repeat after me: a-no-phee-lees.

Siva jumped up and down. 'A. No. Phi. Liss. A. No. Phi. Liss.'

Raman gathered him in his arms. 'Yes. Don't forget. Then when you are older you will be a mosquito scientist just like your father.'

On every other Sunday Mallika took Siva to Vishnu's house. Although Vishnu was troubled to see his grandson dressed up like a girl he did not voice his angst.

After Mallika left, Vishnu and Siva wandered down Gibbs Road and to the beach. Together they examined all that constituted nature: the sea, mud, trees, stone, sand, insects, birds, animals, people. And all that was spawned by them: cobwebs, nests, homes, gardens, the zoo, the village, and the gods and temples they occupied.

On some days Vishnu took Siva to the lake in the woods. When Siva clapped the birds in the tall trees were startled and ruffled the leaves as they took flight. On other days they were at Pinto's ice cream parlour with four flavours: vanilla, orange, chocolate and pista, where Siva sat with his grandfather on the railing and licked ice cream cones. Next to it, there was the old barber shop with frosted glass windows. Siva peeped through it and watched men with soap on their cheeks, ready for a shave. And beside it, the greengrocers with yesterday's vegetables in small cane baskets in the front, going at a discount. While Vishnu talked to the grocer, Siva dropped the old vegetables into the fresh vegetable bin. And then there was the fruit vendor whose shop smelled like a jelly orchard in the sun.

One Sunday afternoon when they were at the beach Siva asked his grandfather, 'Who am I?'

'What?' Vishnu laughed. 'You are *you*.'

'Appa says I am Siva but Amma says I am Tara and makes me wear frocks. I want to be Tara. When I am Tara Amma is very happy.'

Vishnu said, 'No kanna, you can't be Tara. You are Siva.'

'Then why Amma says I am Tara? Who is Tara?'

'Tara was your twin sister. She was born with you. She looked just like you.'

'Where is she?'

'She went away, kanna.'

'Where did she go?

'To paradise.'

'What is pa-ra-die-s?'

Vishnu held Siva's chin and looked into his eyes. 'It's a lovely island in the sky.'

'When will she come back?'

'She won't come back now.'

'So I won't see her?'

'No. But if you close your eyes and think of her you will hear her voice in your ears.'

Siva was in the garden, following a large green chameleon that emerged out of a hole in a tree. It was bright had green at first, then sun-bleached, then stone-brown. The chameleon hopped off the tree, scrambled down the low stonewall to the stairs at the back of the house. It leaped up on a step and stopped. It cocked its head and looked up at Siva, swishing its tail in a friendly fashion. Then with a change of colour, it disappeared into a hole in the wall.

Siva climbed the stairs to the top of the house. Up on the terrace he tried the door in the corner. It opened into a small landing. He climbed up another flight of steps to the attic. There was a hole in the roof where the tiles had fallen off. Birds flew in and out through the hole. The attic was home to many insects. Siva crept about like them, trying not to make any sound.

Siva often went to the attic. It was from there that he called out to Tara, far away in pa-ra-die-s. 'Look at the new frock Amma got me. You like it?'

He would get a plate of goodies for her to eat and as he ate them he talked to Tara. He talked to her about the hide-and-seek game the clouds and the sun played each day. He told her about the moon and the stars, which were torchlights in the sky, and how the soiled sky had a shower in the rain and when it was clean a rainbow popped out of its mouth like a multicoloured smile.

On some days Siva was in the attic with the comic books Raman had got him. He read aloud to Tara the yarns, plots and woes of the Li'l Bad Wolf, Bugs Bunny, Donald Duck and Uncle Scrooge, Mickey Mouse and Goofy, and tried to talk like them.

When a cobweb stuck to the soft hair on Siva's arm he heard Tara whisper in his ear,

Whazz this?

'Webs. Cob-webs. Th' spider makezz' em,' Siva replied.

Whazze make 'em out of?

'Spit.'

Kin ah make 'em wiz mah spit?

'No.'

'Wy not?'

'Becazz you-a not a spider.'

But whazzit make webs for?

'Like th' birds build the-a nests.'

It livezz in th' web, yeah?

'Yeah. It asso traps othe' insectz in it.'

Wy?

'It likez to eat 'em.'

Argh. Thass auful!

'Thass how it iz on eartz.'

Then Siva lay under the hole in the roof and watched the blue sky. He saw a plane flying past. He saw its huge belly. He saw bird-bellies flying. It was so different seeing the big sky in the open and seeing it through the hole in the roof. The sky became so small that it belonged only to Tara and him: their bright-blue sky with planes and birds that flew on their bellies.

Whenever Siva needed to be with Tara, he hid in the attic. It was Tara's and his womb-world, their own pa-ra-die-s on earth, with a tiny sky.

Mallika had made semolina laddoos. She gave one to Siva. He ran to the back of the house where new anthills had cropped up. He dropped tiny bits of the sweet around the anthill, and then watched ants scurry out of nowhere.

'Come, come,' Siva called out to them, 'come and eat sweet laddoo,' he said holding his breath lest he blew the ants away. As the ants moved with their sweet burden, Siva plucked a hair from his head and with his cheek against the ground, he gently nudged each ant on its way with the strand of hair. 'Go, go,' he whispered as he guided them to the anthill.

But the next morning Siva came upon a dying caterpillar; the garden was full of them. Many had wandered out because of the heat, Vishnu had told him. This one's numerous legs were raised to the sky above, and it was wiggling its life away leg by leg. Ants perambulated around the dying creature in mock Brahmin ritual, nibbling at it.

'Shoo,' Siva shouted at the ants, 'shoo.' Then he breathed hard and blew them off the scene of extinction. He looked at the caterpillar, sadness in his eyes.

Ammamai called out to Siva. She was in the kitchen sorting mangoes from a basket. 'You haven't eaten yet,' she said to Siva when he came into the kitchen. She sat down on the floor with a plate of food. Siva sat beside her. He had the dead caterpillar in his hand.

'Why does everything have to die?' he asked Ammamai.

She rolled the rice, sambhar and vegetables into a small ball and pressed it into his mouth. 'Now eat your food and I'll tell you a story about death,' she said.

'See, at first, when the gods built the world, there was no death. So creatures and people went on and on being born. Soon the earth was full. So many people in it with so many problems and desires that the gods could not attend to them all.

'So what to do? The gods thought and thought and then introduced Time. Now the young ones grew old, the old ones grew older, and the older ones grew still older.' She put a ball of rice into Siva's mouth. 'The tired ones wanted to rest. Those with pain in their bones cried out. The gods became worried.

So they came up with the plan of death. They made categories, and then decided who should live and for how long. They made germs live the longest, flowers the shortest and trees, birds, beasts and people in proportion to their work on earth.'

She fed Siva more rice 'So, Siva, that is how death came on earth,' Ammamai concluded. She put the plate away, cut a ripe mango and gave him a piece.

'But Tara was so young. Why did God make Tara die?'

Ammamai shielded her eyes with her hand and shaking her head she said, 'How I wish Tara had lived. Everything would have been all right.' She uncovered her eyes and looked at her grandson. 'But I knew Tara would die the moment she was born. She was so weak. And yellow like this mango. I know who will die soon and who will die later. You see, the gods drop the children from heaven with special smells and return dates stamped on their foreheads.'

She sniffed a mango. 'See, like this mango. The children who have to die smell over-ripe.'

Ammamai's eyes filled with tears. She bundled her sari and raised it to her mouth.

'Ammamai, why are you crying?' Siva asked. He blew air into his palms and pressed them to her eyes. 'Now your hurt will go away.'

Sixteen

MALLI WAS TALL, MUCH TOO tall for her age. Her skin had a pearly translucent quality and was stretched tightly over her bones. Her face was oval and pale, brightened by her eyes that had tints of blue-green in them. Her smile, the most charming feature of her face, brought out two dimples on the same cheek. Her curly hair hung loose around her face and neck. She looked just like her mother.

Whenever Mallika saw Malli she felt she had somehow betrayed Nayantara. She didn't know why. But one thing she knew, it had to do with her child. More often these days when she looked at Siva she failed to see her Tara in him. Moreover, one evening, in a fit of rage Raman had discarded all the frocks.

Mallika became remote and absent. There was a weight on top of her, something that pressed down on her life. It was as if darkness were coming upon her. She grew cheerless and confused. For most of the time she remained closeted in her room.

Ammamai was sitting in the veranda, fanning her face with a magazine. Not far from her Siva, in an old pair of shorts and a white T-shirt with stains on it, was on the floor, colouring a sketch of a house he had drawn. When he looked up he saw Saroja and Malli walk through the gates.

Saroja gave Ammamai the box of sweets she had brought with her. Malli stood before Siva and swinging to and fro she said, 'It's my birthday today. I am seven years old.'

'Appy b'day, Malli,' Siva said.

'See, Saroja-patti got me this dress.'

It was a white frock with layered frills of soft chiffon and lace, mother-of-pearl buttons and a broad white satin sash.

Ammamai looked at Malli and cracked her knuckles on either side of her head. 'I see the resemblance now; she has her mother's face-cut,' she said to Saroja, and under her breath she muttered, 'poor girl.'

Ammamai yelled out to Mani to get coffee and coconut barfi that she had made that morning.

'Where's Mallika?' Saroja enquired.

'In her room. She's not too well.'

'What's wrong?'

'Nothing,' Ammamai said with a wave of her hand, 'just moods. She gets like this now and then. She was indisposed the last time you came, remember. How is Malli's father?'

'Siddhartha moved to LA.'

'L. A? Where is this L. A?'

'America,'

'Aichichoo, so far away?'

'He got a good job there.'

'At least when he was in Madras he could come to see his daughter often, but now … How long will you look after his daughter?'

'She's Nayantara's daughter too,' Saroja said.

'Appa says when I am older I can live with him,' Malli said turning towards Ammamai. 'Can Siva come home with us now?'

'Okay,' Ammamai said, 'and I'll send Mallika to fetch him if she is feeling any better. Or Mani can fetch him.'

Malli looked back at Siva. He had drawn a little girl and a boy next to the house and coloured them. He pointed to the boy and said, 'This is me.'

'And this is me?' Malli asked pointing to the girl.

'No. That is Tara.' He pointed to the house, 'And this is Para-die-s.'

'Patti, make Siva a butterfly kite,' Malli said when they were home.

Saroja took Siva's shoes off and placed his bare foot over a sheet of white tissue paper. She outlined the shape of his foot on the paper and cut out six footprints. She arranged them in the shape of twin wings, pasted them together with a stick in the middle and tied a string to the stick.

'Here, Siva, a white butterfly kite,' Saroja said. 'Go out and fly it and I'll get you something to eat.'

Malli held Siva's hand and ran into the garden at the back.

'How to fly?' Siva asked.

'Hold the kite and walk back, more back, more. Okay, stop.' Malli yanked the string and shouted, 'Let go of the kite, Siva.'

She pulled the string harder and with a fluttering sound the kite soared high into the sky. She let Siva hold the string and when he did the kite spun and swirled.

'Pull it, pull it,' Malli yelled.

The kite dived.

'Oh no,' Malli cried.

The kite plunged and got caught in the electrical lines.

'Look what you did, Siva. We lost the kite.'

'That's okay, Siva,' Saroja said, bringing two wedges of watermelon on a plate. She left it on the table in the veranda and went back into the house.

'I'll show you something,' Malli said and out of a wooden box in the veranda she held up a thick glass object with a steel handle.

'This is a magic glass. My father got it for me.' She showed Siva how things became bigger when seen through it.

Siva looked at the watermelon wedge through the glass and he could see its pink skin and tiny threads that held the red juice. The seeds looked like big beetles with a white moustache. He lay under the peepal tree and looked at it. Its bark looked like the crocodile's skin he had seen when Vishnu-tata took him to the zoo. Behind the rough, dirty skin he could see the pink baby skin. The tree trunk looked bigger and closer through the glass, and he saw the greenbones of the big leaves. Then he looked at the sky through the magnifying glass.

'Vishnu-tata says Tara is up there in the island in the sky,' he said.

'Siva! Don't do that.' Saroja came rushing to his side. She snatched the magnifying glass from his hand.

Saroja took a piece of paper from the table, she placed the magnifying glass over it until the sun's splinter went through and made a glowing dot on the paper. Then the dot turned yellow, and then brown and then whoosh, it caught fire.

'Don't play with the glass in the sun,' Saroja said, 'it will burn you. Malli, why don't you play in your room; it's getting hot. Go now.'

Malli took Siva up to her room. She emptied a plastic bag on the bed.

'Look at all the things my father sent me,' she said.

There was an assortment of things: hairclips, a fancy brooch, a box of felt pens, a sketchbook with a butterfly on it, a doll with shiny blonde hair and a powder-blue frock embellished with pearl buttons and a white lace collar.

Malli picked up the doll and said, 'Let's play Pretend.'

Siva frowned, 'Pre-tend?'

'You are the boy and I am the girl. We get married and this is our baby,' she said holding the doll to her chest. 'You go to office and I will cook and clean the house. And when you come home tired in the evening I will feed you nice food, okay? And then one day I will die in a car accident and you will be left alone. So you will go to office and come home in the evening and cook and clean the house and look after our baby.'

She pointed to two corners of her room. 'This is our home and that will be your office. And that is the road where I will die. Let's play. It will be fun. You wait here. I'll get some food from the kitchen.'

No sooner had Malli left the room than Siva undressed and compelled by something mysterious within him he pulled the blue frock over his head and slipped his thin arms through its sleeves. He buttoned the frock and tied the sash tight around his waist. He pirouetted round and round, his arms stretched above his head like a little ballerina.

'Why are you dressed in my frock?' Malli asked Siva when she came back.

'I will be the girl.'

Malli giggled. 'How can you be the girl, stupid? You are a boy.'

'I will be Tara.'

'If you are the girl also we can't play then.'

'Why?'

'Silly-silly-silly,' she slapped his chest. 'If we are both girls then how can we get married and have a baby? You have to be the boy.'

'Then I don't want to play,' Siva said.

'Go then, don't play.' Malli stuck out out her tongue at him. 'Give back my frock, stupid. I want my frock back. It's my frock.'

'Malli, why are you shouting like that?' Saroja called out. 'If you don't stop screaming I am coming up and I will take Siva home.'

Siva hurriedly changed back into his clothes.

'Here take your frock,' he said, holding the dress out to Malli.

'If you don't want to play, then go home,' Malli said sternly.

'Oo-ke-ee, we play,' Siva said with a sigh of resignation. 'What do I have to do?'

Just then Saroja asked them to come down. 'I have to go to the market. I'll buy you ice cream.'

Malli and Siva went to the market with Saroja. She got them ice cream cones from Pinto's.

Malli looked down the street. She saw a woman dressed in a bright-red sari walking towards them. Her face was like a man's.

'Look, there's girl-boy,' Malli said.

Siva turned around to see. 'Who?'

'Kamala, the girl-boy.'

'Girl-boy?'

'Yes. She is both, girl and boy.'

'How?'

'Because, because, she was a boy first but became a girl.'

'Can I become a girl?'

'No silly.'

'Why not?'

'Because you are a boy-boy, stupid.'

Siva stared at Kamala when she walked over to them. Her hair had greyed in places.

'Hello princess,' she blew kisses at Malli. 'And you are Mallika-ma's son, no?'

'He is Siva,' Malli said.

Kamala pinched Siva's cheek. 'Such a sweet face, like a girl's,' she said making kissing sounds with her lips. And then she walked away.

Malli held Siva's hand and pulled him across the road.

'Whererewe going? Whererewe going?' Siva asked.

'To the palm reader. There he is.'

'Who's a palm reader?'

'He can tell what's going to happen to us.'

'I thought only God can do that. Ammamai said God makes everyone and then decides what will happen to them.'

'He is the Playing-God man then. Come on.'

Siva looked at the Playing-God man with deep curiosity. He was matchstick thin and he breathed with a pneumatic hiss. His face was tired, very tired. He seemed to Siva as though he was dying.

Did gods die also? It was an important question, he decided, and it needed to be asked. For the sake of the flowers, trees, insects, animals, his mother, father, Ammamai, Vishnu-tata, Malli, Tara and himself.

If God died what would happen to them?

The Playing-God man had hung up a number of square charts on the wall behind him. On the ground in front of him were more charts and charms of many kinds. Malli sat down and showed him her palm.

'Tell me, who will I marry?'

The Playing-God man faintly smiled at her and hissed through his nostrils. 'You have to wait ma, you are too young to marry.'

'Look in your chart; tell me who I'll marry when I am older.'

'So impatient you are to get married, ma.' He picked up a chart from the ground, blew the dust from it, peered into the squares and said, 'You will marry a nice young boy.'

'That much I also know,' she said laughing into the Playing-God man's face.

Malli held Siva's hand. 'Him? Will I marry him? He's nice, sometimes.'

The Playing-God man sneezed; he pinched his nose between his fingers, blew hard and wiped his fingers on the sleeve of his shirt. He looked up at Siva and smiled, showing all his crooked teeth.

'Yes-yes, nice boy, yes. When you are older, I am sure you will marry him.'

'See I told you,' Malli told Siva. 'I knew when I am older I'll marry you and we will have a baby. And then I will die.'

Siva asked the Playing-God man his burning question. 'When will you die?'

The Playing-God man breathed long and hard, then he choked and coughed and his chest made a rainthunder sound.

'I think he's going to die now,' Malli said. She heard her grandmother call out to her. 'Let's go.' She stood up and holding Siva's arm ran across the road to Saroja who was waving to them.

'What were you doing?' Saroja asked Malli.

'The palm-reader said I will marry Siva.'

Saroja laughed. 'There's a lot of time for that. Come on, let's go home.'

'When will the Gods die?' Siva asked.

Saroja patted Siva's head. 'The Gods will die when you want them to, kanna.'

Siva looked up at her. 'Ammamai said that we die when the Gods want us to. Tara died because God wanted her to die.'

'No. kanna, that's not true.' Saroja patted his head once again. "Come along now, let's go home.'

As they approached the house, Mallika was waiting in the veranda. Malli ran to her.

'Mallika-aunty it's my birthday today,' she said.

'I remember.' Mallika looked at Malli. She looked so much like her mother. 'Happy birthday Tara,' she whispered.

Malli turned to Siva. 'Will you come to my house tomorrow?'

'Yes,' Siva said. 'And we will play a new game of Pretend.'

'Who will we be?'

'God.'

Malli screwed up her nose. 'I don't know how to be God.'

'It's easy,' Siva said. 'First we will make people and then decide who should live and for how long.'

Mallika shared her room with Siva. A few weeks before Siva started school, Raman said to him. 'You cannot sleep in your mother's room, Siva.' He had asked Mani to move Siva's things to the small room next to the stairs. 'You will sleep in your own room.'

'No,' Siva cried. 'I want to sleep with Amma. I don't want to sleep alone. I am scared.'

Raman patted Siva's head. 'Don't be silly. Aren't you Appa's big boy now?'

Siva stood on his toes. 'Yes, I am Appa's big boy.'

Mallika seemed pleased with the new sleeping arrangement. As the weeks passed, there were nights when Siva's screams brought Raman rushing to his bedside and at other times Ammamai was surprised to see Siva asleep next to her on her bed.

It was Siva's birthday. His star birthday, Ammamai told him. He was seven. When he asked Ammamai what 'star birthday' was, she explained, 'The calendar was made by the English to keep dates to control people all over the world. English birthdays are according to the calendar. But Hindus are born under stars. We have a special group of stars for each of us. Yours Siva, is called Uthradum. And when these stars come in the sky, it is your birthday.'

Mallika went missing from the morning. Ammamai looked for her everywhere. She asked Mani, 'Ye da, Mani, did you see Mallika?'

'No Amma.'

'And you Munniamma? Did you see her?'

Munniamma continued scrubbing the vessel. 'She must be in her room Amma.'

'What do you think I have? Eyes or buttons? That's the first place I looked in. I wonder where she has gone. It is Siva's birthday. It is Tara's birth anniversary, or, should I say, death. We always go to the temple. She can't have forgotten today. And where is Siva?'

Siva was in the balcony outside Mallika's room waiting for her. The previous year, on his birthday Mallika had got him a frock and cake and candies and she had pretended he was Tara.

Mallika returned half an hour later with Malli. She put down some packages on the bed, then she went back to the door and locked it.

'Where's Siva?' Malli asked.

Mallika put her finger to her lips. 'Sshh. See what I have got you.'

She opened one of the packets and took out a frock. She dressed Malli in it. 'You look so sweet Tara,' she sighed.

'I am Malli, not Tara,' Malli giggled.

'You are my sweet sweet Tara. And I love you.'

Mallika set out paper plates and cups, plastic forks and a knife, candies and potato wafers on the bed. From a box she lifted out a cake, pink and white with red roses on it. From another box she removed six candles, planted them in a circle on the cake and lit them.

'Now blow them out, Tara.'

When Malli blew the candles out Mallika cut the cake and held a wedge to Malli's mouth. She shut her eyes and began to sing: 'Happy birthday to you … Happy birthday dearest Tara …'

Siva watched them from the balcony. Ten thousand ants nibbled at Siva's heart. He was his mother's Tara; not Malli. Making as little noise as possible he walked up behind Mallika picked up a piece of cake and bit into it. A dollop of icing stuck to his nose.

Malli giggled. Mallika opened her eyes. She looked at Siva as though she didn't recognise him. Her eyes grew large and round. She slapped Siva hard on his face. Bits of cake flew out of his mouth.

Siva ran out of the room, down the stairs and all the way to Ammamai in the kitchen. He cried, cake all over his face.

'Why does Amma hate me?' His eyes filled with tears.

'She doesn't hate you, kanna,' Ammamai said wiping his face with a towel. 'She doesn't know how to love.'

Seventeen

Ammamai shook Siva awake early one morning. It was still dark.

'Wake up, it's Chitirai Vishu. It's the New Year. Wake up, wake up, but don't open your eyes yet. Keep them shut tight.'

She led Siva, still half asleep, down the steps to the prayer room. She pushed him down on the floor in front of a large mirror and said, 'Go on, open your eyes, kanna. Look at all the things.'

Siva opened his eyes. Reflected in the mirror he saw a silver bowl of rice, bowls of payasam and sweets, fruits heaped on a silver plate, gold necklaces on a silk cloth, a bowl full of silver coins and a pile of books.

Ammamai said, 'It's the New Year today brand new, shiny like a new coin. Now look at all the things here, one by one, and soak your eyes with them. You will be blessed with an abundance of food, wealth and wisdom.'

Ammamai held out a parcel of brown paper and said, 'Here, Appa has got you new clothes. After you bathe, wear them. Now pray to God; ask him for whatever you want.' She got up and went into the kitchen.

In the light of the lamp Siva made faces at his reflection: iiii-yeeee-oooooo. When he was finished with face-making, he closed his eyes and prayed a picture-prayer: he imagined himself as Tara with his mother's arms around him and he heard her breathless whisper, 'I love you.' Then with his eyes open he prayed with his thought-words. 'I want to be Tara,' he thought, 'and I want Amma to love me.'

He filled his pocket with coins, stuffed his mouth with the sweets, picked up the unopened parcel, and ran up to the bathroom.

After he had bathed, Siva wrapped a towel around his waist, and with the parcel he went to his mother's room to look for her. She wasn't there.

Siva put the parcel on the floor and stood in front of the mirror. He let the towel slip, and nervously, he looked at his nude self.

Whazz that?

What?

Tha' thing, hangin'.

'That's my little thing.'

Iz lookz funny.

'You don't have one?'

Corz not.

'Why not?'

'Cauze am a garl, silly.

I want to be a girl too.

Like me?

Yes, like you.

Then be me.

Siva picked the parcel up from the floor and tore it open. Folded in it was a pair of brown shorts and a pale blue shirt with tiny aeroplanes on it.

Siva walked to his mother's cupboard and, opening the shutters wide, he picked out the silk skirt, pale blue like the sky, and a blouse, mud-red as the earth. He had seen them a few days ago; his mother, he was certain, had got them for Malli.

Siva dressed up in the skirt and the blouse and stood in front of the mirror.

Ya. Yu look so pretty.

'Just like you?'

Ya, juz like me.

Siva saw Mani's reflection in the mirror and he turned around.

Mani stood at the door, grinning. He went up to Siva, put his arm around his waist and swirled him around. The warmth of Siva's body existed Mani.

Ammamai called out to him from below. Giving Siva a quick twirl around once more, Mani blew a kiss in the air and scrambled past Mallika down the stairs.

Mallika walked into the room dressed in a new peacock-blue sari with golden dots. Her hair was knotted into a bun with a string of flowers in it. She smelled of jasmine and incense.

'Look Amma, I am Tara,' Siva said.

Mallika's eyes, bright as ever, stared back at her son with a peculiar, fixed intensity, and feelings she had crushed surfaced and overwhelmed her. She rushed to Siva and drew him into her arms and kissed the top of his head. She combed his hair, gathering it into a tiny ponytail. Then she plucked the string of flowers from her hair and pinned it on Siva's hair.

'Mallika!' Raman was the door. 'Why is he dressed in those clothes? Where are …' Then his gaze fell on the clothes lying on the floor. Raman walked to his son, plucked the flowers from his hair and tore them to bits. Siva tried to resist but Raman slapped him hard on his face.

'Stop, don't you dare hit my Tara!' Mallika screamed and caught hold of Raman's arm, her nails digging into his skin.

Raman caught her by her shoulders and shook her violently. 'Tara? Tara? Have you gone absolutely mad, Mallika? Look at him. He is Siva.'

Mallika turned to look at Siva. She stared at his face in a confused manner. Hearing Raman's voice, Ammamai came charging into the room.

'Why are you shouting at her, Raman,' she said. 'It is the New Year.'

'What New Year? Just look at your grandson. He looks like some eunuch.' Raman dragged Siva into the bathroom and locked him in.

Siva banged the door with his fists. 'Appa, Appa, open the door. Let me out,' he cried.

A little later when Raman had gone to his study Ammamai opened the door and held out the clothes Raman had got Siva.

'Here kanna, change into these and go and say sorry to your father. And don't wear girls' clothes any more, understand? It's not funny. Not funny at all.'

Ammamai waited until Siva had changed and picking up the discarded clothes, muttering to herself she walked away.

Siva dashed to Mallika's room. She was sitting on the bed. She looked up at Siva with red eyes. She started, and seemed to shudder. Siva reached forward his hand and tentatively touched her arm.

'Don't touch me,' Mallika spat at him.

'Why are you angry, Amma?' Siva wrapped his arms around her thighs and buried his face in the folds of her sari.

Mallika plucked his arms off of her one by one and pushed him away. She breathed heavily and averted her face.

'I am not your amma. I don't know who your mother is.' She shoved Siva out of the room and shut the door.

Siva heard a heavy crash and he looked at the door with new fear. But fear of what? He didn't quite know.

He was in the attic one evening when from the rear window he spied Kamala. She hurried through the trees clutching a bag. Siva scrambled down the stairs, out of the gate and down the mudpath. He ran through the trees. When he reached the lake he hid behind a bush and watched Kamala swimming in the water.

After some time Kamala swam to the shore, hoisted her naked masculine body out of the water and climbed out. Her long hair was loose and her face was without the usual make-up. She walked to the old chakka tree, picked up the towel under it and dried her body and hair with it. Then she plucked her sari and petticoat off the branch where she had hung them and tied them around her waist. She put on her blouse and adjusted the balls of cloth in the cups. She shook out her hair and rubbed it dry with her hands. Then she saw Siva peeping from behind the bush.

'How long have you been standing there, you naughty boy?' Kamala laughed. 'Come here. Siva, that's your name, right?'

She lifted up a large watermelon and knife from her bag under the tree. Holding the fruit between her feet she cut it in half, then slowly sawed a disc, and then two more. Siva watched her; Ammamai cut watermelons in slices, or wedges, or cubes, but never in rounds. Kamala handed a fruit disc to Siva.

Siva lay under the chakka tree and watched the sun poke splinters at him through the watermelon disc. The sunrays looked like tiny lights caught inside red teardrops. He stretched his tongue out and licked the juice that trickled on his face.

He poked through the centre of the disc with his tongue and made a hole. Then with his tongue he broke the fruit and ate it so that the hole in the centre got bigger and bigger and bigger until there was only a ring left. Kamala lay close to him so she could see through the ring. Siva looked through the hole and the sky grew small and round and belonged only to them. Their own pa-ra-die-s.

'How did you become a girl-boy?' Siva asked Kamala.

She arched an eyebrow. 'When the baby is a tiny little thing in the mother's womb it is always a girl first. Then as the mother's stomach grows, the baby grows in it and if it has to be a boy then it grows as a boy but only bit by bit. But some babies take a long time to become boys and the mother gets terrible pain and so the baby is born even before it is fully a boy. His heart is still a girl's. So the girl inside him feels trapped and very sad.'

Kamala hesitated. 'I was born a boy,' she explained, 'like you, Siva. But I was not fully a boy. One day I was looking into the mirror and I saw the face of a young girl. I could hear her talking to me. I wanted so much to be her. I knew I would be happy if I could be her. So I became her.' She raised her arms and shrugged. 'That's how I became a girl-boy.'

When Siva returned home Ammamai was in the veranda. 'Where did you go?' she asked.

Burrowing his nose into his grandmother's chest Siva asked, 'Ammamai, when I was in Amma's stomach was I a little girl first?'

'Of course not!' Ammamai held him closer. 'You were a cute little boy.'

'Was I born before time?'

Ammamai patted his head and laughed. 'Aiyooo I remember those days. We were waiting-waiting for you. Kanna, you were in your mother's stomach for ten long months. Too long. Too long, I would say.'

'Ammamai, was I fully a boy when I was born?'

Ammamai slapped Siva's back. 'What-what rubbish you are asking eh? What's got into that stupid head of yours, kanna?' She looked at her grandson and her face softened. She opened her arms wide. Siva snuggled into them.

Eighteen

In the days, weeks and months it took to make up the following years, Mallika was deeper into Malli and ignored Siva. As for Siva, he was deeply miserable. A large part of his misery was simply because of not knowing why he was miserable.

Although he was twelve he looked younger. He was lean and wiry, almost girl-like, with a sweet face. Malli had grown closer to him. At first she had seen in him a brother – a sibling she didn't possess. Later he became her most true friend.

Malli and Siva were drenched by the time they reached Siva's home from school. 'Look at you,' Mallika exclaimed when she saw Malli, 'soaking wet.' Holding her hand she took Malli to her room. Siva followed behind them. Mallika dried Malli's hair with a towel and took out a new dress from the cupboard. 'Look what I got for you, Malli.'

She glanced at Malli's small breasts with a keen eye. 'It's time I got you a bra. You are a big girl now,' Mallika said in a voice full of tenderness. 'Here, change into this frock. You will catch a terrible cold. Tomorrow we will go shopping for your bra.'

Siva watched them, a stiff and pained expression growing on his face. He picked up the towel from the bed and dried his hair.

Mallika said to Malli, 'I have made bakodam especially for you. I'll go and get it.' She hurried down the stairs.

Malli peeled away her uniform. Siva curiously stared at the two mounds of flesh on her chest. He felt his own flat chest and his mouth formed a grimace.

Malli giggled. 'You want to touch them.' Clasping Siva's hand she pressed his fingers to her breast. 'See, I am a big girl now, Siva,' she beamed.

Next day after school when Mallika told Malli she was taking her shopping, Siva asked his mother, 'Can I come too?'

Mallika turned to face him, eyes ablaze. 'You?' she laughed, her mouth curving into a sneer. 'No need.'

At home, Siva changed out of his uniform and stood in the balcony. It was his favourite place, from where he peeped at the world, outside-in. And deep into himself, inside-out. He thought of his mother and Malli together and the dark tension of his emotions intensified and his thoughts congealed into an aching knot in his throat.

Was it possible that his mother was someone else? As soon as he had this thought, a chill spread right through to his chest, arms, loins, the back of his thighs, and to his toes. He stood still, doused by an anguish of want, animal-like in its intensity.

A pigeon perched on the railing, distracting Siva from his troubled thoughts. Siva clapped his hands and the bird flew far away into the clouds.

Almost an hour later when he heard Malli's voice he ran into his mother's room. Standing at the door he saw three bras on the bed: pink, white and beige, with tiny bows and a lace trim. Mallika was explaining to Malli how a bra was to be worn. She hugged Malli and breathlessly said, 'Now you are my grown-up Tara.'

When it was time for Malli to go home, Siva pinched the pink bra from her bag. Later, after dinner, he stood naked before the mirror with the bra. He smelled it; it smelled of moist husk in the monsoon. He pressed it against his cheek, then held it against his chest and looked into the mirror. He stared at his reflection for a long time. Then he felt the irrepressible feeling inside him surface.

Siva wore the bra the way Mallika had explained to Malli. He clasped the hooks in front of him, turned the bra around and slid his arms into the straps. It hung on his shoulders like a pair of collapsible tents. He stuffed several handkerchiefs into the cups of the bra. He stroked his arms and his chest, his stomach and his thighs in a fit of anxiety, as though he needed to reaffirm that they existed or that those parts of his body belonged to him. He bent closer to the mirror and peered at his face, as if examining an exotic insect. A few strands of sweaty hair hung down over his forehead, sticking to his skin. Then puckering his lips he kissed his reflection in the mirror.

'My grown-up Tara,' Siva said mimicking his mother's breathless voice.

Mallika had been summoned by Miss Gracy Thomas, Siva's schoolteacher, but she did not to go to see her. As for Raman, he was out of town.

Miss Thomas was a Malayali Christian, so English came naturally to her but she spoke it with a Malayali accent. She wore her hair backcombed into a ball at the nape of her neck, which made her look severe. Her face was taut with a permanently angry expression. She was the head teacher of the secondary section.

Besides teaching English, Miss Thomas was in charge of the library, of general discipline and personal hygiene. Quite frequently she made surprise visits to the girls' room and demanded to see their handkerchiefs. She examined their hair, teeth and nails.

Miss Thomas was a devout Catholic and in charge of the Catechism class. Every Tuesday and Friday soon after the morning assembly she wore a sombre face as she talked to the children. But because of a new government rule, Catechism ceased to be compulsory for non-Christians. So every Tuesday and Friday the non-Christian children had one hour free. They were meant to spend this time in the library. But very often the boys were out in the playground and the girls were in the girls' room. And Siva was with the girls. This fact troubled Miss Thomas.

At first Siva was thrilled by the girls' friendship and trust. But as months pressed on, it occurred to him that their ready acceptance was because his presence didn't bother them. He was not dissimilar; he was almost one of them.

However, for the boys in school Siva was the butt of ridicule. They mimicked him, swinging their hips as they walked behind him, stroking the air with their hand as they talked, adjusting a lock of hair behind their ear now and then, and touching their cheeks in a sweet caress.

It bothered Siva. It bothered Malli more.

'Don't mind these boys, Siva,' she told him, 'they are horrible.'

The girls clung together. They did not mix as casually with the boys as they did before, though they couldn't stop talking about them. They giggled and laughed and spoke in whispers.

They began to sprout hair on their arms and legs and in their armpits. They envied Siva's hairless, slender body, his pinched waist and the way it arched into hips.

Once, one of the girls stole her brother's razor and brought it to school. After class, some of the girls collected in the girls' room, lathered their arms and legs with Lux Beauty soap, and shaved them clean.

That night, in the upstairs bathroom, with his father's razor, Siva shaved the little fuzz there was on his arms and legs.

Siva noticed some of the girls had begun to display breasts, which they flaunted as trophies. They were rapidly turning into little women. Their cheeks and foreheads were breaking out in a crop of pimples whereas the boys were growing soft coconut fuzz on their upper lips.

But Siva remained as he was. No breasts, no fuzz.

The girls had planned to go out after school, first for a movie and then to a restaurant for dinner. They had come prepared with a change of clothes.

'Look, what I got,' one of the girls said holding up a pink pouch with make-up. Siva walked into the girls' room just then. The girls had forgotten to tell him about their plan.

'We're going to the movies,' a girl announced. 'You want to come?'

Malli teased him. 'If you are going with us then you have to wear a frock,' she said.

Goaded by the girls' screams and insistent clapping, Siva put on Malli's new dress. It was too big for him. He fastened the red belt tightly around his waist, and then Malli tied his hair into a tiny ponytail with the red ribbon from her hair.

'Now the make-up,' a girl said and the others set up a chorus: 'Make-up make-up make-up.'

From the pink pouch Malli plucked the eyeliner, rouge and lipstick. She brushed two rounds of rouge on Siva's cheeks, drew the liner over his eyes and, lastly, applied the lipstick.

One of the girls said, 'Now dance for us, Siva.'

The girls clapped and raising his arms above his head Siva pirouetted round and round and round.

Miss Thomas, who was passing by in the corridor and had heard the cheering and clapping, peeped into the room and saw Siva. She stood frozen in the doorway, horror and disgust on her face.

'Get out! Girls, get out at once. You stay here, Siva.' She chewed on her lower lip then, making up her mind, she picked up Siva's uniform from the floor.

'Pick up your bag, Siva.'

Siva bent down to pick his bag up and looking through his legs to see if Miss Thomas was watching him, he quickly took the make-up pouch from the window sill and shoved it into his bag. Miss Thomas yanked his arm and dragged him towards her room. The boys in the corridor whistled as they walked past.

'Back, get back into your class, all of you hooligans!' Miss Thomas yelled at them.

She sat behind her desk and looked at Siva with scorn. Siva tilted his head; he looked up from her face to the statue of Jesus Christ nailed to the cross on the wall behind her. The plaster-of-Paris figurine was naked except for a bit of cloth around his groin and the headdress of thorns. While Siva was preoccupied with Jesus he didn't notice that Miss Thomas had walked towards him, until he felt the steel ruler on his back.

The teacher pushed him towards the mirror fixed on the shutter of the cupboard. 'Look at yourself, son. What do you see?'

'Me?'

'See, that's your trouble. You don't see *me*. That's not who you see.' She snorted and clasped her hands in front of her chest. 'You see Jesus, son. This face does not belong to you. It belongs to our Lord Jesus. How can you make Him wear cosmetics? And if you wear cosmetics then your face will become a lie. And Jesus does not want it like that. Remember, Jesus is watching you.'

Miss Thomas used her morning assembly voice. 'So be precisely what God made you, son. And be a man. This is what Jesus wants you to be. Now until your father comes to fetch you, stand in the corner and pray to our Father.'

Siva stood in a corner and in a loud, clear assembly voice, he prayed: 'Our Father, Who Art in Heaven, Hallowed be thy Name ...'

Miss Thomas called Raman on the phone. He arrived half an hour later and she told him what had happened. 'Siva is a brilliant boy,' she said, 'and I have no complaints about his school work. He should be with the boys, playing cricket, cycling and all that. But he spends too much time with the girls. Particularly that Malli. She is a wayward, motherless child and I think she's a very bad influence on Siva. You must talk to him.'

She called out to Siva. When he stood before her, she said, 'Just look at him; he looks like a girl.'

Raman looked at Siva, a curious expression on his face. It was not dissimilar to the one he wore when he squashed a mosquito.

'And sir,' Miss Thomas added, 'you should get his hair cut. Look at it, so long and all over his face.' She held out Siva's uniform and asked him to get dressed at once.

'Did you hear what the teacher said?' Raman asked as Siva got into the car. 'You spend too much time with the girls.'

'But they are my friends.'

'They do different things, you know, these girls. You should cycle, play cricket, do all the things boys do and not sit inside the house and talk all the time, read silly books or be bothered about how you look. That's for girls.' Raman ruffled Siva's hair. 'Now promise me you will stay away from the girls.'

Siva looked at his father and shook his head. 'They are my friends.'

Raman didn't reply. He looked out of the window. A nerve twitched at his temple and his fists were clenched.

On reaching home Raman grabbed Siva by his arm and dragged him into his study. He locked the door and paced up and down the room. 'Tell me Siva, who made you wear the frock?'

'Malli. It was just for fun, Appa.'

'Fun? What fun! Miss Thomas is right. Listen to me, Siva,' Raman said. 'Promise me you will not talk to Malli or go to her house again. And she will not come to our house, understand?'

'But Appa, she's my friend. I will talk to her. I will go to her house.'

Raman went out into the garden, then bounded back into the study and towards Siva, his face thrust forward, holding a stick in the air. He caught Siva by his neck and pushed him forward. Siva shut his eyes, which only intensified the pain on his back when the stick hit it. With each beating, Raman screamed, 'I don't want to see you with Malli! And you will not go to her house again! Did you hear? And she will not come here. Understand?'

Siva remained silent. The heaving and sighing of his body was tragic. His head fell forward and he wept.

'Do you understand?' Raman screamed as he yanked Siva to face him.

Siva looked at his father. He saw the wrath on his face and the disgust in his eyes. 'I don't want you to meet that Malli again. Do you understand?'

'I will meet Malli,' Siva said defiantly.

Raman sucked up from his throat a large gob of spit and spat on Siva's face. Siva stared at his father who he thought looked ridiculous, his mouth and his eyes shaped like capital O-s. Laughter arose from the pit of Siva's stomach. It resonated in his ears. Tears streamed down his face. Laughter and tears, like the sun shining in the rain.

Raman raised the stick. 'If you meet her again I will break your legs.'

Ammamai came rushing to the door. 'Raman, why are you shouting?' Her hands flew to her mouth. 'Aiyayooo, why are you beating him?'

Siva ran out of the room.

Raman raised a finger and shook it. 'I don't want that Malli to come to this house. I don't want Siva to go to her house.'

Ammamai slapped his finger away. 'If that is what you want then why don't you stay at home and make sure.'

She slapped her head with both her hands. 'Mosquitoes, mosquitoes all the time, you don't know what-what is happening in this house even.'

Mallika was worried. She hadn't seen Malli for a few days. She made rice payasam, which Malli liked a lot, and went to meet her.

Malli hadn't come to school either and Siva went to her house after class. Malli was in bed.

'What's wrong?' Siva asked.

Malli giggled. 'I can't tell you. It's a girl thing.'

'Okay. Then don't tell. I am going home.'

'I got my period, stupid.'

'Period?'

'Yes, period. Once a month it bleeds from here.' She stuck her hand between her legs.

'Oh my God. Are you going to die?'

'No, stupid. All girls get it. Ask your mother. She came to my house in the morning. She got payasam and fed me with her own hand. And she told me not to go to school.' Malli pulled up her knees to her chest and winced.

'When will I get it?' Siva asked

'Stupid, only girls get it.'

Siva ran out of the house. But he didn't go home. He walked through the woods, disturbed. He looked up at the palm trees that waved their fronds in the wind, and the big fat trees that spread their arms on and on, and the flowering trees that smelled nice, and the fruit trees that the birds liked so much, and the leaves that rustled in the breeze and sounded like a little girl in a starched silk skirt, running.

Siva lay under the parijat tree, took a storybook out of his schoolbag and began to read it. Sweet flowers fell on the open page. He watched a row of red ants climb on the page – plump 'i's' with circled dots. They loafed letter to letter, word to word, and between lines, disfiguring words, sentences and punctuation.

Siva dozed off. He woke up with a start when an ant bit him on the earlobe. He searched his mind for nagging thoughts. Suddenly he knew what it was that had been bothering him.

He rushed home. He slashed his finger with his father's razor blade. He let the cut bleed and smeared the blood on his underwear and ran up to his mother's room. He held out his underwear to her. 'Look Amma, I got my period.'

Mallika looked at the stained garment. Her face recoiled in panic and then her eyes became hazy. She stared at Siva; Tara's eyes stared back at her.

A mad wild look entered Mallika's eyes. As though in a dream, she held Siva in her arms and kissed his cheeks. 'Oh Tara, my sweet Tara,' she cooed.

She pulled out an old trunk from under the bed. She looked through the silk saris she had stored in it and lifted out her wedding sari, scarlet-red with a gold zari border. She draped it around Siva. On a sudden impulse Siva darted out of the room and returned with the make-up kit.

'Where did you get this?' Mallika asked.

'Malli gave it to me,' Siva lied.

Mallika seemed to be lost in thought. She remembered the day, a long time ago, when Nayantara had made up her face. Almost in a trance, out of the pouch she picked out a stick of lip-colour, a box of blush-on, eyeliner and face powder.

Mallika made up Siva's eyes, his cheeks and lips. With her finger she stroked his lips to press the colour in. 'Now smack your lips.' Siva licked his lips. 'Not like that, Tara,' Mallika laughed and pressed her lips to Siva's, smacking the colour in.

She smeared kohl in his eyes and dotted his forehead with red pottu. She blew kisses in the air.

'Oh Tara,' she said. 'You are a big girl now.'

So engrossed was Mallika that she didn't hear Raman come in.

It required no more than two long strides for Raman to be standing next to them. It was as though a dam had burst within him and he couldn't hold back the deluge of rage.

Siva ran to the corner of the room. With his hands covering his face, he turned to face his father. Through the slits between his fingers, he saw Raman clench his teeth, the muscle of his jaw twitching. Raman strode across the room and slapped him hard across his face. Some of the lip-colour stained the back of his hand and Raman rubbed his hand on his shirt as though it was infected with some incurable disease.

Siva didn't flinch. He gaped at his father's face and registered the three capital O-s. He laughed; it was a strange sort of high-pitched laughter.

This enraged Raman even more. 'What are you laughing like that for, you jackass?' He raised his hand in the air to hit Siva again, but Mallika grabbed it in a swift movement of her hand and pressed it to Raman's chest. For her size, she displayed substantial strength. Raman yanked his hand free, and stood motionless for a minute as though he had been stung.

'Mallika, you are making an utter fool of our son.' With sadness in his eyes Raman looked at Siva, 'Please don't be like this, son,' he said, then turned around and walked through the door.

Mallika felt her heart beating as blood rushed to her face. She bounded to Siva and gathered him in her arms, holding him close. Siva burst into tears.

'Ssh, ssh, Tara,' Mallika whishpered. 'I love you.'

Book Four

Nineteen

THE EVENING AIR WAS MOIST and heavy. The clouds looked like dirty rags hung on an invisible clothesline. Siva and Malli walked to the lake. They sat down on the bank. Around the sweet hedge, fireflies danced and cruised the evening air in fine, semolina lines of light.

Siva sighed, not because of the fireflies, but because he could feel the warmth of Malli's thigh pressed next to his as they sat side by side. A giant firefly seemed to stir in his heart; it flapped its wings and forced his breath out in a whistle.

Malli sniffed and rubbed her nose with the back of her hand. Siva looked at her, perplexed.

'Are you crying, Malli?'

'Appa wants me to live with him in America. He's coming to get me next week.'

Siva's eyes reflected the pain she felt. Malli cupped Siva's face with her hands, then ever so gently she kissed his cheeks one by one. She looked into his eyes and then kissed them, one, the other, as if to wipe his hurt away.

'I'll be back for holidays.'

Siva covered his face with his hands, and as he spoke there was despair in his voice.

'So you *are* going away.'

Malli threw her arms around his neck and pulling him closer, kissed him fleetingly on his lips. Her lips were soft and smelled of sweet flowers and spice, and her breath was warm like the summer breeze.

Siva was overcome with shyness and an unfamiliar thrill. He touched his lips. The giant firefly fluttered in his heart once more and a surge of desire consumed him.

'Promise you will write to me?'

'I promise.'

Siva turned into a shadow. He walked stealthily, his body pressed against the walls, from room to room, up and down the stairs, his head bent low, as though his eyes were tied with strings to his toes.

He hardly spoke to anyone. Each day he waited for Malli's letter.

'Did any letter from Malli come, Ammamai?' Siva asked her one afternoon.

Ammamai shook her head. 'No letter came, pa.'

'Why has she not written, Ammamai?'

'I don't know, kanna.'

'She promised.'

'Maybe she has forgotten you.' Ammamai patted Siva's head. 'You should forget her.'

Siva couldn't forget Malli. He hid himself in the attic after school. He lay under the hole in the roof and watched the blue sky. He saw a plane flying past. He saw its huge belly. He saw bird-bellies flying. He thought of Malli. And once he believed he heard Tara whisper in his ears.

Ammamai was in the veranda one evening fanning her face with the palm-leaf fan. Munniamma came rushing through the gates with a bag of vegetables. 'There you are. How long does it take you to get vegetables,' Ammamai glowered.

'I stopped at Vishnu-aiyah's house. He's very sick.'

'What's wrong with him?'

'Coughing-coughing all day long. He is very weak. He said he didn't have much time left. Poor man. You must send Mallika to him.'

Ammamai sighed and then looked up at Munniamma with a scowl. 'Are you going to stand here till he coughs his last breath? Go, tell Mallika about her father at once.'

Munniamma ran up to Mallika's room. A cold fear gripped Mallika when she heard about her father. Was he dying? Mallika was terrified and bewildered.

'You must go to him at once, ma,' Munniamma said. 'Come, let's go.'

Mallika packed a small suitcase and left the house with Munniamma.

Ammamai was still in the veranda when Raman returned home. She looked tired and forlorn.

'What's the matter, ma? Are you not well?' Raman asked her.

'I am all right. It's Vishnu who is not well. Mallika has gone to his house for some days.'

'Good,' Raman said. 'She should stay there as long as it takes.

'How can you even say such a thing,' Ammamai retorted.

Raman's eyes grew weary. 'Both Mallika and that Malli should stay away from my son.'

It was Siva's birthday a week later; he was thirteen. Ammamai had made chakka payasam for him and Raman had got him new clothes. But Siva was filled with gloom. He missed Malli; he missed his mother who was still in his grandfather's house. Not once had she called him. Not even on his birthday.

He went to bed early that evening. In his dream he saw Tara. When she spoke her voice was sweet like the note of a flute. Hand in hand, like two lost children, they wandered together in a paradise of their own making.

They stood on a cliff looking down at the sea. The rock cracked below Tara's feet. She tripped and fell and her voice cried out to him: S-i-v-a.

Siva lunged towards Tara and grabbed her hand just before her body was pitched forward. He could see her face contort, horror in her eyes. Siva tightened his fingers around her hand, but he couldn't hold on. Tara fell into the sea below.

Mallika came up behind him. She screamed. 'You killed my Tara.'

Siva woke up. He tried to recollect his dream, but remembered nothing. Only a long breathing and blankness and a feeling twitched in his head.

Even as he was half asleep, Siva, he tried to reassemble his thoughts. He felt an overwhelming fear, a memory of something soft and zigzaggy, like melted tar with tyre-marks. His eyelids seemed to be glued together.

Then he heard Tara's voice in his ears.

Wy didyu let me die?

Siva started to feel nervous, strangely nervous. It wasn't something he could understand clearly, it was as though his body was too small; he felt hemmed in. He felt his heart twitch; it seemed to have a life of its own, not his.

Siva felt sharp pangs in his limbs, so acute that he could hardly walk or sometimes even stand. He did not know where the pain came from nor why; it seemed not to have anything to do with his self, his body.

He was in the clutch of some mystifying *thing* - the voice in his head – Tara's voice. It talked to him; it told him what to think, what to do and how to do it, and helplessly, he surrendered to it.

He couldn't eat, sleep or think his own thoughts. But now and again when he was able to formulate his thoughts they unfolded as questions and answers.

'Where are you, Tara?'

Ere.

'Are you inside me?'

Ya.

'Are you alive?'

Ya.

'Am I you?'

Ya.

Siva stood at the door of his father's study. Everything in it appeared needlessly solid and foreboding to Siva. His father sat at the desk. On it was a heap of books, hardbound, leatherbound, all gloomy and dark. The room was relatively dark too; only one light behind his father spread a steady glow that illuminated the unnoticeable bald patch on his head and the paper he was reading. An elliptical shadow cast by his head covered a large portion of the paper.

'Appa,' Siva called out to his father. And then again, 'Appa.'

Raman turned and looked up at his son. He noticed how thin he had grown: ribs like a lobster's cage, frightened eyes in a tiny sparrow face. It seemed to Raman that Siva had grown shorter. He had lost height and weight.

'What is it, Siva?' Raman asked.

Siva pushed his head against the door and raised his hand to his eyes, closed them with his thumb and forefinger to stop his tears, then wrapped his arms around his body. His body shook with convulsions of fear, anger, loneliness and the frustration of not knowing what was wrong with him.

'I don't feel well,' Siva muttered.

'Come here,' Raman pointed to the chair, 'and sit down, son.'

Siva walked to the chair and sank in it.

'Now tell me what's wrong with you.'

'I hear a voice in my head.'

'Voice in your head? What voice?'

'Tara's.'

'Tara's?'

Siva gloomily stared at his feet. He rotated one foot, and then the other. Then he explained as best as he could what he felt and although he sounded, even to his own ears, incredibly foolish, he asked his father, 'Who am I?'

Raman walked over to his son. Siva looked sideways at his father. His face thrust forward a little and his eyes were suspended in distress, in a torture of madness, as he stared straight into his father's eyes. 'Am I Tara?'

Raman held Siva's arms and lifted him from the chair. He put both his arms around him and his hands trembled as he drew his son closer to him. Father and son held each other close for comfort. Raman dropped his head and his shoulders jerked with little sharp twitches because of the deep regret he felt.

Siva rested his head on his father's chest and blurted, 'I am scared, Appa.'

'Don't be scared, Siva,' Raman said. His eyelids trembled with the *sorry* in his eyes. 'Go to your room, lie down and rest.'

Siva walked away. Raman called out to Ammamai. She came rushing out of the kitchen.

'What's the matter now? What do you want?' Ammamai asked.

Raman felt a curious tossing in his stomach. He wiped his brow with his hand. 'I think Siva's very sick.'

'What's wrong with him?'

'He has gone mad. He's sick in his head.'

'What do you mean?'

He thinks he is Tara.'

'Tara?'

'Yes. Tara. He has really gone mad.'

Ammamai started to weep, the end of her sari pressed to her mouth.

'It's all because of that Elizabeth's ghost. She has cursed our family.'

'Don't be silly, ma and stop crying. I must go to the doctor.'

Raman immediately rushed to Dr Kuruvilla's clinic. The waiting room was crowded and it was not any different from the railway platform. Entire families had accompanied their sick ones and they talked incessantly, not about the illnesses but about politics, films and prices of land, petrol and tomatoes. Some of them stood around the water cooler, filling water in small paper cups and drinking it with unexpected thirst. Raman's throat was dry and his lips stuck together.

He was shown into the consulting room. He sat down in front of the doctor and looked at him from under furrowed brows and heavy eyes.

Dr Kuruvilla's face was sphinx-like. Black hair bristled up on one side of his head, which was otherwise full of grey. As always he was dressed in a suit and tie. He intently listened to what Raman had to say about Siva, all the time fiddling with the ring on his finger. It had a large red ruby, the size of a one-rupee coin, the kind that is worn to ward off evil.

The doctor clasped his hands, and stated, 'Siva has, I think, taken on the burden of being the replacement child. Therefore, in his mind, he is Tara.'

He glanced down at his hands clutched in front of his chest. His face was set and expressionless. 'Siva needs to see a specialist. I could refer you to a doctor in Madras. A psychoanalyst.'

'Psychoanalyst?' Raman asked in deep, bitter displeasure.

'Yes. I am certain the psychoanalyst will be able to help Siva.' The doctor put his hand to his brow. 'From what you have told me I understand that Mallika blames Siva for her daughter's death. The difficult task is to purge the identity of Tara from Siva's mind and, what is more important, from his mother's mind. You must not forget that she suffers as much as Siva. Each time she sees Siva she is reminded of Tara. And every time Siva sees his mother he wants to be Tara. It would do Siva and Mallika good to be away from each other for some time. It's the only way Mallika can get over her grief and Siva can preserve his own identity. And yes, it may be a good idea if he stops going to school. Children can be very cruel. They will tease him at school and it is possible they already do. Or on the other hand they may avoid him altogether and this will damage his mind further.'

Dr Kuruvilla removed his spectacles, blew on the lenses, wiped them with a handkerchief, and put them back on. He shut his eyes for a moment and then said, 'Twinless twins often experience severe psychological problems. They are reminded of their dead twin every time they look in the mirror, and the pain of loss consumes them. In very serious cases, the surviving twin even contemplates killing himself so he can be with his dead twin.'

Raman was a man whose life had been filled with the small activities of mosquitoes. They were his world. Without knowing it, he had been sucked into the activities of his mother, his wife and their son, and their collective emotions. He found the balance of his life suddenly losing its fulcrum. He had not known before that everything around him could break down, that he himself could break down. He raised his hands to his face and did.

Twenty

EARLY RAINS MOISTENED THE DRY summer air. The clouds were soaked and heavy. Siva stood by the window in his room looking up at the rain. Hyphenated lines in the sky, vertical-vertical, and as the wind moved through the rain, slanting-slanting. He looked at the grey folds of the sky, which seemed like the waves in the sea. The peepal tree outside the gate went sis-sis in the breeze. The dark clouds floated away and the sky no longer mimicked the sea.

Siva thought about Malli; she hadn't written to him. He thought of that evening when she had kissed him. He wanted to take pleasure in those moments; he wanted to live with them each day. And he couldn't, unless she wrote to him, unless she returned to him. So he had for a long time locked these memories in his heart for safekeeping, trying not to let them into his mind.

Now he opened his heart to himself as if it was a small but full purse with a tiny clasp ready to burst open. He felt his heart beating; blood rushed to his face. He held his cheeks with his hands, shut his eyes and then he heard Tara's voice.

Whazz zhat sound?

Siva looked at the peepal tree outside the gate.

'The tree in the wind.'

How dozit feel, za wind.

'Wet.'

Wot iz wet?

'Rain.'

Rain? Whazz iz made of?

'Water.'

Whazz wata?

'The pond is full of water.'

Whazz zhat sound?

'It is the gate.'

Whoz zhat?

'Ammamai.'

Who?

'Grandmother.'

An zhat?

Siva stuck his head out of the window. He saw a woman walking down the mudpath.

'That is Kamala.'

Siva walked through the woods to the lake. He sat down on the grassy bank and waved out to Kamala in the water.

'Take your clothes off and jump in,' she yelled.

Siva looked down at the water. He stared at his reflection in it and then he screamed.

Kamala scrambled out of the water. She dressed hurriedly and sat down beside Siva. 'What's the matter? Why did you scream like that?'

Siva looked close to tears.

'I saw her eyes looking back at me,' he said.

'Whose eyes?'

'Tara's.'

'She's dead, Siva.'

'She is inside me.'

Kamala gathered Siva in her arms. 'Oh my sweet,' she said. 'Is that who you are? Tara?' She pressed his head against her chest. 'Ask Kamala; I know what you are going through. Like me, Siva, you are a girl trapped in a boy's body. You are Tara.'

'I am Tara?' Siva felt light and giddy.

'Yes princess, you have been lost all these years. You are Tara, not Siva.' Kamala clasped her hands. 'Don't worry; I will look after you from now on, Siva,' she said then corrected herself, 'Tara. I am going to Madras in two days. You must come away with me.'

Siva didn't know if it was because of her voice or what she said but something stirred in him then. All the misgivings he had shackled deep inside him seemed to surface and float as if on water, uncontrolled and flowing.

The evening light cast an eerie stain on the wall in Siva's room. He was alone. Mani had gone to meet his uncle in the market and Ammamai had gone to see Vishnu who was in a bad way. Siva felt restless and strangely inadequate. He undressed and looked at his reflection in the mirror.

You are Tara, he remembered Kamala say. *You are a girl trapped in a boy's body.*

He had a boy's body all right. But his thoughts and the voice in his head were unmistakably a girl's. Was he like Kamala: a girl-boy? Is that who he was? Siva's breath came out in spurts, as though he had run up a long flight of stairs. He had an unbearable sense of his own hopelessness. He pressed his hands against his eyes and tried to quell the longing.

With the raging thirst of an alcoholic who had been forbidden a drink for a long time, Siva pulled out Malli's bra and his mother's red sari with the gold border that he had hidden deep inside his cupboard. He dressed up. A warm butter-like feeling spread through him; his toes and fingers quivered and he could hear his heart beat in his ears.

He didn't hear Mani come up the stairs. Mani stood at the door with a large sweet lime and a knife. He raised one brow, nodded appreciatively and whistled.

'You look pretty.' He tossed the fruit in the air, caught it but it slipped out of his hand and rolled towards Siva. Mani walked to Siva, picked up the fruit and cut it in half. He chuckled. 'These will make you more pretty.' And then pulling down Siva's blouse, Mani stuffed the fruit cups inside the bra Siva had on. He pressed the sweet lime halves against Siva's nipples, moving them slowly in circles. Citrus juice trickled down Siva's bare stomach. Mani bent down and licked the juice. His tongue felt warm on Siva's skin and Siva's thoughts plunged into a vague and sensuous confusion. His body went taut and his breath seemed to burst out of his nostrils. Fluid surged deep inside, drowning him. He shivered with an unfamiliar thrill and fear; it was like standing on the edge of a cliff. Every moment seemed drawn out and electric with meaning. But he couldn't decode precisely what it was.

Mani dropped his lungi and took his shirt off. He pushed Siva on the bed, climbed over him and rubbed his body against Siva's slowly, cat-like. Siva felt frightened, though not because of fear – it was out of a sneaking pleasure that he had not experienced before. But along with it he also felt a palpable disgust.

A door banged shut downstairs. 'Sssh,' Mani said in Siva's ear, 'it's only some window banging in the wind.' He pulled off the end of the sari and began to lick Siva's neck.

Ammamai called out to Mani from downstairs. He raised his body, a praying mantis, and clicked his lizard tongue. He put his clothes on and ran out of the room.

Siva felt an acute sadness, like the dull ache in one's throat after a terrible loss. He looked up at the ceiling and pondered over, one by one, the feelings that could move him to twin heights of pleasure and loathing.

He built imaginary cliffs in his mind so he couldn't see himself. Herself. Him/Her/Self. Higher. Darker. He felt a gnawing pain and borne with it, like an identical twin, fear. The fear of unknowing. Of not knowing who he was. Or what was wrong with him. Or what was inside him. The salt of his tears poured out of his eyes.

This is how Ammamai found Siva. Weeping. With fruit-halves inside the bra-cups and juice-stains on his belly. She opened her mouth, then quickly closed it. She slapped her forehead several times and then banged it against the wall. A thin wail emanated from her throat. Her lips quivered with each wail.

Siva ran up to her and put his arms around her waist. She turned on him and hit him with both her fists. She didn't say a word, but continued wailing as she repeatedly slapped him. She pulled the sari off, removed the bra, flung the fruit-halves on the floor, then said, 'Why didn't you die instead of Tara,' and walked out.

Siva packed a small bag that evening.

Siva was with Kamala on the late night train to Madras.

The train carriage rocked with the rhythm of iron upon iron; a hidden metronome directed them. How carefully the railway sleepers were laid at equal distances. Turum turum turum turum turum. Sometimes the distance between the sleepers didn't match. The sound was different then: turrururm turrururm turrururm turrururm.

Siva shut his eyes. He rocked with the train. Front-back-front-back. Small movements. Like the sound of pigeons when they made those throat-sounds: guturu guturu guturu.

Siva pressed his back to the seat. He stopped moving. He looked at his toes. They were edged with black dust from the platform. Dirt got in his eyes. He inhaled the smell of the evening. Somewhat scorched, as though the train was burning through nightblue thermocole. His stomach made sounds. Fear sounds: buru buru buru. He slept.

Through the next day the train travelled past forests and hills, past waterless rivers, and through dusty towns with peeling walls that were decorated with paintings of gods, urinators pissing between them. It was late evening when the train reached Madras.

Kamala and Siva took a bus to the eunuch colony. It was far away from the station; almost where the city ended.

Tall arecanut palms veiled the slum. It had no name; it was an anthill of eunuchs carrying their fate stamped on their heads and their burden between their legs. They were everywhere: peeping out of doors, leaning over fences, walking down the beach, gossiping, laughing, scratching and combing each other's hair.

Kamala and Siva walked down the market road strewn with debris: wood fibres, stone dust and plastic bags thin like sausage skins, garbage oozing out of them. A radio blared a film song, and then jingles for toothpaste and balm. The huts, huddled close together, smelled of old leather – a pungent musty smell.

Siva was nauseous. He pinched his nose with his fingers and walked with Kamala to the Guru's house.

The Guru was short and fat and her thick, pouting lips were painted ruby-red. A large black mole above them sprouted three strands of hair. Fake diamond studs glittered in her nose and ears. Her teeth were stained yellow with too much tobacco. She was old.

'Ah there you are Kamala,' the Guru said. 'You have forgotten poor old me or what eh? It's been almost a year.'

'This is Tara,' Kamala said.

The Guru surveyed Siva with piercing eyes and a solemn pout. She held his chin, tilted his face and ran her hands over his body. She shook her head at first, then her eyes filled with pleasure.

'He's very pretty,' she said smiling. 'He will grow into a beautiful woman.' She laughed; spit from her mouth landed at Siva's feet. The Guru indulged in a side business of providing beautiful eunuchs to film-makers and to men who needed to be amused.

Siva's eyes, like a deer's, darted warily. The Guru slapped her forehead. 'Why does he look so scared? As though fate has dealt him a severe blow henh?' She clapped her hands. 'Kamala, take this sad creature away and feed him. Fatten him up. He must have something to call hips if he has to be a woman. Even goats are fed and fattened before they are slaughtered. You had better get him a nice skirt and blouse.'

Kamala held Siva around his waist and as she led him out of the room, the Guru shouted after them, 'And wipe that fear from his eyes. It's a tough life for eunuchs. Make him understand this.'

Next day Kamala got Siva a red pavadai with gold buttis on it and a green blouse. It cost her nearly a hundred rupees. She dressed Siva in the new clothes. 'You can't be dressed like a boy now. You are Tara, remember?'

In the following weeks Siva worked in the Guru's house with Arun, a dark, skinny boy with a scraggy moustache. He had come to the colony a few months before Siva.

Arun and Siva swept the floor, swabbed, cleaned utensils, fetched water and, in the evening, pressed the Guru's legs. By night-time Siva was exhausted. He lay down beside Arun in the shack and cried.

Once, Arun put his arm around Siva and pulled him close to him. His breathing grew heavy and there was a silly expression on his face. When Siva looked at him, his eyes looked like the flourpaste that Munniamma would boil, letting it bubble and pop till it became hazy and opaque. Arun grabbed Siva's hand and pressed it to his bulging crotch. Siva pulled his hand away; he crawled to Kamala and lay down next to her.

Siva had been at the colony for over a month. Kamala found him weeping one night.

'Why are you crying?'

'I want to go home.'

'This is your home now. Tomorrow is the New Year. I will take you to the city. Go to sleep.'

But Siva couldn't sleep that night. The voice in his head was loud and shrill. He covered his ears with his hands, thought of Malli and shut his eyes tight.

'Come Siva, I'll help you get dressed,' Arun told Siva the next morning.

'For God's sake do not call him Siva,' Kamala said. 'Remember his name is Tara.'

Arun dressed Siva in his red silk skirt with gold buttis and a yellow blouse too big for him. He made Siva sit on the floor and combed his hair. It had grown long, and he gathered it into a tight ponytail. He twisted a string of jasmine around it. He rubbed talcum powder on Siva's face and smeared bright-pink lip colour on his lips. He rubbed rouge on his cheeks and pinched them to soak the blush in. With his middle finger he stained Siva's eyes with kohl.

Arun pushed Siva in front of the mirror. 'See how pretty you look, my kanmani.' Arun made a kissing sound with his lips.

Siva studied his face in the mirror. A wiry hair grew out of his nostril. He pulled at it hard.

Aooou.

The hair stuck to its root so Siva pulled harder.

Aachooo.

Siva heard the voice in his head sneeze.

His nose turned red, his eyes, watery. Siva stared at himself in the mirror. Was this really who he was? He felt terrified. At that moment however, another feeling overwhelmed him.

'I am hungry,' he said, bunching up his skirt.

'Stop crushing your skirt,' Kamala said. She was dressed in a brocaded silk sari and had on fake gold jewellery. Her hair was plaited with scented oil, her eyes were blackened with kohl and her cheeks were a bruised rouge-red. With a lurid lipstick she stencilled a pout on her lips, and wiped off lipstick from her tooth with a swirl of her tongue. 'You better get dressed,' she said to Arun.

'First let me put these flowers in your hair.' Arun looped a string of jasmine into Kamala's hair. 'There, you look beautiful now.' Arun cracked his knuckles on either side of his head.

'Oh come on you flatterer!' With a delicate wave of her hand Kamala slapped Arun's rump. She looked at her gold-rimmed men's wristwatch and then looked in her purse for small change. She didn't have any. She held out a twenty-rupee note to Siva.

'Here, go buy some fruit and come back soon. And don't forget to give me back the change.'

Siva walked down the lane. The stalls on either side were festooned with glittering tinsel and arranged in them was a profusion of glass bangles, cheap jewellery, cosmetics, brooches and hairpins, saris, a variety of panties and bras with stiff pointed tips, and blouses and petticoats. Film music blared through speakers that were perched on stands. The place was thronged with brightly attired eunuchs with counterfeit breasts and hairy thighs.

Siva walked to a fruit stall and bought a large papaya. Kamala took the fruit from his hands when he returned. She cut it into halves, discarded the globs of slippery white and black seeds, then cut one half into two. 'The youngest gets the biggest piece,' she said as she gave Siva the other half.

Siva walked to the window and sat on the ledge. He scooped the flesh with his fingers and stuffed it into his mouth, making sure the juice didn't drip on his skirt. He liked papaya more than any other fruit. He licked his fingers clean.

Not far from him, across the lane, an old man sat on the ground holding a cord. The other end of the cord was tied to a monkey's neck.

'Dance, monkey, dance,' the keeper shouted and as he sang, the monkey danced around him. Suddenly the animal stopped, threw its hands up in the air and looked at Siva.

Siva remembered the day a monkey had chased Malli and how terrified she was. They had been eating corncobs by the lake. 'Malli, throw the cob,' Siva had screamed and Malli had flung it up in the air. The monkey grabbed it, and bounded through the trees.

The thought of Malli sent a cold shiver down his spine. Every emotion, every sentiment seemed numbed for the moment. She had said she would be back during the holidays. It was holidays now. He wondered if she had come back. How would she know where to find him?

Him? Siva looked down at his clothes and recoiled. He looked at the papaya in his hand, juice oozing out of the wound that he had made in it with his fingers. He stabbed the papaya repeatedly with his thumb until it leaked out its orange-yellow blood.

Kamala stared at him. 'Tara! What are you doing?' she said.

'I don't want to be Tara,' he said. 'I am Siva.'

'Stop this nonsense,' Kamala retorted. 'You *are* Tara. Now let's go, it is time.'

They took a bus to the city and got off near the Madras Station. They wandered through the market. Kamala pestered shopkeepers and the people on the streets for money. Arun and Siva stood by a lamp post watching her.

'Watch me carefully,' Kamala said when she walked up to them, 'you must learn to beg. This is what you will have to do for a living.' She counted the money she had earned and put it in her purse.

It was late in the evening when they returned to the slum.

Siva was tired. When he was asleep Kamala and Arun sat under the tall peepal tree outside their shack.

Kamala leant against the trunk and sighed. 'I must take Tara away from here. She's so unhappy.'

'Where will you go?'

'I don't know yet.'

'Are you from Madras?'

'No. From Kanchipuram.'

'You could take Tara there. And me too.'

'No. I can't.' Kamala sat very still. There was a trace of redness on her cheeks and her nostrils flared and words spurted out of her mouth as though she could not control them.

'My mother was a whore,' Kamala said. 'Because of my father. He made her do it, the motherfucker. He brought his friends and relatives. Taxi drivers. Bloody traders. He took money from all of them. Then got drunk. Bastard.' The little muscle beside her left eye twitched madly and she was close to tears.

'My name was Kamal. I was a boy. My father told me I was his son, as though it was any comfort. I watched each night from where I slept. Men came and went and I wondered which one could have been my father. My fucking mother didn't even know!

'One morning I woke up and found my mother flying. I saw her feet first, not on the floor but dangling mid-air. I looked up at her: her head was several inches below the fan. My father walked into the room and screamed. I can never forget that nerve-racking scream. I was twelve.

'My father stayed at home all day. He never had a job. I did. Not far from our house was a taxi stand. I washed taxis in the morning and in the evening I worked in a cheap hotel. I cleaned utensils and plates till midnight. During the day I had to do my fucking mother's chores at home – washing, cleaning and cooking.

'I returned from the hotel late one night. I was tired. I noticed my father sitting in the corner. I hadn't cooked any dinner. The previous night he had beaten me and taken away all the money I had. There was no money to buy anything to cook. "There's no food," I told him and sat down on my mat.

'"We have to feed our hunger then, don't we?" he said walking over; he sat down next to me. He stank of sour rum and sweat.

'He put his arms around my waist and pushed me to the floor. He pulled my shorts down and began to touch me. I was frightened. Then like a raging beast he brought his body heavily on top of mine and slammed into me.

'Pain bolted out of my ears and numbed my brain. All of a sudden it started to rain. I was confused but I distinctly remember the fermented smell. Rum? I opened my eyes and stared at the mirror against the wall in front of me. It was an old mirror I had picked up from the street and it was broken on the top. Through the sweat pouring all over my eyes I saw the motherfucker pissing on me. And then the mirror seemed to merge with the floor, until it faded.'

Kamala laughed. 'Silly of me, isn't it? At that moment I thought I smelled something else: pungent and aromatic. I was not wrong. My father had brought mutton biryani. He had opened the packet and was stuffing the rice into his mouth as I watched him. He must have been terribly hungry. It must have been expensive biryani; it had black kismis in it. I don't know why I remember this. But I do. This is how it started.'

The sobs smothered Kamala now; her breast heaved and her throat trembled visibly. 'Each night I lay awake in bed terrified that he would assault me again. Soon I knew when he would: his footsteps were light and mean, and he always brought biryani. I could smell it, with my eyes closed, from a long distance: the fragrant rice, the curried mutton in it and the black kismis.

'I gave up resisting. It was a way of obliterating my self from myself. After that it became a simple routine. He just called me to his bed. And I went. And later we ate biryani together.'

Kamala wiped her eyes with the end of her sari. 'I have never forgotten the stench of that biryani. Whenever I smell it, I am reminded of him.'

She laughed, but her eyes were moist. 'From time to time I need biryani to remind me of those fucking nights, not that I can ever forget. I need to torture myself enough to want to kill that motherfucker.' Kamala's face seemed to tighten slightly and then to sag. 'One day I will … I will kill him before he dies.'

An owl hooted in the distance. Kamala continued the rest of Kamal's story. One evening Kamal had returned home with strings of jasmine and after bolting the door he dressed up in his mother's old sari. He put on lipstick that smelled of stale oil, and kohl that had hardened like rock. He lay in bed imagining how perversely some man must have fucked his mother to give birth to a body such as his.

At around this time, Kamal got friendly with an inseparable pair of eunuchs. They called themselves Sweety-Cutie. They had come to the hotel where he worked. The next day Kamal did not go to work; instead he went to them. They dressed him up like them and took him to the market.

After that day his disgust for his father took on another shape. He realised that the depth of his misery was not entirely because of him, or his mother. They were but two festering boils on his inner thigh, filled with foul pus, whose smell reminded him he was not an orphan.

Kamal's ache was deeper, duller, devoid of even a familiar stink. It was connected to an unfathomable part of him – that core of his being that had misgivings about who he was. Or was not. He was fifteen.

A week later, Kamal left home with Sweety-Cutie. They boarded a bus, got off some miles outside Madras and ambled their way to the slum. Sweety-Cutie took Kamal to the Guru, who castrated him with a knife. Amidst joyful songs and rituals, Kamal was renamed Kamala.

Despite the pain Kamala felt happy. Frequently her hands stroked her crotch, searched the missing lump of flesh, as the tongue would seek a fallen tooth.

They locked her in the room for forty days. She was allowed outside only when it was dark and when no one could see her.

After that Kamala had to learn to be girl-like. All along she had thought this would be easy. But now with a woman's body she was still reacting like a man. When she had to leave the room she felt very strange because she came to it dressed as a man, and was leaving it in a sari.

After nearly six weeks, Kamala saw all the other eunuchs. She tried to imagine how they felt between their legs – if they had the same feelings as her, or if they could imagine having a penis, as she did. She tried to walk like a woman but it was difficult. When she was a man people teased her because she sauntered like a woman, so delicately, but now when she walked she felt ungainly and her feet fell heavily on the ground. And she couldn't pee properly while squatting. Her face was round and soft like a woman's before but now that she had turned into one, her face seemed angular and hard; her eyes popped out of their sockets and her beard was coarse.

Sweety-Cutie got Kamala her first boyfriend. He was a tailor. He made her a sexy red blouse. Kamala could never forget her first night with him, having sex as a woman. She couldn't remember exactly how he looked but she remembered the touch of his hands, warm between her legs, and she knew she'd have been excited, if there had been something to excite.

Arun let out a deep sigh. He reached out and clutched Kamala's hand.

'So here I am,' Kamala said.

Siva felt someone shake him awake that night. It was Kamala. Her tone was terse as she whispered, 'I had a bad dream. I think my father is dying. I have to go to see him.'

Siva clung to her arm. 'Take me with you. Don't leave me here.'

'I can't,' Kamala said firmly. 'I'll be back soon.'

Dawn broke open and light seeped into the room. Siva woke up suddenly as if from a dream. He looked around the hut for Kamala. She had gone.

That afternoon the Guru ordered one of the older eunuchs to lock Arun in a dark room. Several times through the day one of the eunuchs fed Arun opium and milk to keep him intoxicated.

Late at night, the Guru pulled Arun out of the room and forced him down on a stone table. The other eunuchs were gathered around them. Siva hid behind one of them and watched.

The Guru tied a cord tightly around Arun's testicles. Two eunuchs held Arun down as, in one swift movement, the Guru severed his penis and testicles with a sharp knife. She bled the cut to drain every drop of Arun's manhood. She inserted a wooden plug shaped like a wine cork into the wound, leaving an aperture. Then she poured hot oil over the gash and pressed a pad of herb paste on it to heal it. Siva watched them, his hands pressed to his crotch.

Next evening all the eunuchs dressed up in their finery. One of them combed Siva's hair, fixed a string of jasmine in it and painted his face. Then as the mob of eunuchs clapped and made ululating sounds out of the depths of their throats, the Guru forced Arun down on a the large pestle of a grinding stone until he bled from the anus. The drops of blood were taken to signify the first menstruation. The initiation was complete. Arun was now a woman. She was named Aruna.

Siva was terrified. Arun's tortured screams rang in his ears as he stumbled back to the hut. Because of the shock and fear of what he had witnessed, that *thing* that lived in Siva's body, that *thing* that thought his thoughts, that *thing* that spoke to him, the girlish *thing* in him moved away for the time being.

He still had the change from the money Kamala had given him. He removed it from under his mattress and ran into the oncoming dusk.

Twenty-one

SIVA BOARDED THE BUS TO Madras Station. When it reached the terminus he got off and strolled down the street. He looked at shop windows, at the mannequins dressed in fancy clothes. He stopped at a fast-food restaurant with a large glass window through which he could see people eating. He was hungry, but he knew the money he had left wasn't enough to eat in the restaurant. He walked towards a roadside vendor and watched him make dosas. The man looked at Siva curiously. 'Hey girl, what do you want?' Siva showed him the coins he had left. 'Ha, that's not even enough to buy chutney. Run along now. Go home. I don't run a charity service.'

Siva sat down on the pavement under a tree. A crowd of people streamed out of the cinema hall nearby. They gathered around the vendor and ate the dosas he fried for them. Then a woman rode up on a motorbike. Her hair was cut short and she wore a red T-shirt, trackpants and sneakers. She parked her bike and walked up to the vendor with a tiffin carrier. She was tall and muscular, and walked with a swagger. The vendor filled a container with sambhar, another with chutney. He started to fry dosas and put them in the top container. The woman saw Siva watching them.

'Who's that young girl? A relative of yours?'

'Chi. Of course not. She has been here for some time. She looks hungry but she doesn't have much money.'

The woman walked up to Siva. 'What's your name, girl?' she asked.

He was about to say Siva, but then he looked at his clothes and hesitated. 'Tara,' he replied.

'How old are you, Tara?'

'Thirteen. No, fourteen.'

'You look much younger. What are you doing here alone? Are you lost? Where do you live?'

'Machilipatnam.' Siva said looking down at his toes. Arun had painted them red. 'I want to go back.'

'The railway station is at the end of this road. There is a late train to Machilipatnam.' She looked at her watch. 'Do you have no money?' She counted some notes. 'Here, that's all I can spare. This will buy you the ticket and a meal.' She turned to the vendor. 'Venkat, fry her a dosa, will you? Add it to my bill.'

The vendor clicked his tongue. 'You have a weak heart, ma. Thousands of girls run away from home. They all crowd this city and become tarts. Look at her face, chi, so much make-up.'

'Never mind,' the woman said, 'feed her. And show her the way to the station.' She collected the tiffin carrier, waved to Siva and rode away.

The vendor handed Siva a plate with two dosas. When Siva had eaten them, the vendor packed his belongings and started to roll his cart down the lane. Siva walked behind him. When they passed the railway station, the vendor stopped, pointed to it and trundled on.

An old man helped Siva buy the ticket and walked him to a bench on the platform. 'You sit here, girl. The train to Machilipatnam is two hours late.'

Siva sat on the bench and waited. An hour later, he stretched out on the bench and within minutes, he was fast asleep. He woke up when he heard a tapping sound. It was a policeman, tapping the bench with his staff.

Siva looked up at him sleepily. 'If you want to sleep here, girl, then it will cost you ten rupees a night. Nothing in this world is free. Get that? What's a young girl like you doing here eh?'

'I am waiting for the train to Machilipatnam.'

'Left an hour ago,' the policeman said. He shook his head. 'So you missed your train eh?' He took out a packet of cigarettes and lit one. 'You can lie down here tonight. But don't sleep. It's not safe,' he said and walked away whistling a tune.

Siva tried to stay awake but couldn't. When he awoke it was well past dawn; he went back to the vendor. Early office-goers crowded the stall. The vendor whistled at him.

'Hey, missed your train or what? Well, don't stand there gawking about. Come here and clean these plates.'

Siva washed the plates with water from a bucket. He wiped them dry with a soiled towel the vendor handed out to him. A truck drew up. The driver got out and stumbled towards the cart. He was short and bulky with small piercing eyes. He stank of rum. He slapped the vendor on the back and laughed, looking at Siva.

'Who's this?'

'I don't know. She's been here since last night. She's from Machilipatnam she says, but I don't know what she's doing here in Madras. She was to take the train last night.'

He held out a plate of dosas. Siva took it from him and sat down under the tree to eat.

The driver glanced at Siva. 'Pretty young thing she is eh?' he laughed again, then looked at his watch. 'I am going to Machilipatnam in about an hour. I can pick her up on my way.'

He turned to Siva. 'Would you like to come?' Then with a smile he added, 'My name is Selvam.'

He returned two hours later and yelled out to Siva. 'What are you waiting for eh?' the vendor asked. 'Selvam is giving you a free ride, go. You can't stay alone in this city. It's dangerous.'

They sped down the highway. Selvam talked. He sang. He was nice. It was past 6 when they stopped between rows of trucks, at Paradise India Hotel. It was a dingy eatery with a newly painted signboard, red and yellow, lit by a tubelight. Its windows were fixed with blue nylon netting to keep insects out.

A blue-light fly-killer was fixed on one of the green walls inside. The flies were lured to it like a drunk to another drunk, and then with a spark and a ping they were incinerated.

The aroma of coffee filtered the hot air inside. Selvam greeted the owner, a rotund man with a scary moustache and red eyes. He sat near the entrance, surrounded by large bottles of biscuits and sweets. Behind him several dozens of bananas hung from a rod. He yelled out to a boy. Several boys in vests and khaki shorts ran between the tables. One of them splashed water on a table, wiped it with a dirty rag, then beckoned Selvam to sit at it. The place was crowded with truck drivers gorging the last meal of the day before they set off, with full bellies, to drive through the night.

The combined smells of boiled rice, fermented curd, spicy curry and chutney spun invisible cocoons around Siva's nose and mouth. His stomach churned. He swallowed his spit.

Selvam ordered two meals of rice and curry and coffee. Siva looked around. On one wall were three photographs of the chief gods and their respective wives: Shiva-Parvathi, Vishnu-Laxmi, and Brahma-Saraswati. Each of the wives was equally buxom, their full breasts covered by see-through silks. Their faces were candy-pink and their lips, blood-red. White and pink plastic flower garlands hung around them. On the adjacent wall were the leaders of the nation similarly garlanded: a young ebullient Pandit Nehru, a sweetly smiling Mahatma Gandhi, and a tired-looking Indira Gandhi.

Bleached lizards moved from the leaders to the gods and back; they clicked their tongues and smacked their mouths in anticipation. But most of the insects ended up in the blue electric mouth.

A young boy brought their meals and coffee. He set two steel bowls in front of Siva. The smaller bowl sat upside down in the larger one. Like a deft juggler the boy lifted the small bowl, and coffee spilled into the larger bowl at the bottom. He poured the coffee from one bowl to another several times until it frothed.

A man walked up to them. He patted Selvam on his back and whistled at Siva. 'You pluck them young, don't you Selva? He bent forward and stroked Siva's cheek. 'With skin smooth as velvet.'

Selvam grabbed his wrist and yanked his arm away. 'Leave her alone. She's my sister's daughter.'

The man arched an eyebrow. 'Niece eh? And one so tender?' He laughed.

Selvam's tone was terse, 'Did you not hear what I said? Leave her alone.' He turned to Siva and said, 'Come on, drink up your coffee and let's go.'

They hit the road again. Siva sat close to Selvam. When the truck lurched Siva was plummeted against Selvam; his head rested on his arm. He did not move away. Selvam bent down and kissed his head. 'You must be tired,' he said. 'Go to sleep, girl. We have a long way to go.'

It was past 8 when Siva awoke and a blanket of dusk had spread over them. Selvam swerved the truck into a dirt road. All around them in the fields the crops grew tall.

'Sugarcane,' Selvam informed Siva as the blades of the tall grass sssssed in the breeze. He stopped not far from a shack. Several drivers were sitting around a table outside it. They were drinking and smoking. Selvam waved out to them.

One man with purpled cheeks and the look of an alcoholic stared at the scribbled menu board in front of the door. He swayed and the stench of cheap rum hula-hooped around his body. Passers-by made a loop around him to dodge the stink.

'Mutton curry and rice plate,' he said aloud. A woman passed by him; she had hitched up her sari and her ankles were visible. She wore silver anklets that jingled as she walked. She carried a steel tray. The drunk put his fingers in his mouth and whistled. He unzipped his trousers and scratched his balls. 'Tch, tch, those melon breasts. Sridevi's breasts.'

The drunk followed the woman. He walked like she walked, hips swaying, chest strutting out. He whistled again and walked alongside her, muttering obscenities. She swung at him with her tray. He held her wrist tight for a minute; with his other hand he squeezed her breast. She laughed and hit his head. He let go of her hand. As she turned he plunged his hand between her buttocks.

Selvam and Siva walked into the shack and sat down at the counter. Selvam ordered a plate of onion pakoras and an orange drink for Siva. The drunk came in shortly and sat down beside Siva. 'Mutton curry and rice plate,' he muttered to the man behind the counter. He scratched his face. 'No. Make it chikan curry and rice plate,' he said.

'No chikan, only mutton curry, meat bhajji, meat roast, fish curry, potato curry, puri, roti and rice plate,' the man behind the counter replied. He was short and extremely lean. He seemed nervous and his hands shook.

'Chikan,' the drunk insisted.

The woman returned. She stood behind the counter in front of the drunk. The palav of her sari had slipped off her shoulder; her blouse was cut low. 'Did you not hear what my brother said?' She screeched. 'No chikan, only mutton.'

'Chikan, I want chikan.' The drunk banged the counter.

The woman said something to her brother. He ran off and minutes later returned with a bowl of chicken curry and a plate of rice. The curry was a bowlful of fatty broth, piled high with bones.

'Eat.' The woman pushed the bowl towards the drunk. 'And then get out.'

In the meanwhile Selvam had taken out a quarter bottle of brandy from his pocket. He took a long thirsty swig from it. The drunk was watching the woman's cleavage through an empty glass. She didn't seem to care. And each time she stood before him the man breathed hard and drooled.

He mumbled, 'Left tit, right tit, in-between tits, tit-tits,' and laughed.

Siva munched a pakora, then looked around him and then down at his clothes. He wished he had his pants and shirt on. Amidst the burly men in the shack he felt an urgent need to be a man like them. Suddenly, the drunk leaned across the bar and pushed his hand into the woman's blouse. He lost his balance and fell against Siva. Siva hit his head hard against the counter and fell to the floor.

Selvam picked him up and, holding his arm, he led him out of the door. He walked him towards a crop of trees in the field. He sat down on a boulder and pulled Siva towards him. The drunk and some of the other truck drivers who had followed them, staggered close, tipsy and boisterous. The drunk caught Siva's shoulders and crushed him against his chest. Cranked up by the other men's hooting and whistling, he yanked Siva's blouse off.

Selvam laughed. The drunk pinned Siva against a tree, plucked his skirt off and slipped down his underwear. Then said, 'What have you brought with you, Selva?'

Selvam looked at Siva, stunned. The truck drivers' guffaws enraged him. He pulled Siva by his hair. 'What are you doing dressed up in a skirt you mother-fucking eunuch?' He slapped Siva hard across his face, then boxed his eye and then his ear. Siva fell down. Selvam kicked Siva's ribs repeatedly, screaming obscenities. Then with the heel of his shoe he kicked him on his nose and pain rose in Siva's nose like the aroma of an onion: a tart, pungent ache. He passed out. But before he did he saw Selvam pick his clothes up and, amidst the laughter of the drivers, walk away.

When Siva came to it was morning. He felt a smarting in his belly and doubling up, he vomited. He stared at the orgy of muck: fermenting pakoras and chutney that he had eaten the previous night, gastric fluids, a hideous medley of this and that. He looked at it with dismay. He threw up again.

Slowly Siva got to his feet. He stumbled towards the main road. He found his clothes under a bush. His hands were shaking as he put them on. His head felt shrivelled up, pickle-like under a hot sun. He collapsed in a heap.

A truck driver who had stopped for a leak found Siva. He shook him awake but Siva couldn't speak. The driver yelled out to a young boy. 'Come here, quickly! Poor girl, she's a mess.' Together they carried Siva to the truck and put him in the back. Siva passed out once more.

'You must be hungry,' the driver said when Siva woke up. It was evening. 'In another twenty minutes we will reach Machilipatnam.

Twenty-two

THE NIGHT SIVA RAN AWAY Ammamai didn't realise he was missing until late next morning. 'Have you seen Siva?' she asked Mani.

'No,' Mani said averting his eyes. 'Maybe he has gone to Vishnu-aiyah,' he suggested. 'Or perhaps he has gone to Saroja-ma's house.'

'Go at once and bring him back,' Ammamai said to Munniamma. But Munniamma returned half an hour later without Siva.

'I am sure Siva will come back,' Mani said. 'Where can he go?' He looked anxious.

Vishnu telephoned several times to enquire about Siva and Saroja came to see Ammamai late in the afternoon. 'Don't worry, ma,' Saroja said. 'I am sure he will come back. Have you contacted Raman?'

'No,' Ammamai said. 'I'll tell him when he returns home tomorrow.' Then with a sigh she added, 'By then I am sure Siva will be back.'

Raman returned late in the evening. Ammamai who was waiting for him in the veranda had fallen asleep on the pai. Raman shook her by her shoulder. 'Why are you sleeping here?'

Ammamai slumped on the floor and repeatedly slapping her head with her hands she wailed. Raman held her shoulder with both his hands and vigorously shook her several times. 'What is wrong? Why are you crying like this?'

Ammamai looked up at him, 'Siva has gone,' she cried. 'We have looked everywhere. He's gone.'

'Gone? Why?'

'I shouldn't have shouted at him.'

'Why did you shout at him, Amma? You know he's not well.'

'I found him dressed in his mother's clothes. I was so upset and angry. So I shouted at him. It's my fault he went away.'

'Don't blame yourself. It's not your fault, Amma. If it's anybody's fault it is Mallika's.'

Together with Mani, Raman went in search of his son. It was nearly dawn when they returned. Exhausted and worried Raman informed the police. Even after a week the police could find no trace of Siva.

Vishnu's condition had deteriorated ever since Siva's disappearance. One morning he asked Mallika to take him to her mother's grave. They left in a taxi. Vishnu held Mallika's hand and climbed to the top of a hill. It was a glorious day, more than Mallika could have wished for – the sunshine and the cool breeze smelling of flowers. If she could ever imagine a beautiful place, this was it. If she could ever imagine a happy morning, this was it. If only Tara had been there with her, it would have been the happiest moment of all.

They sat down on a rock. Vishnu looked at Mallika with a certain pinched look in his face, and fear in his eyes.

'Grief is dangerous, Mallika,' he said 'It ruins everything you have. You lost your mother, your daughter and then your friend Nayantara. You haven't been able to forget your pain. You still miss her, don't you?'

'Nayantara?'

'No. Tara.'

'I wish she was alive. I wish Siva had died. I hate him,' Mallika said vehemently.

Vishnu put his arm around her shoulder. 'You don't hate him, Mallika. You can't feel any love. You loved too much, too soon.'

'It is because of Siva that Tara died.'

Vishnu coughed violently. He patted his chest and said, 'Tara didn't die because of Siva.' This voice turned pitiful. 'Just as your mother didn't die because of you, Mallika.'

Mallika's face convulsed. 'But you always told me she died because of me.'

Vishnu held her hand and confessed, 'That is true. Every time I saw you I wished you hadn't been born. And when you were older and looked just like your mother I learnt to love you though it was not you I loved but your mother that I saw in you. It took me years to come to my senses, to realise you were my flesh and blood, that you were all I had, and that if I had lost my wife, you had lost your mother.'

Mallika's shoulders grieved. Vishnu held her face in his hands. 'Don't repeat the mistake I made, ma. Promise me you will look after Siva. God only knows where he is now, poor boy. He lost his twin sister even before he had seen her. Think how unhappy he must be.'

A dusty haze darkened the sky. The trees threshed the wind and made a dry, rasping sound. Vishnu watched Mallika's face soften, as large drops of rain floated down from the skies and they seemed to him to wash away all her tears. Soon, streams appeared all over the ground and built up rapidly. Here and there the wounds on the soil bled with reddish sludge. Resembling inverted commas, they twisted along their way and ended in puddles.

Vishnu was drenched, and so was Mallika. They walked down the hill, her hand holding his. They returned home.

Vishnu sat on his bed in the dark. He was not afraid of darkness. He would be rid of it soon. He knew. He took his violin out of its case and played a melancholy tune.

Mallika found him dead the next morning. She picked up his violin from his bed, wiped it with the end of her sari and put it back in its case. She shut the clasps one at a time. She covered his corpse with a sheet and then informed Ammamai and Saroja.

Mallika systematically packed her father's things in two trunks. She felt a whirlwind of emotions on the tip of her tongue; she tasted each one: sweet, sour, bitter. And then in a big gulp she swallowed her spit. Her mouth was dry, bereft of taste. After many years she felt an eerie calm.

The garden, that afternoon, was filled with people besides Ammamai, Raman, Saroja, Munniamma and Mani. Eager crows sat on the trees. Raman stood at the door and watched Mallika by her father's corpse on the floor. He was touched by an unfamiliar emotion. For the first time he felt sorry for her.

Mallika pressed her father's feet beneath the sheet, mistaking them for his knees. The body had shrunk. It smelled of an old, slightly damp towel that had been stored in a trunk and discovered after many seasons. It was the stench of a man who had lived alone for too long.

Outside, when the pundit lit the ritual fire, Raman sat in front of it. Mallika sat next to him. Saroja gave Mallika a large vessel of boiled rice and Mallika emptied it next to the pundit. Then she got up and ran to the nearest tree and cried into its bark. The pundit directed the steam from the boiled rice towards heaven, pushing it with his hand. He coaxed it in Tamil, 'Po-po.' He blew after it phonetically: phoo phoo. The steam rose, moistened the leaves, soaked the air above, then with a loss of spirit, it tumbled downwards, wrapping itself around the people who had gathered. The pundit slapped the rice into a perfect square, cut it into three horizontal sections, sprinkled sesame and water on it, and offered it to three generations of the deceased.

When the funeral rituals were over at the house Raman and Mani carried the corpse to the cremation ghat along the river. The pundit followed behind them carrying a clay pot filled with water.

At the ghat Raman and Mani set the corpse on a heap of firewood. The pundit made a hole in the clay pot and raised it to Raman's shoulder. The water dripped from the pot as Raman circled the pyre. Once. Twice. Thrice. On the pundit's signal Raman crashed the pot on the ground and then lit the pyre.

The pundit chanted aloud as the pyre burned. When the last embers had died, the pundit collected the ashes in an urn and handed it to Raman.

Mallika lay in her father's bed staring at a spot on the ceiling. Raman stood at the door holding the urn of ashes in his hands.

Saroja walked up behind Raman. 'Mallika, Raman is back, ma,' she said. 'What do you want to do with your father's ashes, my child?'

Mallika turned and looked at Raman. Her eyes were vacant. She got out of bed. 'Please take me to the market,' she said.

Raman didn't speak a word to Mallika as they walked down Gibbs Road. He didn't know what to say to her. Of the children they had shared, one had died and the other had disappeared. What could he possibly say?

Mallika stopped at Ranga Roses and bought some flowers and from Yusuf's pet shop next door, a cage of love birds.

On top of the hill, under the Parijat tree Mallika sprinkled her father's ashes on the spot where her mother's were mixed with the earth. She covered the ground with flowers and let out the birds one by one. They flapped their wings, then flew into a seamless sky.

Saroja was waiting in Vishnu's house when Raman brought Mallika back.

'You go home now, Raman, Saroja said, 'you must be tired. I will stay with Mallika here tonight.'

After Raman left Saroja led Mallika to the garden at the back. She put her arms around Mallika's shoulders, drawing her close. Loss, to each of them, was more poignant than death itself. There didn't seem to be any use for words. Tears sufficed.

Saroja and Mallika sat on the steps. Mallika didn't utter a word. Saroja was silent. They were lost in thought. Loss, to each of them, was more poignant than death itself. Mallika's face was covered in a white, cold sweat of pain. She wretchedly said, 'My mother died, Tara died, then Nayantara, and now my father has left me. Why do the gods want to punish me like this?'

'The gods have nothing to do with all this, Mallika,' Saroja replied. 'Gods exist only in our minds, because we are afraid, and they keep us afraid. You must learn to be strong.'

She looked up at the sky and added, 'Can you see those seven stars, Mallika? At the beginning of this world there was only a big round of white light. It was much bigger than the sun. Around it everything was dark. Then a little bit of light broke from it, and was hurled into the sky. It tore into seven bits. They became the seven stars, the saptarishi, the seven minds of the universe. Out of the special energy of these seven stars people's minds were made. And out of people's minds the gods were made up because people were afraid. Remember this, the mind was created even before the world was, or the gods were. So as long as you feel fear, create your own fleet of gods. Bribe them with flowers and coconuts; yes they like coconuts but they like money even more. Then when you are no longer afraid, let all the gods go. Release them. Like this.' She clapped her hands thrice. 'Po, po, po.'

Mallika looked up at the sky. Saroja held her hand. 'You must go back home tomorrow.'

'This is my home.'

'This was your home, Mallika. You must return to Raman's house. And you must be there when Siva returns. He is your flesh and blood. He is all you have left now. I wonder where he is. Poor boy.'

That night as Mallika sat alone in her room the bitterness she had cradled since she was a girl seemed to leave her. She thought of Siva. She had tied him to the death of Tara. She had despised him. Now she felt nothing, neither hate nor love. All she felt was intense regret.

Raman found it very hard to sleep that night. He slept at early dawn, though fitfully. When he opened his eyes he wanted to flee back to sleep, to close his eyes and shut his thoughts. He felt a dull throbbing under his eyelids, and deep in his heart.

His eyes closed tight, he started to think. Now that Mallika's father had died, he would have to bring her home. But what would happen if Siva returned? Siva had run away because of her. He was sick because of her. He had gone mad because of her. He'd have to tell her the truth – that she couldn't come home. But what would he say to her? What would she say?

Raman woke up. It was still early. He dressed hurriedly and went to Mallika's house. The front door was ajar.

Raman walked in and looked for his wife but he didn't call out her name, he simply couldn't bring himself to do this.

Not finding her anywhere inside the house Raman stepped into the garden. He saw Mallika watering the flowerbeds.

Mallika looked up and seeing him she walked along the hedge to where he stood.

'How are you? Are you okay? Raman asked.

'How could I be okay?' Mallika's voice shook. 'First I lose my daughter and now my son. It's because of me that Siva ran away.'

Her sudden confession unnerved Raman. He clasped his hands in front of him and locked the fingers in. He seemed uneasy; he didn't know what to say.

He cleared his throat. 'Mallika, I, I think, I mean, your father is no more and I, I,...'

Mallika's eyes didn't waver as she looked at Raman. She shook her head. 'No,' she said, 'I am not coming back.'

The utter relief that Raman felt at that moment brought tears to his eyes.

Mallika reached out and touched his arm. There was a veiled expression in her eyes, something curiously persuasive.

It doused Raman with guilt.

'It's not my fault Mallika,' Raman began.

'What's not your fault?'

'It's not my fault that Tara died.' Tears streamed down his cheeks. 'She was my daughter too.'

Kamala returned to Madras and was shocked to hear from Aruna that Siva had run away.

'He must have gone back home. It's for the best,' she said somewhat relieved.

Aruna screwed up her eyes. 'Where did you go?'

Kamala's face was tight. There was an excess of saliva in her mouth; it sputtered at the corner of her lips and caught the light. She sat down, her back against the wall. She undid her hair and let it loose, then she hitched up her sari and crossed her hairy legs in front of her. Moments passed, then scrunching her sari and holding it between her knees, she confessed, 'I went to see my father. I had to reach him before he died.'

Kamala crossed her arms across her chest. 'He was half his size. Raw rum had cratered his cheeks and his eyes bulged out of their sockets. When he held my hand, his fingers felt cold and moist like the underside of a toad.'

Kamala scratched her hair, plucked a fat louse from it, then crushed it between two fingernails. She made a sound with her tongue like a slurp. 'I looked after him for a week, revelling in the satisfaction of his dependence on me. I fed him mutton biryani every day, bathed him, and as he slept, sang songs to him and watched the tears roll down and collect in the well of his cheeks. Then when I thought he had cried enough I bought special mutton biryani with black kismis. I set the plate on my father's chest so that the smell would drift to his nostrils and remind him of those days we spent together. Then deliberately and slowly I fed him. He died that night. He had wet the bed. He stank of piss and sour rum.'

Kamala wiped her face with the end of her sari. 'I made a mistake,' she said, 'a terrible mistake and I've been living it all my life.' There was something definite and purposeful in the way she spoke. 'I am a fake. In my heart where my feelings are stored, I am a woman. In my head where my thoughts are shaped, I am a woman. But in this body, I am a man. And deep in my conscience I am utterly indefinable. Because I never look there, I betray myself. I hold on to a fate not entirely my own.

All these years the effort I took to be a woman meant I was being cruel to the man in me. But I made a choice and now I have to live the lie.'

'Will you go back to Machilipatnam?' Aruna asked.

Kamala sighed. 'I will go back to my father's home. I will live there now.'

It was past 7 when the truck reached Machilipatnam.

Siva got off but he could hardly walk. The driver and his attendant held him by both his arms and walked him down the market street. Siva pointed in the opposite direction but when he tried to speak they couldn't understand what he was saying. Siva pulled his arms away, turned back and stumbled on.

Mani and Munniamma were at the gate when they saw Siva walking towards Victorian Villa. Mani rushed to Siva, held him by his shoulders. 'Thank God you are back.'

Munniamma ran into the house shouting for Ammamai. When Ammamai came to the door and saw Siva standing outside, badly bruised and dressed in a tattered skirt and blouse, she was aghast. She didn't say a word; instead she wrapped her arms around him.

'Take Siva to his room, Munniamma,' Ammamai said urgently, 'I must inform his father.'

Holding Siva by his arm Munniamma pulled him up the stairs to his room. Siva collapsed on the bed. Munniamma cleaned the cuts and bruises on his arms, legs and face then rubbed ointment on them. She helped him into fresh clothes, and into bed.

Ammamai burst into the room with a plate of dosas. She sat beside Siva on the bed and fed him. Tears streamed down his face.

'Don't cry Siva,'' Ammamai said, 'don't cry.'

'I am so sorry…' Siva said.

'You are home. That's all that matters,' Ammamai said.

When Raman arrived Ammamai was waiting for him on the steps of the veranda. Seeing him her tears descended like rain.

'Poor boy he's become so thin, just skin and bones,' she said between sobs. 'And he is bruised all over. Who did this to him?'

Raman rushed to her and bending low he put his arms around her shoulders. 'Don't cry amma.' Then straightening up he asked, 'Have you told Mallika?'

'No. I have told no one. And I told Mani and Munniamma not tell anyone.'

'Where is he?' In a gentler tone he asks, 'Where is my son?'

'He's sleeping,' Ammamai said. 'Don't scold him. And don't tell him about Vishnu's death. He won't be able to handle it. I have told Mani and Munniamma not to breathe a word about Vishnu to Siva.'

Raman turned around and bounded up the steps to Siva's room.

Twenty-three

IT WAS A MONTH SINCE Siva had returned home. Each day went by at a snail's pace for him, almost heavily as though the hours of the day had been anchored to a rocky mountain. Ammamai and Raman, Mani and Munniamma fussed over him and although he got better, sadness had made a permanent hole in his heart. He thought Vishnu-tata. Why had he not come to see him? He thought of his mother and wished he could see her. But what would she say to her? What would she say to him? As for Tara, she still occupied his mind. Only one person could make him feel good, he knew, make him feel himself, make him feel whole.

When Ammamai had gone to the temple one evening and he had the chance, Siva went to Saroja's house. Saroja couldn't help staring at him; he looked as though he had stepped out of a tragic picture. Her eyes pricked with the hurt of it all. 'Come, Siva,' she said and holding his arm she led him inside and into the garden at the back. They sat down on the steps.

Siva reached up and scratched the lobe of his ear. 'Why did Malli never write to me?' His question was direct, as if he didn't have the inclination to ask it any differently. And didn't care any more if the answer to his question wounded him.

Saroja didn't want to lie to him. She held his hand and stroked it with the other. 'She wrote to you, Siva. She told me she did.

She wrote to you many times. Maybe your father didn't want you to get her letters.'

Siva's face turned white. His eyes lost their colour as he peered at Saroja. 'No, that's not true. Appa would never do such a thing.' Then his eyes became dark and focused. He took in a long breath.

Siva stood up and ran out of the house. The thought of his father pained him; it was an acute sensation, like a pebble in his shoe. It hurt him as he walked home.

'Siva, Siva,' someone called out to him as he crossed the road. He turned back and saw Mallika. It was the first time she had called him by his name. She walked up to him. For a moment she looked as though she wasn't sure what she ought to do. She moved forward and opened her mouth as though to say something, then she reached out and touched his hand. Her eyes were gentle. She tried to smile but couldn't; the end of her nose trembled.

'I, I, I am sorry,' Mallika hesitated as words got stuck in her throat. She blurted, 'Your grandfather died, Siva.' She raised her hand to stroke his head but Siva pushed it away. He turned and ran. He heard Mallika calling out to him but he didn't stop.

Siva stumbled home. As soon as he was in his room, he sat on the bed and stared at the wall in front of him. The paint on the wall, yellowed in patches, looked as if it was watermarked with burned edges. An old photograph of Vishnu and him hung on the wall above the desk. He had been ten the day the photograph was taken in Sunrise Studios. The lizard that peeped from behind the photoframe was mottled with blue veins.

Siva's eyelids twitched and his face contracted. He lay down in bed. He fixed his eyes on a fan-blade that had a dent on it. It turned slowly and then with a loud whir the fan began to rotate faster. Siva was not surprised; this had happened many times before and on one such occasion when he was with Malli, he had flung a book at the fan, dimpling one of its blades.

He covered his eyes with his hands. He opened his mouth as if to yawn but no yawn came out of it; only a sigh – a long hiss, a disturbed breath. More than ever before he wished Malli was with him. Had Malli really written to him?

Raman came to call him for dinner, 'I don't want to eat,' Siva said. 'I am feeling sick.' He patted his stomach.

'It must be something you ate, Siva,' Raman said. 'Don't worry son, you will be fine in the morning.' He looked at Siva with kindness and affection. 'You get well soon, kanna, and next week we will go on a trip to Madras.' He had fixed an appointment with the psychoanalyst that Dr Kuruvilla had suggested.

When Raman turned to go, Siva asked, 'Appa, did you take Malli's letters?'

Raman's shoulders fell. Siva saw his arms tense up. Raman turned to face Siva, but did not look at him. 'Go to sleep, you must get better,' he said and walked away. Siva stared at his father's back until he disappeared out of the door.

He felt a fury that lay knotted deep inside him; it effervesced to his gullet and tasted sour on his tongue. Suddenly the typhoon in his lungs raged, the air in his head swelled, and a hiss blew out of his nostrils. After dinner, after Raman had gone to his room, Siva tiptoed down the stairs to his study. He pushed open the door carefully.

He looked in the top drawer. There were rolls of papers secured with rubber bands. He took the rubber bands off and spread the sheets on the table. They were his father's notes; they looked important. He put them back. At the bottom of the drawer he found a notebook with squashed portraits of mosquitoes and besides each, a note in his father's handwriting.

In the lower drawer he found a brown paper packet. Siva looked inside it; it contained Malli's letters. There were many. He took the notebook and letters and went up to his room. He arranged the letters according to their dates on the bed. He read them chronologically, frowning, smiling and laughing now and then. He kissed each letter after he had read it and folded it carefully. The last but one letter was dated a month ago. Malli had written in it that she had something important to tell him.

Siva trembled with excitement as he opened the last letter. It was dated two days before he ran away. It was the longest letter – eight pages long. 'I have great news.' Malli wrote at the start of the letter. The remainder of the letter contained detailed accounts of Richard and how they had met and loved. 'I love him, Siva,' she had written, 'and I know you will like him very much. He's in New York and I will see him in two days! Can you imagine?'

Siva didn't read any more. He repeated aloud the last line he had read.

Can you imagine?

Can you imagine?

Can you imagine?

They had met near the lake the evening Malli had kissed his cheeks one by one and then his eyes. Fireflies had dotted the night sky. Impulsively Malli had kissed him on his lips. He had run his tongue over his lips, testing, tasting, as though he was licking a new flavour of ice cream. It was an unusual flavour. He had liked it. He remembered.

Yes, *I can imagine*, Siva muttered to himself. Then exhausted, hurt, wounded, he covered his face with his hands and tried to cry. But the tears didn't come. Instead he heard Tara's voice.

'Go away. Please leave me alone,' he cried.

Siva opened the windows next morning to admit a heavy-eyed dawn. He inhaled the crisp air deep into his lungs. He dressed impatiently and into a bag he stuffed his mother's sari that he had stored in the cupboard, his father's mosquito notebook and Malli's letters. His eyes fell on the photograph of Vishnu and him on the wall. He reached inside the drawer of the desk and retrieved an old one-rupee good-luck coin his grandfather had given him. He stuffed it into his trouser pocket and stealthily he walked out of the main door.

He walked down Gibbs Road, his eyes intent on his feet. There were a few people on the street already, but it seemed as though they moved away from him. He noticed some of them staring at him and then whispering to each other as he passed them. In the intricately choreographed community of Machilipatnam, Siva's unexpected appearance had an electrical effect.

He passed what used to be a bookshop. He looked up at the sign painted in the colours of an upside-down taxi, black on yellow: Sweeties Saloon. Hairpieces displayed in its window rolled down in ringlets or were piled high on pink plastic heads. It was a beauty parlour run by two Chinese girls. Their names appeared on the sign: Lin & Jin.

MacOnly's golden twin arcs bloomed into a large M over its roof. A board attached to it read:

No Beef
No Pork
Muttan on Fridays
Waterless Chickans Always
MacOnly
Hambuggas
Be Eating
Being Happy

The morning sun hardened, crisping the air. Siva walked to the beach. In the minaret far behind him, the muezzin tapped into a loudspeaker, 'Testing-testing one-two-three-four,' then wailed into the moist atmosphere, 'La ilaha ila allah.' From the Shiva temple the devotees chanted 'Shiva-Shiva-Shiva …' A cripple sang in a mellifluous voice.

Siva closed his eyes, trembling inwardly. When he opened them he saw the crippled beggar; he had a scarf around his neck and a tattered straw hat, possibly discarded by a foreign tourist, perched on his head. The beggar smiled and then with a benevolent nod he displayed the knob of his leg, unevenly stitched. Clutching his leg, he crawled towards Siva. 'One rupee,' he said. 'Give me one rupee, give-give.' Siva dashed across the sand. Baby crabs sprang sideways in rapid camera-shutter clicks.

A runaway paper wrapped itself around Siva's leg. He peeled it off and looked at it. It had pink and blue lines on it. At the top of the page was inscribed a capital A and somewhere in the middle a capital Z. Presumably the paper had belonged to a child learning alphabets. And it had devised a way of memorising them, which was to start with the beginning and end and fill in all the letters in between. A cackle got caught in Siva's throat and made a rasping sound. His life too, he thought, had a definable beginning and end.

The paper slipped from his hand and the breeze scooped it up, then it dipped and soared aloft like the white butterfly kite on invisible wings. Siva watched it and for that moment, he forgot the bitter ache in his heart. Only for a moment.

But in that moment he knew what he had to do. His lips trembled and his knees buckled; his feet sank into the sand. He discarded his slippers and looked down at his bare feet and his hands. He counted his toes and fingers, ten of each and as normal as they could be. He felt an unaccustomed sense of relief.

Siva heard a familiar drone and he slapped his cheek. He scrutinised the squashed mosquito on his palm. He unzipped his bag and plucked out his father's notebook. He flung it far into the air. It fluttered open and, following an invisible arc, plunged into the water. He took out Malli's letters and hurled them into the sea. They sank for a moment then resurfaced, and each wave tugged at each page, slapped it this way and that, as though they were slices of his life. The pages washed ashore, only to be sucked back, page after page. Slice by slice. All of his lives.

Siva removed Mallika's sari from the bag from, the red one with the zari border. He unfolded it and wrapped it around himself. For the last pretence.

A distinct smell engulfed him. A familiar smell. A childhood smell. Mother's smell. Tara's smell.

He retrieved the good-luck coin from his pocket. Once when he couldn't decide which ice cream flavour he wanted to have, Vishnu had groped in his trouser pocket and held up the good-luck coin. 'This should help you decide,' he said. He had tossed it in the air, caught it and closed his hand into a fist. 'Heads, it's vanilla; tails, chocolate. Okay? But never forget,' Vishnu added, 'coins work only for choosing between small things and not big things.' Siva had had a chocolate ice cream that evening, he remembered.

Siva pressed the coin into his fist, holding back his tears. 'This is a small thing,' he said to himself, then chucked it in the air. The coin zipped overhead, caught the light of the sun, winked and flipped, then like a shooting star, it fell on the sand at his feet. Heads. He picked the coin up and flung it into the sea.

With every nerve in his mind Siva obliterated each thought. He was empty now. Empty in his heart. Empty in his mind. He was in an empty place. Through the resounding emptiness all he could feel was the wind sweeping in from the sea, moistening his face, murmuring in his ears, innocent nothings. That moment had about it a certain private quality; without compromise it belonged to him. Only to him.

The sun shone on the water. The sea resembled one big blob of mercury. Folding and then folding again, hissing, crashing, splashing before him. And from far away Siva heard Tara's voice.

Siva, whe-a yu.

Siva looked up for the island in the sky. He saw it deep in the sea.

In a wild hurry, as though he couldn't wait, as though the mercury-sea was waiting for him, and the island was pining for him, and Tara was calling out to him, Siva walked into the sea.

Twenty-four

SIVA'S BODY CRASHED AGAINST THE rocks and washed ashore. The crippled beggar discovered the spray-soaked corpse. It had swollen and flies hummed over the deep gash on its head.

Pundits performed the last rites in the front garden of the Victorian Villa. Ammamai stared at the pond and she believed she could hear a ghostly hissing sound. She covered her ears with her hands and tears streamed down her cheeks. Her tongue felt thick, and bitter from the taste of fate.

When it was time to take the body to the pyre, Raman slapped his head with both his fists. 'Why? Why?'

Malli, who had flown down as soon as she heard the news, stood clutching Saroja's hand. Her face was frozen and her eyes were red and swollen.

Not far from them Mallika pressed her face against the trunk of a tree and began to cry: a pandemonium of hissing, wailing, howling. Tears streamed down her face.

'Cry ma, you must cry,' Munniamma said sobbing as she pressed Mallika's shoulders. 'Cry it all out, ma. It's not good for you to keep your grief inside.'

Mallika was surprised to see Munniamma at her door a week later. Ammamai had been unwell since Siva's death. She got breathless while talking, and when she cleared her throat it made a wet sound like a death cough. She had sent Munniamma to fetch Mallika.

Ammamai clutched Mallika's hand when she came to see her. 'Please come back home, Mallika, please look after me.'

Mallika did not move back but she spent most of the day with Ammamai.

No one spoke of Siva. Not Ammamai, not Raman nor Mallika, not even Munniamma or Mani. Talking about him was hurtful. Raman had framed the photograph of Siva and Vishnu and set it on a table in the living room. Each day Mallika put a garland of fresh flowers around it and lit incense sticks.

It was a full moon night and Mallika and Ammamai sat in the veranda. Ammamai held her head in both her hands and sighed. 'Why don't the gods take me away? Why do they want to punish me like this?'

Mallika clapped her hands thrice and said, 'Po, po, po.'

'What are you doing, Mallika?'

'Gods don't exist, Amma,' Mallika said, 'we make them up in our minds.' She told Ammamai what Saroja had told her. 'And when you are no longer afraid, do this.' She clapped her hands again and said, 'Po, po, po.'

Ammamai darted into the house and rummaged through her trunk. She took a silk sari out of it, an old blouse, a blue velvet jewellery box and a silver container in which she had kept jars of kohl and pottu. She slipped her arms through the sleeves of the blouse, draped the sari around her and put on her jewellery piece by piece. She smeared kohl in her eyes and dotted her forehead with red pottu.

Mallika gawked at her, her mouth open wide.

Ammamai laughed. 'I am going to a new world shortly,' she said, 'make certain I don't reach there dressed like a widow.'

Ammamai sat down on the steps and looked up at the moon. She clapped her hands and in a loud and clear voice she said, 'Po, po, po.'

Victorian Villa was silent that night. The streetlamp cast shadows on the ground. The branches of the neem tree, like the watery arms of a ghost made an eerie noise. Ammamai breathed heavily through the night and her heart raced, until at dawn, it stopped.

Mallika rubbed sandalwood paste on Ammamai's forehead, then poured drops of Ganga water into her mouth. She tied a piece of white muslin under Ammamai's chin and around her head and with strips of cloth she tied Ammamai's thumbs together and then her big toes.

Mallika dressed Ammamai in a red silk saree and all her jewellery. She put a pottu on her forehead and flowers in her hair. Then with the help of Saroja and Munniamma she lifted the dead bride on to a palanquin.

By the end of the day Raman and Mallika had immersed Ammamai's ashes in the river with a prayer.

They were back in the garden of Victorian Villa. Mosquitoes whined around them.

Mallika held Raman's hand in both hers and squeezed it. 'I must go home,' she said.

'But Mallika, this is your home.'

Mallika walked away.

Mallika's house was filled with music. Every morning she coiled her hair into a bun and stuck parijat flowers in it. She smeared red pottu on her forehead and lined her eyes with kohl. Then she sang. Music became her home.

She sang for the radio, music concerts and festivals, just as her mother had done. One evening as Mallika walked home from the radio station she heard angry shouts from the market. She hurried home and shut all the windows and locked the front door.

Riots had broken out once again. A crowd churned around Good Morning Café. The shop sign had been painted over with black paint. Idlis like white saucers were all over the floor of the restaurant.

Nayak, the owner shouted at the men dressed in saffron-coloured clothes belonging to the Hindu Nationalist Party.

'I'll get you for this,' Nayak said twisting his hair, 'you scoundrels, I'll get you for this.' His voice was firm but came out in a squeak when he tried to raise it.

One of the men screamed back at him, 'Change your restaurant's name to a Hindu name. No English names here.'

'This was my great grandfather's restaurant,' Nayak shouted. 'It has always been called Good Morning Café. And over my dead body will I change its name.'

The man sneered at him. 'I'll see how you don't change the name.' He bent towards Nayak and, with a flick of his wrist, yanked at Nayak's white veshti. And even as Nayak stood mortified, his hands covering his crotch, the man threw the veshti on a branch of a tree. It hung gently oscillating like a truce flag.

Further down Gibbs Road, the glass windows of Liberty Shoes were smashed. Next to it, in Novelty Store, the candy-pink mannequins were broken and ribbons and brooches and other fancy items were strewn on the pavement. The glass windows of Queen's, a ladies tailoring shop, were also cracked. Pinto's Ice Cream Centre was in a mess.

Sweeties Saloon and MacOnly's were in flames. Eros Cinema had also been burnt down. The men of the Hindu Nationalist Party had rammed into the earth a large red sign: 'No English. Only the language of the soil. Only Telugu.' Ironically the sign was in English.

A gang of saffron-clothed men walked to Victorian Villa. One of them fixed a cardboard sign on the gatepost covering the name Victorian Villa, and scribbled the new name in red on the cardboard: Ram Vilas.

Mani, who saw them from the kitchen window, rushed to the gates. He caught hold of one of the men by his neck and squeezed hard. As the man started to scream, another man drove a knife into Mani's waist. Mani gasped in pain, stumbled and fell.

'No English. No English names!' the men screamed with their fists raised in the air, and marched away. Using his hands Mani dragged his body through the gates and then collapsed.

Raman heard about the riots and rushed home. He found Mani lying in a heap near the pond, the knife sticking out of his waist. He had lost a lot of blood, but he was conscious. Raman rushed him to the hospital in the car. On the way, between gasps and moans, Mani told Raman what had happened.

Late into the night, the saffron-clad fanatics set fire to the Elizabeth Gibbs Institute and Victoria Dyes factory. A part of the institute was badly damaged by the fire; the dye factory was totally burnt down.

Mani succumbed to his injury a week later. Munniamma said to Raman, 'You must leave this house. It is haunted. By that Eliss-bet Gib ghost. I told Ammamai the minute I met her. But she wouldn't listen to me. It's the ghost who has killed everyone. First Tara, then Siva, Ammamai and now Mani. Even the dog was not spared by her. I am too scared to work here. You must go away, saar.'

Mallika was startled to see Raman at her door the next evening.

'Is everything okay?'

'I am going back to London soon,' Raman said. 'Come with me.'

'Take care, Raman.'

It was the first time Mallika had called Raman by his name. Until now she had only addressed him cryptically as 'Listen, look here, see.'

Before the month was over, due to pressure and threats from the Hindu Nationalist Party all the roads and buildings in Machilipatnam with English names were given Hindu names. Gibbs Road was renamed Sri Krishna Road and the institute was called Mahatma Gandhi Institute. As for Victoria Dyes, there was nothing left of it to rename.

English history and language were deeply entrenched on the tongues and minds of the local people; they could not so easily be erased. Even after twenty years, people still call the main road, Gibbs Road, and the institute, Elizabeth Gibbs Institute.

A leading hotel chain that bought over Victorian Villa converted it into a boutique hotel. In the main hall hangs a large painting of George Gibbs framed in glass. The light from the chandelier is reflected in George's eyes and it seems as though he is watching.

Eighteen months after Victoria Dyes burnt down Saroja had built a home for destitute children in the old premises. She had named the home after her daughter: Nayantara.

Munniamma worked at the home. There were a number of handicapped children amongst the destitute ones. Four of them couldn't see and two couldn't hear. One was crippled, another deformed.

Mallika often spent time with them. Slowly through the children she learned what it meant to feel utterly lost. She made it her heart's purpose to protect them, to ensure that in their separate world they never succumbed to loneliness like Siva had. A clinging loneliness that stuck and did not dry. One so difficult to peel off, like undried bark – a loneliness she knew only too well.

So Mallika collected all the children together with or without their eyes, ears, legs and fingers. She taught music to them, she sang songs, because she believed that in this way she could soothe them of the fear that arose from the undersides of their inadequacies, which made them seem sad and unwanted. And different.

It was little Ajit's birthday that day. He was blind. He had incredibly thick eyelashes, and his eyes were deep but absent, which reminded Mallika of an entire universe lost in a small space.

She sat down on the floor in front of Ajit. From a box she lifted out a cake, pink and white with red roses on it. From another box she took out six candles. She planted them in a circle on the cake and lit them.

'Now blow them out Ajit.'

When Ajit blew the candles out Mallika cut the cake and held a wedge to Ajit's mouth. 'Happy birthday, Ajit,' she said looking into his blank eyes. She pulled him close to her bosom.

Ajit started humming softly. Mallika held his finger and put it on the top of her forehead, then slowly ran it over the ridge of her nose, down its tip, over her lips, her chin and all the way down her neck to the hole-like hollow under it. Then she curled Ajit's finger into the hollow, sheltered and safe.

Mallika was in the garden at the back of her house reading once more the letter she had got from Raman. He had written to her occasionally with news of his work. His research was fruitful, he wrote in the recent letter. He had been successful in micro-injecting new genes into mosquito embryos. He had created a new strain of mosquito, which could be used to make anti-malaria vaccines. His invention had brought him considerable prestige and was called the Raman Technique.

'Please come here,' he wrote. 'It is terrible what happened to you, to us. Please come, Mallika. I need you.'

Mallika felt the workings of love. She understood, perhaps for the first time, that love was not contained in its final conclusion but in its continuation; and that it grew painfully, whole growing from part, consuming every bit of emotion and spirit between two people. This was the essence of loving, which made living worthwhile: the agony of the birth and passage of love, undismayed by any eventuality or any end, and in which alternatives ceased to be. A love so momentary, it could last a lifetime.

Mallika folded the letter and brushed it against her lips.

Acknowledgement

This book wouldn't have existed without Dom Moraes who believed in my writing and amma who taught me all things Tamil, and let me be who I am.

I would like to thank, in no particular order, Nisha Da Cunha, Githa Hariharan, Shanta Gokhale, Ravi Singh, Ayush Ahuja, Ayeesha Menon, Lyn Andrade, Deveshee Dutt and Kavita Bhanot for reading the first draft.

Kulsum Jamal, Murthy, Kalyani and Anshu offered me with place and space to edit the book, and Steve Hopkins provided lilting music and Pradeep, his support, to them my sincere thanks.

Renuka Chatterjee helped me find my way through the book. Saugata Mukherjee, my editor at HarperCollins, re-read the manuscripts at different stages, did not ask too many questions and was unbelievably patient. And all of those who, in my good days and bad, raised a glass of wine with me. Renuka and Saugata did too. Thank you.

My children, Ayush and Anshu filled my world as did this book.

I am grateful to my agent, Wendy Goldman Rohm, who cast her meticulous eyes over my words. She knew when to push me and when to let me be.

Let my book be…